Paula Spencer

Paula Spencer

Roddy Doyle

ISIS
LARGE PRINT
Oxford

First published in Great Britain 2006
by
Jonathan Cape,
one of the publishers in
The Random House Group Ltd.

Published in Large Print 2007 by ISIS Publishing Ltd.,
7 Centremead, Osney Mead, Oxford OX2 0ES
by arrangement with
The Random House Group Ltd.

British Library Cataloguing in Publication Data
Doyle, Roddy, 1958–
  Paula Spencer. – Large print ed.
  1. Recovering alcoholics – Fiction
  2. Widows – Fiction
  3. Women domestics – Fiction
  4. Dublin – Ireland – Social conditions – Fiction
  5. Large type books
  I. Title
  823.9'14 [F]

ISBN 978–0–7531–7724–2 (hb)
ISBN 978–0–7531–7725–9 (pb)

Printed and bound in Great Britain by
T. J. International Ltd., Padstow, Cornwall

This book is dedicated to
Aideen, Pamela and Shane

Acknowledgements

The author and publishers are grateful for permission to reprint lines from the following:

"Vertigo", words and music by David Evans, Adam Clayton, Paul Hewson and Laurence Mullen. Reprinted by kind permission of Blue Mountain Music Limited.

"I Should Be So Lucky", written and composed by Stock/Aitken/Waterman. Published by Mike Stock Publishing Ltd/Universal Music Publishing Ltd/All Boys Music Ltd (BMG). Used by permission. All rights reserved.

She copes. A lot of the time. Most of the time. She copes. And sometimes she doesn't. Cope. At all.

This is one of the bad days.

She could feel it coming. From the minute she woke up. One of those days. It hasn't let her down.

She'll be forty-eight in a few weeks. She doesn't care about that. Not really.

It's more than four months since she had a drink. Four months and five days. One of those months was February. That's why she started measuring the time in months. She could jump three days. But it's a leap year; she had to give one back. Four months, five days. A third of a year. Half a pregnancy, nearly.

A long time.

The drink is only one thing.

She's on her way home from work. She's walking from the station. There's no energy in her. Nothing in her legs. Just pain. Ache. The thing the drink gets down to.

But the drink is only part of it. She's coped well with the drink. She wants a drink. She doesn't want a drink. She doesn't want a drink. She fights it. She wins. She's proud of that. She's pleased. She'll keep going. She knows she will.

But sometimes she wakes up, knowing the one thing. She's alone.

She still has Jack. Paula wakes him every morning. He's a great sleeper. It's a long time now since he was up before her. She's proud of that too. She sits on his bed. She ruffles his hair. Ruffles — that's the word. A head made for ruffling. Jack will break hearts.

And she still has Leanne. Mad Leanne. Mad, funny. Mad, good. Mad, brainy. Mad, lovely — and frightening.

They're not small any more, not kids. Leanne is twenty-two. Jack is nearly sixteen. Leanne has boyfriends. Paula hasn't met any of them. Jack, she doesn't know about. He tells her nothing. He's been taller than her since he was twelve. She checks his clothes for girl-smells but all she can smell is Jack. He's still her baby.

It's not a long walk from the station. It just feels that way tonight. God, she's tired. She's been tired all day. Tired and dark.

This place has changed.

She's not interested tonight. She just wants to get home. The ache is in her ankles. The ground is hard. Every footstep cracks her.

Paula Spencer. That's who she is.

She wants a drink.

The house is empty.

She can feel it before she shuts the door behind her. Bad.

She needs the company. She needs distraction. They've left the lights on, and the telly. But she knows.

2

She can feel it. The door is louder. Her bag drops like a brick. There's no one in.

Get used to it, she tells herself.

She's finished. That's how it often feels. She never looked forward to it. The freedom. The time. She doesn't want it.

She isn't hungry. She never really is.

She stands in front of the telly. Her coat is half off. It's one of those house programmes. She usually likes them. But not tonight. A couple looking around their new kitchen. They're delighted, opening all the presses.

Fuck them.

She turns away. But stops. Their fridge, on the telly. It's the same as Paula's. Mrs Happy opens it. And closes it. Smiling. Paula had hers before them. A present from Nicola. The fridge. And the telly. Both presents.

Nicola is her eldest.

Paula goes into the kitchen. The fridge is there.

— You were on the telly, she says.

She feels stupid. Talking to the fridge. She hated that film, *Shirley Valentine*, when Shirley talked to the wall. Hello, wall. She fuckin' hated it. It got better, the film, but that bit killed it for her. At her worst, her lowest, Paula never spoke to a wall or anything else that wasn't human. And now she's talking to the fridge. Sober, hard-working, reliable — she's all these things these days, and she's talking to the fridge.

It's a good fridge, though. It takes up half the kitchen. It's one of those big silver, two-door jobs. Ridiculous. Twenty years too late. She opens it the way

3

film stars open the curtains. Daylight! Ta-dah! Empty. What was Nicola thinking of? The stupid bitch. How to make a poor woman feel poorer. Buy her a big fridge. Fill that, loser. The stupid bitch. What was she thinking?

But that's not fair. She knows it's not. Nicola meant well; she always does. All the presents. She's showing off a bit. But that's fine with Paula. She's proud to have a daughter who can fling a bit of money around. The pride takes care of the humiliation, every time. Kills it stone dead.

She's not hungry. But she'd like something to eat. Something nice. It shocked her, a while back — not long ago. She was in Carmel, her sister's house. Chatting, just the pair of them that afternoon. Denise, her other sister, was away somewhere, doing something — she can't remember. And Carmel took one of those Tesco prawn things out of her own big fridge and put it between them on the table. Paula took up a prawn and put it into her mouth — and tasted it.

— Lovely, she said.

— Yeah, said Carmel. — They're great.

Paula hadn't explained it to her. The fact that she was tasting, really tasting something for the first time in — she didn't know how long. Years. She'd liked it. The feeling. And she'd liked the prawns. And other things she's eaten since. Tayto, cheese and onion. Coffee. Some tomatoes. Chicken skin. Smarties. She's tasted them all.

But the fridge is fuckin' empty. She picks up the milk carton. She weighs it. Enough for the morning. She checks the date. It's grand; two days to go.

There's a carrot at the bottom of the fridge. She bends down — she likes raw carrots. Another new taste. But this one is old, and soft. She should bring it to the bin. She lets it drop back into the fridge. There's a jar of mayonnaise in there as well. Half empty. A bit yellow. Left over from last summer. There's a bit of red cheese, and a tub of Dairygold.

There's a packet of waffles in the freezer. There's two left in the packet — Jack's breakfast. There's something else in the back of the freezer, covered in ice, hidden. Stuck there. The package is red — she can see that much. But she doesn't know what it is. She'd have to hack at it with a knife or something. She couldn't be bothered. Anyway, if it was worth eating it wouldn't be there.

She has money, in her coat pocket. Not much, a fiver and some change. She could go and get bread, more milk. The Spar is still open. But she knows she can't. Her shoes are off.

Tomorrow is payday. Always a good day. Excitement, a bit. Pride, a bit. New clothes, maybe. Food. A good dinner. A half-full fridge. A video.

But tomorrow is tomorrow. Fuckin' miles and hours away.

Cornflakes.

The secret of the Spencer family's success.

She fills a cup with cornflakes. A bowl when she has milk, a cup when she doesn't. She likes cornflakes, especially the big ones from the top of the packet. But the packet is nearly empty.

Tomorrow.

The telly is no distraction. Another of Nicola's presents. Second-hand; her old one. Nicola has one of these huge flat ones.

This one is grand. The remote works, and that's the main thing. Paula tries to remember a time when she had to get up to change the channel. But she can't. She can't even imagine it.

The old telly is out the back. Smashed. Leanne threw her shoe at it. The heel did the damage. The noise — it exploded.

Leanne.

Leanne scares Paula. The guilt. It's always there. Leanne is twenty-two. Leanne wets her bed. Leanne deals with it. It's terrible.

Her fault. Paula's fault. The whole mess. Most of Leanne's life.

Paula lies back on the couch. She doesn't like going up to bed before Jack comes home. Or Leanne. Although Leanne can come and go as she wants. She tries to get herself comfortable. The couch has collapsed in places. Given up. It's ancient. She had sex with her dead husband on this couch, long before he was killed. That's how ancient it is.

That's another thing. She can't remember sex. Not really. And it doesn't matter. She doesn't think it matters.

Is that true?

Yes. It is. A man. A woman — she thinks, sometimes. She wouldn't want either. Not tonight.

Where's the fuckin' remote?

She hasn't had sex since her husband died. A year before he died; more. She doesn't remember it. She didn't know it would be the last time. Twelve years — thirteen years ago. It's pathetic.

No. It isn't.

She finds the remote behind her; she's sitting on it. She flicks from channel to channel. There's nothing. She's back at number one, RTE. She keeps flicking. Right through all of them again. Sixteen stations. Ads on most. Useless. The lot of them.

You don't measure your life in sex. She knows that now. Fucking. It was riding when she was younger; now it's fucking. She's bang up to date. The more you fuck, the happier you are. That's rubbish. She knows that. Life without her husband has been better than life with him. Sometimes much better. Most times.

Not tonight. Not today. But she knows the bad days. She recognises them. She feels them coming. They're real but they don't often fool her. She feels them going too.

Bullshit. That's just fuckin' bullshit.

That thing. *Big Brother*. God almighty. They're sitting around. One of them's biting his nails. The blondey one with the boobs knows she's being watched. Stupid — of course she does. She's on telly.

Paula had tits like that.

No, she didn't.

Yes, she fuckin' did so.

Jesus, though. *Big Brother*. Is she too old? That's what Leanne says. Paula's too old to understand it. Appreciate it. But Leanne thinks it's shite as well.

— Would you go on it?

— Would in me hole.

Paula smiles; she feels herself smiling. She's never alone. Not really.

More bullshit.

One of them stands up, on *Big Brother*. A good-looking lad. Nice arse on him.

She flicks on. The sound down. It makes more sense.

She turns it off. Back on. Off.

She'd like to sit in the dark. But the light's on and the switch is far away.

Sex.

Sex.

She turns the telly back on.

And off.

He's there — she knows it — before she opens her eyes. She dozed off, and Jack's there. She sees him, and she sees him looking at the floor, under the couch, for the bottle, the glass.

When will that stop?

— Howyeh, Jack.

He looks at her now. He knows. She's sober. He relaxes. She sees it.

— Hi.

— Where were you?

— Out.

— Where?

— Just out, he says.

— Just out, she says back.

She sits up.

— I must have dozed off.

He says nothing.

She stands up. That's for him. I'm fine — look. I'm awake and alert. She can't hug him. She'd love to but she can't. He's too old. And too new. Only in the mornings. She can pat his head, ruffle his hair. But not now.

She doesn't mind. She doesn't really mind. She wishes he'd stayed small, but that's stupid. She loves the way he is. He's up there, taller than her. With his bit of a beard. It's a ridiculous-looking yoke, but it suits him. The brand new man. He'll wake up one day and shave it off. She'll miss it.

She doesn't worry about Jack. His breath is clean. His eyes are clear. He doesn't remember his father. That seems like a good thing. She tells Jack about him. Now and again. Mostly good things. But she's told him she threw him out; she had to. She's told him why.

She copes well. She thinks she does.

— Did you eat? she asks.

— Yeah, he says.

He shrugs.

He probably didn't. She won't press it. He isn't wasting away. Anyway, there's nothing in the house. And he had his lunch. She watched him.

— D'you have your homework done? she asks.

— Yeah.

— All of it?

— Yeah; most of it.

— Ah, Jack.

He smiles.

— I've done everything I need for tomorrow, he says.
— Relax.

She smiles. It's a speech, from Jack.

— Bed? she says.

He shrugs.

— Well, I'm going up, she says.

— Okay.

He sits where she was. He picks up the remote.

— Goodnight, love, she says.

— Night.

She goes into the hall. She's tired. She looks at Jack, through the gap between the door and the frame. The couch is up against the wall. She can see a good bit of his face. He's turned on the telly. She hears him bring the sound up, and down. She reaches in, and turns off the light. She sees him look at the door.

— Goodnight, she says, again.

— Night.

He's lit only by the telly now. He's waiting. For her feet on the stairs. He's sitting up.

She goes on up.

She doesn't worry too much about Jack. She doesn't need to, and she doesn't know why not. A dead father, an alcoholic mother — it's not a great start in life. But he's grand. He seems to be.

She's tired.

She's always tired.

Not true. She's tired at night and that's the way it should be. A hard day's work and that. She likes being tired. Tired and sober — it's different. The sleep is

10

different — it's sleep. Although she doesn't always sleep. But it's grand; it's fine. She's not complaining.

Who'd listen?

She brushes her teeth. The important ones are there. The ones at the front. The missing ones aren't seen, unless she smiles too wide. Then the gaps appear. She brushes them well. Brushing will bring the gone ones back. She can believe that sometimes. The new Paula. She can believe nearly anything. She's a bit hysterical. Not now. But sometimes. So happy. Alive. She brushes for lost time. And teeth. Kicked out of her, some of them. Nights and mornings, when brushing wasn't a priority.

She looks in the mirror. There were times when she didn't look. Years.

She knows this mirror. She isn't fooling herself. Yes, she is. And she doesn't care. If she stands here, this way — she looks good.

She looks good.

This distance, this light. She's a good-looking woman.

But she can't stay here, in the bathroom. One part of the bathroom.

She's a good-looking woman. She takes that with her.

She turns on the bedroom light. There's a mirror here too. She stays clear of that one. She takes off her jeans and lets them drop. They fall off her. She doesn't have to pull them off. They fit.

She pulls back the blanket and sheets. She'd like duvets for the beds. They're on the list. She makes the beds these days. Hers and Jack's. She makes them in the morning. Before she goes to work.

She gets into the bed. It's a good bed. A good mattress. She's puked in this bed and she's pissed in this bed. She can think of that; she can remember waking up to it. She can think back now without curling up, or wanting to. She likes this bed. She remembers. Four years after her husband died, five years after she threw him out, she moved over to the middle.

She lies there. She knows. She won't sleep. Not for a while. Jack is down there. Leanne is out.

It's grand. She lies there. She's a mother. It's the job.

She doesn't feel bad. She knows that, suddenly. She's nicely tired. The heaviness is gone. The ache. Or most of it.

That's Jack. She thinks that. And the nap in front of the telly. But mostly Jack. And it would have been the same with Leanne, if she'd come home before him. Just the contact. It's enough. She believes that, most of the time. She believes it.

She's a mother. Still a mother.

She'd still get up. She knows it. If there was anything to drink in the house, she'd get up now and drink it. She'd knock it back and promise herself a fresh start in the morning, as it soaked the back of her mouth. She knows. She can taste it.

She'd do it.

But there's nothing to drink in the house. And that's fine. It doesn't hurt. The pain is safe, behind other things.

She listens.

Her alarm clock. Paula has an alarm clock. She bought it herself and it often wakes her up. She gets woken by classical music. The music itself is shite but it's a nice way to wake up. At half-seven. Five mornings a week. And sometimes too when Leanne works the weekends. She gets up, to be with her before she goes.

Still a mother.

Leanne often went to school with no breakfast or kiss goodbye.

It's in the past.

She knows that's shite. More than anyone, she knows. You can't leave things behind. They come with you.

You can manage. That's the best you can expect.

She manages.

Jack has pushed the sound up. But she can't make it out. She wonders what he's watching. Something he doesn't want to watch with her.

That's fine. It's okay. It's funny.

She knows she's smiling.

It's strange, about the house. About her life. New fridge, old blankets. Does anyone else around here still have blankets?

Plenty. There's plenty like Paula. Although it's changing, the whole place. One of the old shops is a café now, opened a few weeks ago. An Italian place, real Italians in it. Not chipper Italians. Selling bread and coffee and oil and other expensive stuff Paula would love to load up on. There's a fella that does the bread and pizzas. She's seen him in the window. A dark guy, not that handsome — something about his hands. She doesn't stop to watch. She can't. She can't be caught. She's a widow. She's a big girl. She can't be gawking in windows at middle-aged young fellas.

Hands.

Black hair on the fingers. The hands are on her neck. She feels the fingers. Rubbing gently. Pressing. Her throat is dry. She can't close her mouth. The fingers press harder. She can't cry out, move her mouth. It's dry. Dust, muck. She tries to shout — anything. Whisper, move. She can't.

She wakes. She's awake.

She bit her tongue. Badly. She tastes no blood. But it's sore. It's very sore.

The door.

She's been asleep.

She's awake.

Leanne's home. The door slammed. She doesn't know that. She bit her tongue. That's what woke her. She's awake now. And she heard the door.

Leanne.

She listens.

How long did she sleep? She looks at the clock. Jesus, does she need glasses now as well? She brings her face closer. An hour. A bit more than an hour.

Glasses.

God.

She listens. Leanne is in the kitchen.

Paula won't get up. Leanne would know. Her mother, the alco, checking up on her. Leave the girl alone. She's grand. She's fine. She's fine.

14

Paula listens. She hears nothing. No falling over. Nothing stupid. She needn't be worried.

But she is.

She listens.

She crosses the kitchen. She pulls back the curtain. A big blast of sunlight. It would have killed her a few months ago. Guilty! It's grand now, though. She loves a bit of sun.

She fills the kettle. She turns on the radio. The News is on — the European elections. Boring, Jesus. But she leaves it on.

Royston Brady. His posters are all over the place. Energy. Drive. His head is on every pole. She doesn't like that version of handsome. That Daniel O'Donnell look. The mammy's boy. The country's full of men like that. They do nothing for Paula. The Royston fella's in trouble. They're talking about it on the News. Something he said about his da being abducted by loyalist terrorists. She must have missed something — that's her life. It doesn't make much sense.

She'll be voting for Proinsias De Rossa. She hasn't voted in years. 1977, she thinks. The only time she voted. De Rossa's Labour, and his eyes are gorgeous. And he's nearer Paula's age. He'll be getting her vote, if she gets round to it.

The kettle's going.

She's forty-eight. Today.

She puts two spoons of coffee into the cup. She's thinking of getting a plunger — real coffee. Another thing on her list. Or one of those espresso makers. It would look great, near the window. She's seen them for sale in the new café, on her way past. She's not mad about espresso, though. It's too strong, too druggy.

Dangerous stuff.

She wants a drink.

But she's grand. She looks at her hands, the palms down. They don't look too bad. They look fuckin' dreadful but they're not too bad, considering. Her age, her work. Her life. They should be worse. There are badly mended bones in there. There's bad pain on the wet days.

She listens. No one's getting up.

She listens to the radio. They're still on about the elections. Northern accents, talking about Sinn Féin. She doesn't like Sinn Féin. Her husband loved all that hunger strike stuff. The black armbands, the armed struggle. He was going to march, support the hunger strikers. But he never did. How long ago was that? Years — it must be more than twenty. He didn't march. But he stood still for a minute in the kitchen, a minute's silence, after one of the strikers died. They all stood, Paula and the kids. A few hours after Paula had wiped her own blood off the kitchen floor.

She's seen the posters for their Dublin candidate. Mary Lou McDonald. A nice-looking young one. A big smile on her. She wasn't alive, probably, when all that happened.

Paula should have her own posters. Energy. Drive. She sits up straight in the chair. She reminds herself to do it. Straight-backed Paula Spencer.

She hears feet upstairs.

16

She wonders have they remembered.

It's Jack. She can tell — the time between each step. She imagines him, one foot up, like one of those birds in the water. Calm, waiting.

It's Jack alright, gone into the toilet.

She hears the flush.

She drinks more of the coffee. She can feel it push through her. She can feel it in the hair on her arms.

Jack is coming down.

Leanne is different. Leanne is another bird, one of those little frantic birds. Darting all over the place. Pecking at everything. Her steps are little punches to the floor.

Jack walks in.

— Howyeh, Jack.

— Hi.

— You're up early, she says.

It's June. He's on his holidays. He's usually still in the bed when she goes. She doesn't know when he gets up.

— What has you up?

He looks at the window, at the light.

— Don't know, he says. — Couldn't sleep.

He stands there at the door. His jeans are huge, dragging on the floor. They're down over his arse. She looks at his feet. One of them is off the floor. She smiles.

He moves. It's like he's been kicked, or goosed.

— Oh yeah, he says.

Now he walks in.

— I have a job.

— Ah, great. For the summer, just?

— What? Yeah. Yeah.

— What's the job?

— Lounge-boy.

— Where?

— Finnegan's Wake.

It's the local. Someone bought it a year ago. And the new name went up. Finnegan's Wake. After the famous book.

— What's it like these days? she says.

— Alright; yeah.

— The same crowd?

— Some; yeah. I don't know.

He opens the fridge.

He stood outside that pub when he was a little fella, waiting for her to come out. He stood in the rain. He often did it. She brought crisps out to him, and Coke with a straw. Like it was a treat. There you are, love. More guilt. On her birthday.

Fuck it.

— Would you like a rasher sandwich or something? she says.

— Cool.

She loves that. Coo-il. The way he says it. She looks at the clock. She has loads of time.

She stands up. She gets the pan from the press.

— How did you find out about it?

— What?

— The job, Jack.

— I went in.

— And just asked?

18

He shrugs.

— Yeah.

— Good man. Will you have a uniform?

— A waistcoat, he says. — Black trousers.

— Nice, she says. —With the name on the waistcoat?

— It's a bit cheesy, he says. — I've to buy the trousers.

— I'll pay for them.

— I'll pay you back.

— Grand.

She puts the heat on under the pan.

— Pass the rashers over to me, love.

He doesn't know it's her birthday. He hasn't a clue. It's fine. It's funny. She throws on the rashers. She steps back. They're spitting. She'll have one herself — it's her birthday.

Finnegan's Wake.

The whole area has changed. She's been here since the beginning. It was a farm a few months before they moved in. It was all young families, kids all over the place. Out in the middle of nowhere. No bus of its own. Near the tracks, but no train station. No proper shops, no pub. No church or schools. Nothing but the houses and the people.

— D'you want toast or ordinary?

— Toast.

— Stick it in the toaster, so.

Another present from Nicola. The toaster.

— And a couple of slices for me.

— Okay.

— Thanks.

It had been great back then. It had been so simple.

But that's just rubbish. She knows. It hadn't been great. It had never been great. It's all changed now, anyway, the area — the estate. Or it's changing. It used to be settled. It isn't any more. The café is a start. And the new name on the pub. There's two groups of people living here now. Those who call it the old name and still go in, and those who call it Finnegan's Wake and don't go in.

— What's it like inside? she says.

— What? says Jack. — The pub?

— Yeah.

— Alright.

— I haven't been there in ages.

He says nothing.

— Have they done much to it? she asks.

— Not really, he says. — Just pictures and that.

— The usual, she says. — You can't do much with a place like that.

She came out once and he was standing at the door, in the cold, only his shirt on. She went home with him. She put him into the bed beside her. She cried, once she knew he was asleep. And promised.

Jack knows.

But it's grand.

She doesn't miss it, the pub. Not at all. She hated it.

She hasn't been in a pub since the smoking ban. She wonders what it's like. It's good that Jack will be working smoke-free. She feels good for thinking that.

— D'you smoke, Jack?

She doesn't look at him.

20

— No, he says.

— Never?

— No.

— Ever?

She's no one to be talking.

— I don't like it, he says.

But she's his mother.

— Good, she says.

It's not too late. It's not meaningless.

— Here we go. Plates now, Jack.

He gets the plates. He takes dry ones off the rack beside the sink.

— D'you want butter on your toast?

— Cool; yeah.

— Good lad.

She goes to the fridge. Happy days. She has to move things out of the way to get at the butter. Real butter. Kerrygold.

They sit at the table. They say nothing. They eat their rasher sandwiches.

It's later now.

She's staring at the plate. She can't do anything else. She's afraid to.

She waits.

The house is empty. She thinks she heard the door slammed twice. Leanne and Jack. She doesn't know which of them went first. She thinks they're gone. She's not sure.

Leanne.

Jesus.

She screamed at her. Leanne did. She screamed at Paula. She hit her.

Leanne hit her.

She can still feel the sting. The shock of it.

She slapped her. Across the face. Said sorry.

— It's okay.

Jesus.

She's been sitting here for hours. She thinks she has. She thinks the house is empty.

Today is her birthday. Her daughter has just attacked her.

She won't let herself get corny. She has to be honest.

She stands up now. She looks at the clock. She took it down off the wall a few months ago. It had been stopped for years. She took out the old battery. She brought it down to the shops and asked if they'd any more like it. It was one of the old batteries, one of those huge ones, before Walkmans. But they'd had one and she bought it. She brought it home and put it into the clock. She washed the sides and the glass, and she put it back up on the wall.

She looks at it now.

She's been sitting there for half an hour.

She goes to the kettle.

It's been coming. She knows it has.

She empties the kettle. She fills it with new water.

Leanne is an alcoholic.

But Paula's not sure. She isn't certain. She's a bit of a reformed hoor. Everyone's an alcoholic.

She puts the kettle onto its stand. She presses the switch. She looks out the window.

Leanne came in after Jack. Paula'd heard her getting up. Jack was back up in his room, maybe back in the bed. Full of his rasher sandwich.

Paula listened, as Leanne moved around in her room. She heard her on the stairs. And she was frightened. Of what she was going to see. The signs, the face. Red, wet eyes and broken lips.

The kettle's nearly there. She hears it starting to rumble.

She's pleased with herself. That's odd, and kind of indecent. But it's true. She hasn't let the slap become the thing she can't get past. She's over it. She isn't — but she is.

The kettle clicks itself off.

She throws a teabag into the cup. She pours the water onto it. She watches the colour glide out of the bag. Like red smoke. She likes that colour, before all the water turns that way and darkens. It would look great in her hair. Just a splash of it. A streak down the side.

What does an alcoholic mother say to her alcoholic daughter? It's shocking. It's terrible. But Paula's not falling down on the ground. She's not running away or pretending it's not there, or screaming and making it worse. All the things she's done before and will probably do again.

I am an alcoholic.

She's facing it.

She drinks her tea standing up. She needs the energy that standing gives her, the alertness.

Leanne walked into the kitchen.

It wasn't just the early-morning mess. The mad hair and last night's mascara. It was the colour of her skin. The veins on each side of her nose. The look in the eyes that came straight at Paula, the anger and panic, terror, the whole lot coming at her. It was Paula looking straight back at Paula.

Help.

She understands. She knows.

She knows fuck-all.

It's there in her head before she thinks of it. The putdown. She knows fuck-all. But she does know. She knows hatred when it's coming at her. She knows how to duck it. And she knows the hatred comes out of herself. She needs no help from someone else. Paula knows her stuff. She's done her research.

Leanne walked into the kitchen.

— Jesus, Leanne.

Leanne didn't answer. She went to the fridge. She stood in front of it.

— Leanne.

Leanne stood with her back to Paula. She was waiting.

— Leanne, love.

Paula saw the anger. In the shoulders. Love. The word had nudged her. Like a spike.

— We have to talk about this.

— About what?

— Come on. Sit down. Leanne.

Leanne opened the fridge.

— What?

She talked into the fridge.

— No juice in this fuckin' dump.

— Stop that, said Paula. — Come here.

Leanne turned.

Her little girl. She's not being corny.

— What? said Leanne.

— Look at you, said Paula.

— Look at yourself.

Paula nodded.

— Fair enough, Leanne, she said.

— Fuck off, Ma, would yeh.

— Leanne.

She stepped towards Leanne.

— Leanne, love.

— Stop it!

Before she could get her arms to Leanne. The slap came at her — she could see it coming. But it was gone before she understood.

She sat down. She had to.

— Sorry.

She heard Leanne. She didn't look — she couldn't. She nodded. She managed that.

— Sorry, right?

Paula stared at the plate. And the piece of rind she'd taken out of her mouth a few minutes before. The crumbs, the bit of congealed butter that had dripped from the sandwich. She fixed her eyes to the plate.

It's good. She's confronted it. She's started. We have to talk about this. She's doing what she should do. It's good.

It's fuckin' sick. She's climbing over Leanne so she can feel good about it. Knocking her down to help her up.

25

But that's not true. It's not fair at all. Leanne's in trouble — Paula's fault. But that's not fair either. She's doing her best. She can't go back, to stop it from happening. She can't blame herself for saying Yes when her husband asked her to dance that first time. She can't blame herself for starting to drink. She can, but she won't. She's always blamed herself, for everything. It goes without saying now; it gets her nowhere.

She's doing something. She won't let it go away.

She never thought of Leanne as someone to keep her company. To drink with her at home. The two of them skulling the bottles. They're more like sisters, aren't they? She tried that with Nicola. She bought Nicola a bottle of vodka for Christmas. Wrapped it and all. Nicola was sixteen.

— Happy Christmas, love.

Paula shivers, just thinking about it — letting it in.

— Are you going to open that bottle? she asked her a few days later.

— I gave it to Tony's ma, said Nicola.

Tony was her boyfriend then. Her husband now.

— That was your Christmas present, Nicola.

— Weird present, said Nicola. — Anyway, it's gone.

— Bitch.

She still thumps herself, thinking about it.

It'll never go away. That was as low as she got. But she only knew that later.

It hasn't happened this time.

She's ready.

That's a fuckin' laugh. Leanne didn't lick it off a stone. She grew up with nothing else. And a few good

26

months aren't going to change that. There have been good months before. Paula could count them. They won't add up to much more than a year.

Enough.

She'll do her best.

She puts the cup in the sink. She's late for work. She goes looking for her keys.

It's later again. It's after work. She cleans houses four mornings a week. And she has to work again later. She does offices, five nights.

She's doing the shop. She's going to get a cake as well. Jack and Leanne will see it on the table later, and then they'll remember. If Leanne comes home.

The supermarket hasn't changed. It's still a bare shell of a place. It has none of the fancy stuff that you'd find in Tesco's. It's changed names a few times but it's still the same. The same people go in and out the door at the back, where the offices are. The management team. The women on the check-out are nearly all foreign. That's the only real change.

Paula tried to get a job here once. They told her they'd let her know. A woman with ALICE on her badge interviewed her. She stood in front of Paula, blocking her way, telling her, more or less, to get out of the fuckin' shop.

It's a bare old place. It always has been. They just rip the tops off the boxes and pile them up, on top of each other. The only real shelves are around the sides, on the walls. The aisles are made of pallets and boxes. It's never busy. There are five check-outs but only one of them is open. She's surprised it still does any business.

She walks on to Tesco's when she has the money. It's half an hour. But today she just wants the basics.

The basics. For fuck sake. She could tell you the number of times she's made it past the basics.

It's getting hot. It's been like this for a few days.

Her sisters both have mobile homes. Somewhere near Courtown, near the beach and that. They're always at her to go down. She'd like to. She went there once, when she was a kid. And she went there as well on her honeymoon. She'd love to go back to Courtown. But she feels a bit frail when she isn't at home. She doesn't trust herself. Yet.

Carmel and Denise spend most of the summer down there. Once their kids get their holidays, they pack up and go. She isn't envious — she really isn't. Jack's too old. And he has his summer job. He wouldn't go with her. Leanne went to Spain somewhere, last year. A whole gang of them. She's going nowhere this year. She hasn't mentioned anything. But it's early. It's only the start of June. That would be good. If Leanne came home with the holiday brochures. Last year she'd the whole thing booked before she went back to work after Christmas.

There's an African woman on the check-out. Nigerian, or one of the others. What other African countries do they come from? Paula doesn't know. There are wars everywhere; you could never keep up. It's the first time she's seen a black woman working here. Good luck to her. She's lovely. Her hair up in a scarf. Her long cheekbones. Lovely straight back.

What would Charlo think? she wonders. What would he have said about it? Charlo was her husband. He died before all these people started arriving. Before the Celtic Tiger thing.

She smiles at the African woman. The woman smiles back. Bread, a carton of milk. A half-dozen eggs — she fancies an omelette later. A few tomatoes, two big onions. Cornflakes. Coffee.

It's nice. She knows she has the money. She didn't have to do the arithmetic when she was filling the basket. The euros are in her pocket.

That job. There's nothing to it. Holding the things — the items — over the yoke. Swiping, she thinks it's called. You just swipe them over the little light thing. She'd be well up for that. The cleaning tires her out. It always has. She hates the hours, going to work when people are coming home.

— Please. Twenty euro and thirty-seven cent.

The black girl, the check-out woman.

Lovely voice.

Paula gives her a twenty and a five. She's beautiful. Charlo would have called Paula a lezzer for thinking that, for saying it. It's funny, she doesn't know if he was a racist or not. She hasn't a clue. She'd know these days quickly enough. They're all over the place, the foreigners, the black people. Is that racist? They're all over the place. She doesn't know. She means no harm. It's just a phrase. And she doesn't mind it. She likes looking at all the foreigners. Some of them scare her a bit. The Romanians, the women. They're a bit frightening — wild, like they've come straight out of a war. But most of them are grand.

The woman here gives her the change coin by coin. Onto her hand. Her nails are perfect; she's painted them white.

— Thanks.

— Thank you.

— Bye now.

— Goodbye.

Deep voice.

Paula has her plastic bag with her.

— Lovely day, she says.

— Yes, says the girl.

— You must like it, says Paula.

— Yes.

The woman smiles.

— Where you come from — your home.

— Nigeria, says the woman.

She smiles again.

— It is very sunny there, she says.

— Lovely, says Paula. — Bye again.

— Goodbye.

She stops at the noticeboard. There's nothing about jobs. There isn't much of anything. A dog minder. A little picture of a pup on the card. That wouldn't be for Paula. She's not mad about animals. Maths grinds. Ordinary and Honours Level. That's some teacher doing a nixer. It's a sheet of paper, with the phone number repeated at the bottom, and cut into strips, one strip for each number. It's a mobile number, 086. Paula tears one strip. She puts the little piece of paper in her pocket.

She has no idea why she did that. She has no intention of doing maths, at any level. It was just something small to do. To be involved.

She's collecting phone numbers.

The bag is biting into her fingers. She changes hands. The new Paula. Bringing a plastic bag. Thinking to bring it, a step ahead. She's rarely that skint that she can't afford the 15c bag tax. But she'd never have thought of it before, bringing the bag, before she left the house.

Little things.

The car park here is nearly empty. She'd love a car. She'd love a lot of things. The vegetable place is new. Garden Fresh. Not her garden. It's a wreck. It's another of the things on her list. Do the garden. Do what? She hasn't a clue. Borrow a lawn-mower, cut the grass. Get out into it. Find the time, find the energy, the interest. Become a gardener.

She looks in at Garden Fresh as she passes. It's nice, old-fashioned. There are boxes of fruit tilted on shelves covered with that artificial grass-looking stuff. She hasn't seen that stuff in years.

There's no one in there. No one guarding the stuff — the produce. A few years ago, they'd have been running off with all the fruit and some of the vegetables, the kids around here, her own included. There are hardly any kids now. They're like hers, grown up. A lot of the new people don't have kids. Young couples. Women on their own. Jack's school is nearly empty. There's only twenty in his class. There's a rumour they'll be closing it down. Carmel told her, the bitch. Her own kids went elsewhere. Carmel's buying an apartment in Bulgaria. So she said, this morning. Paula's second call.

— Bulgaria?

She told her after she'd wished Paula a happy birthday.

— Yep.

— Where's Bulgaria?

— Eastern Europe, Paula.

— I know. But where? Do people go there on their holidays?

— Yes, Paula.

— Is there not a war there or something? Orphans?

— Not at all. They're joining the EU in 2007.

She stops at Garden Fresh. She won't go in. There's fruit at the front, and she doesn't know the names. She wouldn't know whether to peel them first or bite straight in. Another day, she'll buy some of them, to try.

The chipper has changed hands, but it's still the chipper. There are two men outside the bookies, having a smoke. They can't smoke inside any more. It's gas. Clean air, paper bags, apartments in Eastern Europe.

She'll get an atlas. She'll buy one.

— What about Courtown? she said, this morning.

— What about it? said Carmel.

— Are you selling it?

— No. Why would I?

— Well. How many holidays can you go on in a year?

— It's an investment, Paula.

32

— Oh. Yeah.

— When Bulgaria joins the EU the value of those apartments will go through the fuckin' roof.

An investment. They used to talk about *EastEnders* and their husbands.

The men outside the bookies are looking at her. They nod. They know her. They knew her husband. They were frightened of him. They were at the funeral. They shook her hand. Sorry for your troubles, Paula.

They're still looking. She can't see them, but she knows. Looking at her arse. Looking at each other.

Not bad for forty-eight.

She's never been in the bookies.

Someone's phone. It's ringing.

It's her fuckin' phone.

She drops the bag. The phone's in one of her pockets. God, it's loud. She's mortified. The men outside the bookies — where's the stupid fuckin' thing? They're so bloody small and loud, and not even a proper ring. Scotland the fuckin' Brave.

Nicola's present, this morning.

— Hello?

She's done it right. Pressed the green button.

— Hiya.

It's Nicola.

—How's the phone?

— Well, it works, love, says Paula; she's sweating now. — I'm fuckin' talking to you.

That sounds mean but Nicola laughs.

Paula couldn't believe it earlier, when she unwrapped the box and saw what was inside.

— Ah, Nicola. Jesus.

— It's just plain, said Nicola. — I can swap it for one of the camera ones if you want.

— Don't be mad, said Paula. — What would I do with one of them?

— Take photographs, actually, said Nicola.

The same Nicola.

Paula was still holding the box, turning it in her hands. The lovely young one on the cover, the phone at the side of her head, laughing into it. The sea behind her, yachts, the sunset.

She opened the box. Took out the phone.

— D'you know how to use it?

— I've used Leanne's, said Paula.

— Is hers like this one?

— This one's nicer, said Paula.

She smiled.

— It's gorgeous.

She's delighted with it. She's been looking at it all morning, holding it. Practising.

— I was just checking, says Nicola now.

— No, says Paula. — It's grand. I love it.

— I'm not far away, says Nicola. — Just up in Donaghmede.

Nicola's a rep for a sports clothes company. All those trainers and T-shirts and outfits. Nicola puts them into the shops. Or a lot of them. She has a company car and all. A lovely little car.

— Will I come down for a cup of tea? says Nicola.

— Ah, no, says Paula. — Better not. I've to go off to work in a minute.

She doesn't feel too guilty. Lying to Nicola with the phone that Nicola has given her.

— Use it whenever you want, Nicola had said, earlier. — Don't worry about the bill.

— God, Nicola, she'd said. — You're amazing.

And Nicola had shown her how to open the phone book, how to put in the few numbers Paula knew or needed — Leanne, Carmel, Denise, the doctor, the Chinese takeaway. Paula began to get a bit angry. She wanted the phone back. Nicola was bullying her, making her go too fast.

— Why would I want that? she said. — The number's on the menu.

— Ah, Ma. Stop being thick.

Nicola must have phoned Carmel and Denise earlier or the day before and told them about the mobile she was giving Paula. Because they'd both phoned her a couple of minutes after Nicola had left. She's a great kid, Nicola, the best. But Paula doesn't want her wrecking her plans.

A car passes. Nicola will hear it. Paula can't pretend she's at home.

— I'm at the shops, she says. — But I'm on my way home. And then I've to go.

— Are you having a nice day anyway?

— Ah, yeah.

— It doesn't sound that brilliant. Shops and work.

— Ah, Jesus, love. I'm forty-eight. I didn't want a Barbie.

— What about Ken?

— Ah now.

She laughs.

— I don't think I'd like Ken that much, she says.

— He's gone an'anyway.

— What?

— Ken, says Nicola. — They've got rid of him.

— Really, says Paula. — Why?

— Don't know, says Nicola. — They're not making him any more. I think.

Nicola has two little girls.

— That's strange, says Paula. — I'd better get going, love.

— Okay. Talk to you.

— Seeyeh, love; thanks.

Talk to you. Where did she get that from?

Leave her alone. Nicola's making something of herself. More than Paula ever did. And Nicola has her problems too.

She's at the café. She's getting nervous. It's ridiculous. She's only going for a cup of coffee. She used to be good at looking at men. She could look straight back at any age, height, shoe size. Charlo knocked it out of her. That must be it. The confidence, the guts — gone. Or maybe you have to be young for it. To hold a look. To stare without fear.

It's nearly empty. She sees that before she gets to the door. Just two people, Italian-looking, sitting at the back. Tiny cups on their table.

The door's open.

She steps in.

The smell is great. All the different bread and the little pizza things. The salami, all the tomato-covered stuff under and over the glass along the counter. It's gorgeous and nerve-racking. Even the cakes. There's nothing that's just round and normal-looking. She knows the names of none of them.

But it's grand. It's why she's here. There's a wet-looking cake that looks like a killer. It'll do.

There's a body behind the glass, waiting for Paula to straighten up.

A small woman, smiling. Dark, Italian. Paula smiles back. This is easy. She doesn't let herself look further, at whoever might be doing the pizzas, away to her left.

— I'm spoilt for choice, says Paula.

The woman smiles.

Paula points at her cake.

— Is there alcohol in that one?

She looks at the woman asking herself, repeating the question in her head. Strange question, she probably thinks.

The woman now points.

— This?

— Yeah, says Paula. — That one.

— No alcohol, says the woman.

— Grand, says Paula.

She's tempted. She could tell the girl that she doesn't want the kids having anything with alcohol in it. But she doesn't.

— You want?

— Yes, please, says Paula.

She doesn't even ask the price.

— And a cup of coffee for here.

The woman smiles.

— You sit, I bring.

— Grand.

Nicest thing she's heard all day. You sit, I bring.

She sits. She looks in the milk jug. There's plenty. She runs her hand over the wood of the table. She can see the methadone clinic across the road. The steel double doors are shut. There's no sign outside or logo. There's no one hanging around. It's the wrong time of the day. But it's in there. She was there herself more than once, looking for John Paul. She stood in that place feeling great because they were junkies and she was only drunk.

There's a cage over the only window. Maybe there's someone over there looking out, a nurse or doctor, looking across where Paula is. Maybe thinking the same thing as Paula. She's on the right side of the street.

She still hasn't looked over at the pizza oven. She isn't that fussed.

The coffee.

— Lovely.

In a lovely cup. Not that cheap china that's half-plastic, that sticks to your lip as you take it away. This one is a beautiful blue, no saucer. And the woman puts the cake, in a box, on the other side of the table.

— Thanks very much.

No mention of money. They know. She won't run off without paying.

Her running days are over.

Scotland the Brave. She's quicker this time.

— Hello?

— It's me.

It's Nicola.

Oh shite, she's caught.

— Hi, love.

It's very quiet, there's a roof over her head — she might get away with it.

— Where are you?

— At home, says Paula. — Just changing my shoes.

— I was thinking I'd bring the kids over later, to wish you a happy birthday and that.

— After work, says Paula. — Lovely. I'd love that.

— Okay. Eight-ish. They've done cards for you.

— Ah. The dotes. Bye, love.

She pushes the red. They'll talk later, while the kids are playing or watching a video. They might talk. Paula doesn't know. They chat but they don't really talk. Nicola looks after Paula. She checks on her — that's what tonight is really about. She was no good to Nicola when Nicola was younger, except as a bad example. But it's better now. She thinks it is — she knows. She wants Nicola to see that.

She adds her milk and tests the coffee.

God, it's lovely.

She thinks of something. She takes out the phone. She turns it off. She presses her fingernail into the hidden button at the top. She's not sure if she's doing it right. But the blue screen goes to black. It's off.

She's a good granny. She loves it. She felt nothing but joy when Nicola told her the news that she was expecting. That was the first time she seriously gave up the drink. She was clean and looking around. And looking after herself. And touching herself, and liking herself. She fell off the wagon that time, badly, but she remembers it as the start. She knew she'd always be trying to give it up. She knew she'd always be fighting.

Vanessa. She was the first. And Gillian, two years later. They're five and three now. Gorgeous young ones. Like their mother.

Like their granny.

And the two other grandchildren. She loves them. She loves it, the whole thing. It's added to her.

She looks away from the window and the truck outside the off-licence. Flavours. That's what it's been called for a while now. Shelves of wine from all over the world but kids still go in looking for cans of Dutch Gold. The bag of cans. She caught Leanne once. She'd hate to see Jack going in, watching him from here, in the sunshine. Having to deal with it. Or ignore it.

There's a new sign in the window. She can read it from here. Dial-A-Can. She won't be putting that one into her mobile.

She looks away, along the counter. To the end of the glass, and the ovens. There's flour in the air over there. Hands with a rolling pin. Good, man's arms. Flattening dough.

It isn't him. It's another man. A goofy-looking poor fella. Mouth dangling a bit over the pizza dough.

Ah well.

The coffee's gorgeous. Paula will come back another day, and the fella she likes might be there. He might even own the place. That might be his wife who brought her the cake. She isn't a bad-looking girl and the Italians always stick together. Look at the two guys down the back. They probably came from miles away just to support their own. And for the taste of home.

Would she do it with a married man? She'd do it with any kind of man.

Not true. She's fussy. Thirty years too late. She's a gas woman. But him being married wouldn't stop her. She doesn't think it would. She'll probably never know.

Enough.

She stands up. Should she go over to pay before she picks up the cake box? To avoid any misunderstanding.

What misunderstanding? They know she isn't going to run.

She leaves the box on the table and her bag of shopping beside it. She leaves the mobile on the table. She doesn't even look at it.

She drops two euro into the tips jar. She hears it land on more coins.

— Thank you, she says.

— Are welcome.

And work. The same as ever. And that's not too bad. It's boring and it gets on her nerves but she actually likes it. She's been doing it for years. She hates the travel. She always did. But it used to be worse, when she was drinking.

She feels fine. She feels good. The usual tiredness and stiffness. But she's calm. She's not desperate for anything. Just the cake. The cake with no alcohol in it. In the fridge at home behind as many things as she could pile in front of it. In case Jack or Leanne are rooting in there. They'd have it for their dinner. Chocolate cake and chips. Knives and forks and all.

They'd pour Bisto on it. They've had stranger dinners. But she knows. Hiding the cake is a waste of time. They'll sniff it out. Kids know. Even grown kids.

They're always kids.

They'll smell it first. One of them will. Whoever's home first. They'll look at it and wonder. And they'll remember. It's her birthday. Their mammy's birthday and they forgot. Then the guilt will get right into them.

Good.

Especially Leanne.

There's more to cake than chocolate.

The mornings when she'd been drinking. They were just fuckin' terrible. Running out of the house, when she could manage it. Not even knowing exactly why. Just knowing she was supposed to. Always catching a bus or train or missing the fuckin' bus or train — she's never worked anywhere she could walk to. She often went to the wrong house on the wrong day. She let herself into one house and she knew when she was pushing the door; she'd done the exact same thing the day before. She wasn't due for another six days. And the houses were miles apart. The wrong direction was a day-long mistake.

Another time, she got sick into a toilet while she was cleaning it. She remembers thinking: God. She remembers thinking: that's handy.

The good old days.

She's nearly done. She usen't to like this open-plan layout. She wanted walls between her and the supervisor, and Charlo and the rest of the world. Now she doesn't care. She isn't interested in hiding. These days she's the supervisor.

Paula's the boss. For two weeks now she's been the boss. It's nothing really. She still has to clean. And that's grand. She'd be bored if she didn't. The money's a bit better. Thirty euro more a week. It's no big deal.

But it's great.

Still though, she'd love a change. It would mean a lot. A start or something.

She's not complaining. She's still delighted.

The boss, Paula's supervisor, came in one day with new bottles of bleach and fresh cloths and mop-heads and the rest. She stopped and had her couple of words with Paula.

— The kids okay, Paula?
— They're grand. Your own?
— Can't keep up with them. I'll tell you though, Paula. Liam's college fees are a killer.
— Yeah, said Paula.
— And the grandkiddies? said the supervisor.
— Lovely, said Paula.
— 'Course they are, said the supervisor.

Give the woman her name. It's Lillian.
— I'll leave you to it so, Paula, said Lillian.
— Okay, said Paula. — Thanks.
— What do you make of the new fella?
— Hristo?
— Yeah.
— He seems grand, said Paula.

She didn't say more; she never would. But Hristo was useless.

— Okay, said Lillian. — See you so, Paula.

She walked away towards the lifts.

— Oh, she said. — I nearly forgot.

She told Paula they needed a supervisor for the fourth and fifth floors because Eileen upstairs was calling it a day. She was waiting for an answer before Paula realised she'd been offered the job.

— God, she said.

— That's a yes, is it, Paula?

— Eh — yes, said Paula. — Yes. Yeah.

Are you sure? she wanted to say. Are you fuckin' serious?

But here she is. Hristo's still useless and she's the boss. She'll sort him out. In her own good time. I insisto, Hristo.

That's another big change, maybe the biggest. The men doing the cleaning work. Nigerians and Romanians. She's not sure if they're legal. She doesn't have to know. She's not paying them. They come and go. They're grand. They're polite. She feels sorry for them. It's not work for a man; she'll never think different. The African lads come in dressed to kill, like businessmen and doctors. They change into their work clothes and back into their suits before they go home. Ashamed. God love them. Handsome lads. They deserve better. But everyone starts at the bottom, she supposes. But that's not true either. She knows it. There's nothing fair about the way things work. She didn't start at the bottom. It was hard work getting there.

But that was then. She's one of the tigers now. She's in charge of two floors.

44

She's nearly finished. She turns off the hoover. The silence is always a little shock. These places should never be empty. Just a few more desks to do.

She's not sure where the Hristo fella's from. Maybe Bulgaria. Maybe it's his home that Carmel is buying. She'd like that. She could introduce him to Carmel. Hristo, Carmel. Carmel, Hristo. You can chat about the EU together.

Now, now.

Nearly done. Then she'll follow them out, her staff, all four of them. She'll escort them off the premises. Then down to Tara Street. She hates that walk. Up to the platform. She hates the wait. Onto the Dart. And home to her cake and family.

Desks never really change. There's always the same stuff on them. The photographs, the clutter or neatness. She can tell each desk — man, man, woman, woman, man. She reckons she'd get ten out of ten. *OK!* in the bin — a girl. Manchester Utd sticker on the computer — a man. Unless it was put there before they sold David Beckham to the other crowd in Spain. Then it might be a young one. She bends down, looks closely at the sticker. It looks new — it's a man's desk. A young lad. Not long out of school. He'll come in one day and peel it off.

Leanne likes Beckham. He does nothing for Paula. He's a nice-looking lad but he looks a bit thick and he walks like he's wearing a nappy. And his white boots. He'll always be a little lad. You see them around, men who didn't quite make it. They get the wrinkles and lose the hair, but they still look like boys. Her husband now, he looked like a man. Charlo would never have worn white boots.

The last bin. She's done.

Hristo's at the lift. He could have been there all the time, waiting for her to make it okay. She couldn't care less. Not tonight. She'll have a good look at his patch tomorrow. She'll inspect. She will supervise.

He smiles at her. He fancies himself. She looks straight back at him. She likes nothing about him. Not one thing. And that's fine. He's looking at a poor oul' one. She can see it in his face.

So fuck him.

— Finished? she says.

— Yes.

— Sure?

He tries to look hurt.

— Yes. Of course.

— Well, she says. — Good.

She'll start being the boss tomorrow.

She waits for the lift.

She's never seen anything like the rain. It falls in sheets, then stops. Minutes later the ground is dry but the air is wet and oily. She's sweating drinks she had years ago. Moving, even thinking, gets her drenched. Her head — Jesus. This isn't fuckin' Ireland. It can't be.

But it is. It's out there. The accents are the right ones. The swearing, laughter, the shouted comments about the weather. It's her country alright.

It was stupid. Fuckin' stupid. She should have thought it through. She should have fuckin' thought.

46

She did it for spite.

It's not the heat. It's not just the heat.

It's everything. She'll go home tomorrow. It's the only thing to do. She's vulnerable here; she's lost. It's ridiculous. If Jack had come with her she'd be better. But that wasn't going to happen. He's too old now to be going on holiday with his mother.

His oul' one.

She's in her sister Denise's mobile home. She's sitting in it while last night's rain rises up around her. She can feel it seep up from the ground beneath the floor.

It's her own fault. She only took up the offer to get back at Carmel. She's stuck here in fluff — rug fluff, cushion fluff, lit by the sun and soggy. She hates the smell of the air freshener.

It's no place for an alcoholic. Alone, restless; alone. Courtown. It isn't even Courtown. It's near Courtown. But not that near. Nearer the beach but still a good walk.

She walked. She went to the beach. She sat like an eejit on her towel with a book. Till her back was sore and she had to stand up. Surrounded by families. But not really. The beach was quiet. The whole place is quiet.

— They're all going foreign, the woman in the mobile next door told her. — It's the smoking ban. They feel like lepers in their own country.

She walked down to the water. She took off her sandals and paddled a bit and felt old. She went back to the towel. She changed her mind as she started to sit down. She just grabbed the towel and the book and kept walking.

She's sitting in a sweatbox. The windows are useless. She doesn't want to leave the door open. The neighbour might come in. She doesn't want that. She reminds Paula of too much.

Mary.

The life and soul of the fuckin' party.

That's not fair. But she only really noticed when she stopped drinking, what fuckin' eejits people can be.

The Mary one next door.

— Come on out and have a can.

— Ah no —

— You deserve it; come on. Stuck in there all by yourself.

Paula knows. Mary couldn't give a fuck about Paula or what she deserves. She wants the company, but she'll drink alone.

— No. Thanks.

— Or a g&t. Or a little vodka. We've all of them with us, Paula.

Paula shut the door. She tried to smile as she did it. She sat down and held the table.

That was two days ago. There isn't the room here for avoiding people. She keeps the door shut.

Her phone's dead. She forgot the charger. She could get another one in Gorey. But she doesn't want to hear the lies. I'm grand; it's lovely; I'm having a great time. And she doesn't want to hear herself whinge. She'll leave it till she gets home.

Tomorrow.

She thinks about Leanne — she tries to. She thinks about Nicola — there's no room; she can't do it. She has her own things, her own problems. She can't get at them either. Her blood is hard. Her blood cuts at the corners.

She stands. She closes the curtains. Now she can walk, she can pace the caravan. Can they see her outside? Her shadow, her silhouette. Does her weight dip and lift the caravan? She doesn't care. She does; she doesn't. She'll walk all night if she has to. She'll stay in here till it's time for the train. She'll get the bus to Gorey just in time. No time to hang around or feel the pull. Those small towns are treacherous. Every fuckin' door's a bar.

She knows already. She's grand; she's fine. She's in charge again, she'll soon be home. She'll clean up, the little that needs doing. She'll pack, she'll go. She can trust herself. She knows she can. She's running from nothing. She's going home. She wants to.

Foreign the next time. She'll go somewhere foreign. Away from drink and familiar accents. Where she won't be alone or it won't matter. She'll save. She'll try. She'll get herself a passport. She had one once, years ago. When she'd thought they'd be going abroad, when there was money and Charlo hadn't hit her in a long time. She'd got herself a passport, the kids' names on it too. And the application form for Charlo. But he'd never filled it in.

She hasn't a clue where it went. It would be out of date now, even if she found it. And the photograph would kill her. Younger, less wrecked. But also sad. Too eager. Too near to Charlo. Too married.

She'll be home this time tomorrow.

She's on her way home from work. The Dart has just left Connolly. She has brochures in her bag. Dell, Gateway, Intel. She went into Peat's on Parnell Street. She spoke to a young lad in a white shirt. He showed her some of the computers. They all looked lovely. She hadn't a clue what he was talking about but she came away with the brochures and the prices. She hasn't mentioned it to Nicola and she won't. This will be hers. Her work is going to pay for it.

The weather's been desperate. Summer, my arse. It's cold. She'll need a coat before the computer. The old one gave up on her this afternoon. The sleeve fell off when she was putting it on. No ripping or anything, it just came away with her arm. The material was worn like paper at her shoulder. No stitching that could have put it back on.

She's always hated sewing.

Shaking fingers.

She threw it out, into the wheelie. And she didn't mind too much. She'll save for a new one. She knows she will.

D'you think it grows on fuckin' trees? That was what Charlo used to say. And she did it once — she looked up into a big tree, in St Anne's Park. When Jack was a little lad in his buggy, and Leanne was with her too. One of those big fat trees, a chestnut or something — she's not good on trees.

50

— Any money up there, love?

— No, said Leanne.

— Ah well. Your daddy must be right, so.

The bitterness was natural. But she should never have dished it out to the kids. More guilt. She didn't do it often. But she did it.

She's human, she's only fuckin' human.

They're moving again. Out of Clontarf station. Over the bridge. She used to clean one of those houses. How long will it be before Leanne is searching the trees for money?

She'll face it. She will — no running away.

— D'you like the White Stripes, Jack? she asks.

Jack looks at her. He has that expression — what's she on about now? She loves that look. He's had it since he was six or seven. It hasn't really changed as he's got older.

He looks at her.

Except in one big way. There's less fear in the look now. He knows she isn't drunk.

He looks at her.

— They're alright, he says.

His music is none of her business. She rarely breaks the rules.

— That sounds lovely. Who is it?

She asked it once, last year.

— Eminem, he said.

She stayed at his bedroom door and listened as Eminem told his mother to bend over and take it like a slut — OKAY, MA? She leaned against the door and smiled in at Jack, like a complete eejit. She watched him squirming. Caught and angry. She was sure the Eminem fella had good reasons for his anger. But she wondered about Jack, why he was listening to that stuff about killing your mother. Not that he wasn't entitled to. But anyway, she copped on. She closed the door and went downstairs.

All mothers feel guilt. She heard some woman on the telly say that. She saw her on that afternoon show on RTE. The woman was smiling. She had glasses on top of her head. She'd written a book about being a mother. For fuck sake.

A month later, she watched Eminem's film with Jack. *8 Mile*, the video. She had to sit there and keep her mouth shut. And watch. The angry young man, the alco ma. Slim Shady is Jack Spencer. And Paula was Kim Basinger. She wondered if he was putting her through it, making her watch what she'd done to him.

It ended.

— What did you think?

— Good, he said.

— Rough, she said.

— Yeah.

— He's a good actor.

— Yeah.

— What did you think of his mother?

— She was in the first Batman film.

— Was she?

— Yeah. When she was younger.

That was all. And that was grand. He rewound it and brought it straight back to the video shop.

She's stayed well away from his music since.

He's standing there now, one leg off the floor. He's scared she's going to say something really stupid.

— I was just wondering, she says. — Because I'm going to see them tomorrow.

— The White Stripes?

— Yeah, she says.

He's amused. He's outraged. He doesn't know what he is — he's confused. Maybe he thinks it's some mad date she's going on. It only dawns on her now. With a biker, or a chap half her age. Going to a gig with a fella.

She rescues him.

— It's just a job, she says.

— What?

— I'm cleaning up after the White Stripes.

— Their hotel?

— No, the place. Where the concert is. Way off, on the southside. Something Park.

— Marlay Park.

— That's right.

He's relaxed; the fear falls off him. She's doing what she should be doing. Cleaning.

— How, like?

— What?

— How do you clean a fuckin' park?

They laugh. He doesn't say fuck very often.

— With a big brush, she says. — How many'll be there?

He shrugs.

— Fifty thousand? I don't know.

— Jesus, she says. — That's a lot of ice-cream wrappers.

— How come? he says.

— What?

— The job, like.

— The money, Jack, she says.

My coat, your computer. She won't go that far. She'll handle her own guilt.

— Okay, he says. — Yeah.

She'd put the word out — Paula's looking for work.

— I have a little job for you, Paula, Lillian told her. — If you're interested. A concert.

It was grand. It didn't clash with other work. The money wasn't bad and they'd get her home when it was over. Once in, she'd be asked again. It could be very useful.

And it's a bit of excitement.

— D'you have any of their CDs, Jack?

— No, he says. — They're on the radio a good bit. "Seven Nation Army".

— I don't think I've heard it.

— It's good.

— I'll listen out for it, she says. — And anyway, I'll hear it myself tomorrow night.

— Will you not be working?

— I will, yeah, but my ears won't be picking up the rubbish.

It takes a while, but he smiles. He's a teenager. She often forgets. He's so old sometimes. Like Nicola was. Like Leanne wasn't. Like John Paul? — she doesn't know. She's not sure what teenagers are. They're probably the sign of a healthy house — a full fridge and teenagers. Hers were all good kids — or absent. They were too good really. Forced to grow up. Teenagers shouldn't have to wash their mother's face and hair. They shouldn't have to peel their own potatoes. They shouldn't get their first alcohol at home. They shouldn't be homeless on their sixteenth birthday. Junkies should never be sixteen.

She watches Jack walk out of the kitchen. She wants to follow him, pull up his jeans at the back.

He's never obnoxious. In a chat with other women about their impossible teenagers, she'd have nothing to say. She'd have to make up something. He's lovely. He organises his own pocket money; he works. He's good in school. He's had nothing pierced. He's made no young one pregnant. She should be very proud of him. She is — and worried.

He's too like a fuckin' saint. She thinks that sometimes. She wants to shake him. She wants him to throw things and hate her. She'd understand it. She'd cope. She doesn't really know his friends. She's not sure if he has any. She'd love to meet a girlfriend. She'd love it if he brought one home. Some gorgeous kid. She'd get a cake.

But she doesn't know his life.

She read a thing in the paper once — someone had left it on the seat on the Dart. *The Irish Times*. About gayness and the absence of the father. The mother made a gaybo out of the son if there wasn't a dad around to stop her. Because of the lack of balance and a male example.

He was some example, Jack's da. A man who beat his wife for seventeen years. In front of Jack and his brother and sisters. But Charlo was Jack's father and he died when Jack was five. So Jack hasn't had a dad. And no other man to show him how to wee standing up, or how to walk like a king, or how to look at a girl quietly.

Jack looks at everything quietly.

She'd love to see a girl.

She's being stupid. He's not gay.

She doesn't care.

He isn't.

She often points out women on the telly and in films.

— She's lovely. Isn't she, Jack?

The young one from *Spiderman*, or any of those kids from *Neighbours*.

— She's alright, he'd say. Or just, — Yeah.

He's useless, hopeless.

She's stupid. No boy wants to talk about girls with his mother. It's different with daughters. She could never follow a film when she was watching it with Leanne, when she was Jack's age.

— Oh, he's massive. Look at his jacket.

Every man from ten to ninety-seven had to get past Leanne. She'd fast-forward to the next fella. Paula watched *Ocean's Eleven* with Leanne but she actually saw about ten minutes of the story. Brad Pitt and George Clooney.

— Brad or George, Ma?

— George.

— No way. Brad.

— D'you not like George?

— I do; Jesus. But Brad. For fuck sake — sorry.

Leanne hasn't a clue.

Watching films with Jack is a waste of time, unless the film is good. It's actually lovely, just the pair of them watching quietly, the odd comment.

— Why did he do that?

— Don't know.

— But —

— Wait.

Jack telling her to wait. Like the dad, the adult. Teaching her to wait, how to watch and listen.

She likes Sean Penn. She'll watch anything with Sean Penn in it.

She'd love to go to the pictures with Jack. Or to the concert tomorrow. She'd love to go places with him, any place. To be able to show her pride, to walk beside him. Look what I've done, look what I've produced.

He's grand. There's nothing to worry about. She missed this part of it when John Paul was Jack's age, so she doesn't really know.

John Paul. Another thing she's had to face. Another one of her lost children. But they're fine, herself and John Paul. They talk. He calls to the house, now and again. She has his mobile number. He has hers. She meets his kids, her other grandchildren.

She can't help it — *other*. As if they're not quite hers. But that's not what she feels. She laughed and cried when she found out about them, when John Paul told her their names. Just like that, they were there and hers. Two more grandchildren. They're gas kids. They're lovely. God though, they scare her.

Marcus and Sapphire.

And their mother — Christ almighty.

Paula wasn't there when they were born. That's the problem — one of the problems. They were there years before she found out. That kills her. She deserves it. She's no right to anything, no natural right — she gave that one away. But no one deserves it. It's savage, ridiculous — they lived four miles away.

She loves them.

John Paul. Her other son. He's good. A good man. He's been through a lot.

There was no fatted calf. But he didn't expect one. It wasn't why he rang the bell. She'll never forget it. Nine years, four months and thirteen days. She opened the door. And he was there. And she didn't know him.

She isn't cleaning up after the gig. It would be too late and too big. She can imagine mountains of rubbish, work for trucks and diggers. She's cleaning up during. Wandering around after brats, picking up their crap. Doing what their mothers wouldn't dream of doing.

She's not complaining. It's money in the bank. Another thing she wants, a bank account.

She waits at the corner. It's August but it's bloody cold. It's always colder near the river.

She'd like that. A bank account. She's never had one. It's always been cash, or none of it. She's always clung to money. There's nothing like the feeling, cash going into her hand. The relief, Jesus, and then the excitement. The fuckin' drug. In your hand. She knows exactly what that means. The weight of it, the reassurance. She needs to know how much she has, exactly how much, now.

She likes the two-euro coins, the way they accumulate. They can become a bit of a fortune while her mind is on the notes. And handing them out; she's always loved that. Watching the little faces as they see what's coming at them in her hand. A two-euro bit for each of the grandkids when they come to the house. That's the rule; they see it that way. They carry the coins around all the time they're there. They don't know how to spend it. In their arses, they don't. But they're not greedy. The coin is a medal. They win it for coming to their granny's.

She'll never get over the terror of having no money, the prison of having nothing. Putting things back up on the supermarket shelves because the tenner in her pocket turned out to be a fiver. Stopping at the front door because the fiver she'd felt in her pocket was gone. Going five days before the next hope of a hand-out from Charlo. A present. That's what the fucker had called it. Buy yourself a few sweets. He'd burned money in front of her eyes. He put it down in front of her, a fortune, solid enough to be a million. He let her look at it. He let her wander the shops and aisles in her head, pushing a trolley with perfect working wheels. He picked it up — she didn't follow; she kept her eyes on the table — and he put a match to the lot. There's waste.

She'll always want cash, but she wants to hold a laser card and join the queue at the Pass machine. I earned the money I'm getting from this wall.

Jack has opened an account. He's been saving most of the money he's earning from work. It came as a shock, the letter in the hall. It wasn't for her. She saw that as she opened it. She stopped. She left it on the kitchen table.

— I had it half open before I realised; sorry.

— It's okay.

It was his first statement. He put it in his back pocket. But it wasn't there when she was putting his jeans in the washing machine. How much does he have? More than her? Of course he does. She's standing on a corner here and she has fuck-all. She actually has €23 and a few cent. Payday's two days away and she should do well tonight. And she might get a bonus, a goodbye present from one of the houses, the one she does on Fridays. They're moving to Prague. She'll be flush. Rolling in it. But her teenage son will still have more than she does.

She'll go to the bank in the morning. It means a walk but she'll do it. She'll open her account. Her own envelope will slap the floor in the hall. Paula Spencer. Private and Confidential.

She's to wait for a minivan outside Tara Street station. She's waiting with the junkies. God love them, and the kids in buggies, their mammies strung out or hurting — Paula doesn't know. John Paul did his hurting out of sight. She never got to hit him with tough love.

— Are you clean now, John Paul?

She asked him that the second time they met, a month after she'd answered the door and found him there, a young man in black jeans and a baseball cap. She thought he was looking for the milk money or something and she was going to put him right. But he moved and then she knew. Just the slightest move. He lifted his hand, and John Paul was in front of her. Back from the dead.

— Alright?

Her son.

And she'd wondered what he wanted. What he was going to take.

— Are you clean now, John Paul?

That second meeting. He looked at her, across the table. He'd left the baseball cap at home or in his van. She could see him clearly. She watched him remembering the kitchen, putting himself back in it.

He looked at her.

— Yeah, he said. — I am. Are you?

He knew. He could see the state of her. This was before she'd stopped drinking, this latest time. He was looking around him and it was coming back. He knew where he'd find the bottles.

But he didn't sneer.

He knew. She knows that now. But she didn't. He knew she was an addict. She didn't. She drank too much. She'd have admitted that. She was an alcoholic. She knew that too. But she didn't know what it meant. She drank too much. The way to deal with it was to drink less. She could give it up any time she wanted.

John Paul looked straight at her. And she realised. It made her want to die or kill him — he expected her to answer.

About time. The minivan stops and the door is slid open. She's climbing in before she feels the heat and she realises that the van is nearly full.

She gets in. There's not much room. Her leg is right against another woman's leg.

— Sorry.

No answer.

She looks around. She's the only white woman.

Someone smiles. She catches herself, smiles back. She turns to face the front. She remembers — she finds her seat belt and puts it on. She has to push and shove. She's like a cranky kid.

— Sorry.

She knows. There'll be no crack on the way. And no singsong coming home. No one speaks. It takes about an hour and it stops being familiar after twenty minutes. Ranelagh, Milltown, Windy Arbour. She doesn't know them. Dundrum. She knows the name — of course she does — but she's never been here before. She looks up at the new bridge for the Luas, where the tram goes right over the road. It's like a different city.

She doesn't feel uncomfortable but it's weird. She's the only white woman. And the only Irish woman — she supposes. The only one born here. The driver's white but he says nothing. He mightn't be Irish either, although he looks it from where she's sitting — his ears are Irish. He doesn't have the radio on, or any music playing. It's so quiet, it's mad. As if they have to stay quiet. As if they're coming up to a border crossing and they'll be caught if they make noise.

She looks out at a shopping centre. She knows the name. Nutgrove. She's heard ads for it on the radio. She can't remember the jingle.

They're going up a steep hill. She can feel it in the engine; she can hear it. It's like the city has ended and they've come right up to the mountains.

She's the only white woman in the van. What would she think if she was outside and the van was passing her now? She doesn't know. She wouldn't make much of it. Just that. The van is full of women and only one of them is white.

She's a failure. She shouldn't be in this van. She should be outside, looking at it going by. On her way home from work. Already home — on her way out again. Irishwomen don't do this work. Only Paula.

That's not true. There's plenty do what she does. Going to work is never failure. Earning the money for her son's computer isn't failure. The money comes from nowhere else.

Ten years ago there wouldn't have been one black woman on this bus — less than ten years. It would have been Paula and women like Paula. Same age, from the same area, same kids. Where are those women now? Carmel used to do cleaning and now she's buying flats in Bulgaria.

Enough.

She's grand. She knows how far she's come. She's not ashamed of work.

They must be getting near. There are Garda at all the corners and gangs of kids, all walking in the same direction.

But it's true. She's been left behind. She knows that. But she's always known it. She was never in front. Except when she first met Charlo and for a while after that. She thought she was winning then. Because she was with Charlo and people got out of his way. He never looked behind him. He never cared what others saw or thought — including her, but she didn't know that then. Anyway, that was the time she thought she was ahead of the pack. And, very quickly, she knew it wasn't like that.

She sits up.

They're going through a gate. They're in the park. She can't hear any music.

This is better. It's honest. She puts in the hours. She gets paid.

Do women her age go backpacking? Go to Australia and that other place — Singapore? Do they go to bed with men whose names they don't want or need to know?

It's looking like serious rain out there. The mountains and trees make the clouds look nearer.

Singapore. My arse.

Honesty. That's what she owns now. She thinks.

— Are you clean now, John Paul? she'd asked him.

— Yeah, he'd said. — I am. Are you?

— No.

He'd nodded.

There were parts of his father sitting there in front of her. The eyes, the forehead, the length of the fingers resting on the table, and the knuckles. But it wasn't

Charlo who'd nodded. There was no sneer or triumph. A good man had nodded back at Paula.

Her son.

She saw him to the door. She went back to the kitchen and she drank a bottle of vodka.

The man stops the van. They're in among other vans and buses, on the grass. It'll be desperate later if it rains, when they're going home. They'll be up their arses in muck.

— Right, says the driver.

He's Irish alright. She was right about his ears.

He turns around.

— Ladies. Out you get.

He thinks he's great. Just now — the power.

— Will you be bringing us back? says Paula.

— Haven't a clue, love.

He's a rat-faced fella, yellowy teeth. There's nothing on his face she'd like to know.

— You might have to walk home, love, he says.

— Fine, she says. — I like a nice walk.

She finds the handle. She opens the door, slides it back. She climbs out. She's stiff. It's cold. The ground is soft and wet. She can feel it in her feet.

She puts on her jacket — Jack's jacket. It's a good warm one, black, for school. He never wears it, unless she stands at the door and tells him to. Anyway, there was nothing else. She's here because she needs a coat of her own. And Jack's computer. It's grand. There's no crest on it or anything. It isn't a school jacket.

She can hear the music now. That bass sound kids seem to love. She can feel it coming from the ground.

She didn't know what bass was in her day. There was a bass player in every band but it didn't seem to matter. It wasn't what she ever heard. Which one of the Beatles played the bass? She still doesn't know.

The African women get out after her. They stand behind her. She's the leader. She doesn't want that but she doesn't want to move too soon, to look as if she's trying to get away. She's stuck. She smiles at two women. They smile back.

— Cold.

They smile.

What's it like for them? Are yis not freezing? It's a reasonable question. What made you come here? But questions like that must piss them off. There are colder places than Ireland. It's Marlay Park, not fuckin' Siberia.

They're not like American black women. The ones you see on the telly and in films. They're blacker; their bodies are a different shape. They're rounder women, bursting with strength. They like wigs, some of them, or bits of wigs — extensions. Going to work with purple hair. These girls have style.

They're young. She's the oul' one again.

— Girls, girls. This way.

Another man. He's waving at them. He's wrapped for worse weather than this. He's Scott of the fuckin' Antarctic. Or the Irish one, the explorer in the Guinness ad, who came back from his adventures and ran a pub. He has a black bag beside him. It's full — she can see that.

It's full of more black bags. He's handing out the bags. He'll be paid more than Paula. She'd bet on it. He dips in and gives her two rolls — twenty serious, heavy-duty bags. She holds a roll in each hand. Plastic bags always feel warm.

He lets go of his own bag and digs into his pockets. He takes out some plastic-covered cards. Laminated — that's the word. He holds out his hands to the women. The cards hang from his fingers. Paula takes one. WHITE STRIPES — STAFF. It's on a thin rope that goes around your neck. She hopes she gets to keep it. She'll leave it on the kitchen table. That'll show them. It'll give them something to be proud of, or envious. Or a bit of a laugh — their groovy ma.

Scott of the Bags points at a path that goes into the woods.

— Down there, girls. That's right. Happy hunting.

Jesus Christ, it's a fairy tale for big people. She's going to get lost in the woods. She's still ahead of the Africans. She goes slowly enough but they won't pass her out. She's the first one into the trees.

She can hear the music now. There's no sign of a house made of gingerbread.

Jack always hated that story. He'd take the book from her and turn the pages till he got to Snow White. Then he'd put the book back into her hands.

— Read it.

On the nights when she could read.

Everything seems well organised. There are big lights, like you'd get at a roadworks, for later when it's dark. But they're lit already. It's already dark. There are

67

barriers at the gaps in the trees, where people might stray and get lost. There are men in fat jackets at every corner and swerve.

It's not very busy. They're the only ones on the path. She hopes it isn't going to be a disaster, that no one will turn up. There'd be nothing to clean up and she'd still get paid. But she wants the experience. She wants to tell Jack all about it. And Carmel and Denise.

And Leanne.

The path is wider now. There's a car behind them. They stand aside. Is this the band on their way to the stage? It goes by slowly and it's only a Ford or something, an ordinary car. Being driven by one of the men in the fat jackets.

The path widens again and they're in front of a field. There's a fence all around it. She can tell. It wasn't there a few days ago. There are four straight lines, steel barriers, like you'd get at a football match for controlling the flow of people. Paula chooses one line and walks down it. The other women are right behind her. She's Mother fuckin' Goose.

A man looks at her staff card. He steps aside.

— Cold enough for you, love? he says.

— Ah, stop.

She smiles.

— What happened to the summer? she says.

— What bleedin' summer?

She walks on.

It's a woman this time, waiting for her. She's staring at Paula's card. She looks at Paula's black bags.

— Over.

She points. She's white but she isn't Irish. She's European or something. One of Carmel's Bulgarians, maybe. She's young. Good-looking but angry — skinny because of it.

— East, she says, still pointing.

That proves she isn't Irish. Just as well she's pointing. Paula wouldn't have a clue. Jack told her once, out in the back garden. One of the times she'd decided to make a proper garden out of it. South-facing, it said on the packet of seeds.

— Jesus, Jack, where's the south?

And he knew. He pointed.

— How do you know?

— Well, he said. — The sea's that way and —

— How do you *know*?

— It just is. So that means the south's behind us.

He pointed his thumb over his shoulder.

— But how do you know? she said.

She didn't doubt him. She knew he was right.

— Geography, he said. — It's easy.

She thought it was great. She watched Jack go to the back door, heading north. She could hear the Dart — and that was west. If she wanted a drink she'd have to head south. She couldn't remember the last time she'd learnt something. Carmel's house was that way, west. America was over the wall, a good long way past Carmel's. It all made sense. She was in the world, surrounded by it.

She never got round to planting the seeds. They're still in their packet, in the press, behind where she puts the sugar bag. She might plant them next year, in the spring.

The woman stops pointing.

— Bring the bags. To here.

Paula is on her own, heading east. There's no one following her now. The field is nearly empty. It would be hard to hide if she wanted to. The stage is huge. She's never seen anything like it. It's like something from a space film. There's no one on it. It's too early for the White Stripes. The crowd is small. It's a mixture of people. Some very young kids with their fathers or mothers — no parents together that Paula can see. Some of them are sitting on big inflatable chairs and sofas. A great idea. They must have bought them somewhere. Now she sees, way over at the end of the field, a hill of inflatable furniture. There's always someone with the right idea, there before anyone else. How do they do it? How do they know? Paula hasn't a clue.

The music is loud and fuckin' terrible but there's no one up on the stage yet.

But there is.

She picks up a cup, one of those big waxy paper ones with the plastic lid, for Coke and that. It's going to be dirty work. They should have given her gloves or something. Her hands are sticky already. Thank God it's too cold for the wasps. She picks up the cup and she hears the voice at the same time as she sees the young one on the stage. She's singing about someone sucking on her tits and wanting to come — something like that, anyway. There's no band, just the young one. And she's not that young either. Paula can see that now

70

on the big screen beside the stage. She's in silver hot pants, and wandering around the stage, like a little animal in a very big cage. She'd be sexy or interesting on the telly but, God love her, she must be fuckin' freezing up there. Whoever she is. She's climbing up the frame at the side of the stage. Anything to stay warm. Paula looks at the parents with their kids. No one's paying much attention to the young one. Imagine being like that and no one cares.

Paula picks up a crisp bag. A cigarette butt — she puts her hand down for it but she stops herself. She'll leave the butts. She'll never fill the bag if she starts picking up butts. Another cup. It's empty but she smells the lager. She drops it into the bag. The smell is on her hands. Around her nose and face. The field is full of plastic cups. She picks up another.

Leanne's there when she gets home. Paula's freezing. She stinks. She's expecting Jack. And it's Leanne.

It's grand.

She sits down.

The telly's on, the sound's down. MTV or something like it. Black ones shaking their arses, fellas with medallions.

— Turn it off, love, will you. I've had my fill of that shite.

— What?

She hears the click. She sees the screen go dead. Leanne did what she was asked. She's not gunning for a fight. She's been sitting and probably worrying. Where was her mother at this hour?

Cleaning the fuckin' mountains.

— Come into the kitchen with me, Leanne. I'm frozen. I need a cup of tea.

— Where were you?

— At a gig.

— What?

— A job, she says. — Come on. I must have walked miles today, and I went fuckin' nowhere.

She makes it; she stands up. Her ears are buzzing. The inner ears, the ones she remembers learning about in school, deep inside her head.

— Where were you?

— Marlay Park.

— Where's that?

Leanne follows her out.

— Up the mountains, says Paula. — Miles away; Jesus.

She looks at the clock in the kitchen. It's two in the morning.

She tells Leanne about her day.

— They made you clean it up?

— No one made me do anything, love. It was a job.

— God though.

— It's grand.

She's getting annoyed. What's wrong with cleaning? Even cleaning a field. But she stops herself. She won't let herself bark. This is good. This is nice.

— I got paid for it, she says. — And I got in for nothing.

— I suppose, says Leanne.

— And I have to say. They were brilliant.

— Who were?

— The White Stripes.

— Don't know them.

— Jack does.

— What sort of stuff do they do?

— I don't know what you'd call it, she says.

She watches Leanne making the tea for her. The big moves, the energy, even when she's just stirring the cup. There's nothing too wrong with that young one. She'll think that for a while. She smells her hands. They're grand. The drink is off them.

It had reminded her of the old stuff. Deep Purple, Led Zeppelin, Rory Gallagher. Good rock from the 70s. Her time. And Charlo's time.

— But, God, it was brilliant. I don't think you'd have liked it though.

— Why wouldn't I of?

— They were hard.

They laugh.

— You're fuckin' mental, says Leanne.

— You've never liked hard music, says Paula.

— Some.

— You used to hate it when I danced around here, when a good one came on the radio.

— That wasn't the music, says Leanne.

— What was it then?

— I don't know.

She does know. And so does Paula. It was the frenzy, the panic, the big fuckin' roar — HELP! A woman stopping madness by meeting it halfway. Leanne saw it. Paula dragged her around the kitchen. You're hurting me; it hurts.

Leanne brings the tea over to Paula.

— It was embarrassing, she says.

And that's fair enough, a bit like Jack.

— An oul' one dancing.

— Jesus, Leanne. I wasn't even forty.

She works it out, does her subtraction.

— About thirty-three, she says. — I was thirty-three. Jesus, that's depressing.

— The tea will help, says Leanne, the wagon.

She sits down, beside Paula.

— Thanks for this, says Paula.

She picks up the cup.

— Were you out?

— Yeah, says Leanne. — Not really. Just for a bit.

They don't look at each other.

— Were they good-looking? says Leanne.

— Who?

Now they can look at each other. They've been at this for years.

— The White Stripes. Who else?

— There's only the two of them, says Paula.

— Are they good-looking?

— One of them's a girl.

— Is he good-looking?

Paula tries to smell the air between them. But her nose is still full of the mountains. Their faces are close. She can't smell anything.

Postpone it. It's late.

— They're brother and sister, she says.

— For fuck sake, Ma. Was he good-looking?

— No, he wasn't. Strictly speaking.

— Ah, says Leanne. — One of those ones.

— He was just brilliant.

— And you'd let him have you up against a barbed-wire fence.

— Ah, Leanne, says Paula.

— Well, you would. Admit it.

— Yeah. I would.

They laugh.

Postpone it.

— And there was you, says Leanne. — Old enough to be his mother.

Paula nods.

— I'm old enough to be most men's mother.

— I wouldn't let that stop me, says Leanne.

She looks at Leanne.

The signs are there, the eyes, the skin. She wants to touch Leanne's face. The warmth, and the smoothness she remembers. She wants to feel Leanne.

Postpone it.

— Where were you yourself? she says.

She yawns. She doesn't need to. She doesn't even want to.

— Nowhere, says Leanne.

— Is that the name of a new pub or something?

— Ha ha.

— Leanne.

— What?

— I'm worried about you.

She wants to run. She wants to turn the table over. To do it before Leanne does.

Leanne's still there, still close. She hasn't moved.

— I've been —

Paula starts again.

— I've been a bit worried.

No explosion. But nothing else.

Leanne is silent, still.

How long have they been like this? Leanne sits still but, actually, she's jumping, frantic. She's out of her seat although she's sitting there.

— Yeah, says Paula. — So. I've said it. So. Leanne?

— I know.

— I'm worried.

— I know. I heard you. You're worried.

She's not looking at Paula.

— Yeah, says Paula.

That's all. It's all she can say. She needs Leanne.

— What about? says Leanne.

— Well, says Paula. — It's —

Jesus.

It's too much.

She's losing control. She knows she's shaking. She's dying for a drink. She wants to laugh. She'll tell Leanne — the happy ending. Later.

She holds the cup with both hands. Something to do; the heat is real.

— I know you might think I'm a hypocrite or something.

Where did that come from?

— I'd understand it if you do.

She puts the cup to her lips.

— Lovely.

That gets nothing.

She sips again. She feels the tea. She feels it crawl across her tongue.

Too much sugar.

— I'm an alcoholic, Leanne.

Leanne's eyes slide off her.

— I know, she says.

— I know you do, love. You've always known. But I've never told you and I should've.

She doesn't cry; she doesn't want — she doesn't need to.

— It doesn't matter, says Leanne.

— It does. But, anyway —

— What?

— Well, she says. — Leanne. Are you?

— What?

— An alcoholic.

— What? Are you mad?

She's stiff-solid now, in front of Paula.

— I am not.

Still there, furious — terrified.

— Good, says Paula.

Leanne says nothing. She doesn't move.

— So, says Paula.

She sips again.

— It's my imagination.

She doesn't want to accuse Leanne. She already has.

— Leanne?

— What?

— Am I imagining it?

— Imagine what you like.

— I've been there, Leanne. I —

— I've been there, Le-annnne —

She fires it back, and it hits. They'd laugh if they saw it on telly.

— Sorry, says Paula.

Leanne's still there.

— Can I ask you something, Leanne?

Another bad line — they're all bad.

— What?

— How —

She goes for the cup — she stops.

— How do you feel when you wake up in the mornings? Most mornings?

Leanne cocks her head. It's not good. She's acting.

She speaks.

— Remember when I woke up once and you were beside me and you were asleep? And your face was stuck to my pillow with your vomit. Do you remember that?

Paula nods.

— Yes, I do.

— Do you? Great. Because I don't feel nearly as bad as that when I wake up in — the mornings. I feel fuckin' great, actually.

Leanne moves. Every part of her jumps, like a puppet whose strings have been tapped. She raises her hand.

And Paula does too, to her face, quickly.

She tries to stop.

She puts her hands down.

— Why did you do that? says Leanne.

— What?

— Did you think I was going to hit you or something?

— No.

— You did.

She raises her hand, fast —

It doesn't happen. Leanne doesn't hit her.

Paula takes her hand from her face.

Leanne stands up. Paula can hear her breathe.

You're your father's daughter. She doesn't say it.

She has to look. It's gone if she doesn't.

She looks up at Leanne. Leanne is looking across at the back door, that direction.

But she looks at Paula now. She looks down at her. Her face is blotched. Her eyes are dirty.

She was never beautiful. Paula can't help thinking that.

She looks at Leanne. She sees the mouth.

— You thought I was going to hit you.

— It was just a reaction. When you raised your hand —

— Like this?

The fingers fly past Paula's eyes.

— Leanne. Stop.

— What? This?

The fingernail stings her nose. She's cut — she must be.

Paula stands — she's not going to be caught.

— What are you doing?

Leanne doesn't answer.

— What gives you the right to do that?

— What gives *you* the right?

— I didn't hit you.

— Not now.

— I never hit you.

Leanne doesn't answer.

— I never hit you. When did I ever hit you?

— He did.

— He hit us all.

— Yeah well, you fuckin' married him.

Paula's fault.

— Ah, for God's sake, she says. — What's this got to do with anything?

— And you did.

— What? Hit you?

Leanne nods. Like a headbutt. Her bottom lip is in her teeth.

— When did I?

— When you were drunk.

She has her; there's no answer.

— You've no fuckin' right to lecture me, says Leanne.

— I know.

— You've no right.

— I know.

— Just, fuck off.

Why should she listen to that? When you were drunk. Why should she have to listen?

If one of them would cry now —

— Is Jack upstairs?

— What?

— Jack. I don't want him to hear this.

— Who fuckin' started it? Accusing me. Of being like you. *You.*

— Stop, Leanne.

— 'Cos Jack will hear? Poor Jack. Jack, Jack, it's always fuckin' Jack!

Leanne loves Jack. She always looked after him for Paula. His little mammy. Paula always called her that and she'd loved it.

Leanne's hands are rolling over each other. Her nails are digging into skin.

— What do you know about me? she says. — What do you fuckin' care?

— You know I —

— I know nothing. Except that you haven't a fuckin' clue. I know that much. And it's more than you fuckin' know. And then you want to tell me I'm an alcoholic?

— And that gives you the right to hit me?

— I'm an alcoholic? Join the fuckin' club. Have a drink, Leanne.

— I never did that, says Paula.

— What?

— I never made you drink with me.

— Well, take a bow. Saint Paula of the alcos. She never made us drink with her.

— Ah, shut up, Leanne.

She could kill the little bitch. Paula's proud of how far she's come. But Leanne is mocking her and it seems so stupid. I never made her drink with me. Come up and get your medal. She wants to drink — her head is hopping. She'd break the bottle over Leanne's head. And the little cunt drones on.

— She made us go to school hungry, she made us wear clothes so that other kids threw twopences at us.

— Shut up.

— She made people move away from us when we sat down in the back of the church because we were late. For my Holy Communion. Because she couldn't get up on time, even though I tried to get you up and even brought you up a cup of tea and got a stain on my dress because of it.

Leanne is giving it all to her. And Paula just wants to slap her. What about now? she wants to yell. What about now? I'm sick of feeling guilty.

Leanne's still at it. Shifting her weight from foot to foot. It's only her hips are moving. And her mouth.

Paula's not listening. Get over it! she wants to yell. Grow up and get out of my house. If it's all that fuckin' bad. Get the fuck out, so I don't have to face you every day and feel guilty all over again.

She knows what her life has been like and what she's had to do to stay alive. And this bitch is kicking away at it, with her stampy little feet.

She's gone. She's not even in the kitchen.

Paula's alone.

It's three in the morning. Three minutes after. Has Leanne been yelling at her for an hour? It's not impossible.

I never made you drink with me.

Pathetic. If that's all she could use to defend herself. When she finally had the chance to take her punishment and listen, then admit and ask forgiveness;

all the conversations she's dreamed about and planned. But all she could say was that. I never.

So.

What's the point?

She won't sit down.

It's all so fuckin' dreadful. She doesn't know what to do. Can she even go to bed? The charge of a drink, the sprint to her head and pain — she'd love it. With ice from the freezer. She'd do it in style. She can taste it — she doesn't need to remember. Then she'd lie down.

But there's nothing in the house. She remembers throwing out the last bottle. Actually, she just dropped it over the back wall. Into someone's garden. It used to be Kellys' but there are other people there now. She doesn't know who. She hasn't seen them. Leanne probably has a bottle hidden. There's a charming thought. Two hours ago she'd have been upset. Now she wants the bottle. They can fight for it and reconcile, in the spill and broken glass.

She's not going to drink. She knows. Even if she found a bottle she'd forgotten about or if Leanne came down with a bottle of Smirnoff and threw the cap in the corner, she wouldn't drink. Not even to win back Leanne.

Win her back? She never had her. She gave her away years ago. She threw Leanne away.

It's one of the interesting discoveries. Sentimentality doesn't have to be soft. She threw Leanne away. An old alco's sentimental shite. She threw Leanne nowhere. She held her tight and slobbered all over her. Your mammy loves you SOOOOOO much.

But it's dreadful. That's rock solid honest. It's fuckin' dreadful. There's no sleeping on this. It's just dreadful.

So why does she feel so good?

She goes up to bed. She leaves the White Stripes staff card on the table.

She's in the café.

The coat will have to wait. Women like Paula don't wear real coats any more. Working-class women. They wear anoraks, snorkel jackets, padded shiny sexless things. That's why she can get away with wearing Jack's. No one knows. Not even Jack. Especially not Jack.

Where would she wear a good coat? She doesn't go out anywhere. She doesn't go to Mass. She doesn't go to the pictures. She's never been in a theatre. Work and the shops — that's it. Her sisters have given up on her. Her last text from Carmel was ages ago and it wasn't a party invitation. She was offering Paula a chicken. *Spare chkn. Wnt?* Paula didn't answer.

Shve it up yr arse.

She'll get the coat when Christmas is out of the way. A long one with a big collar. Soft — cashmere, or something like that. A coat that Melanie Griffith would wear, letting it slide off her shoulders to the rug, showing she's wearing nothing underneath. What film was that in? She doesn't know but she can see the coat. She can see Melanie Griffith's shoulders. She'd kiss them.

Where's Melanie Griffith these days? Paula always liked her.

The vegetable place across the way didn't last long. It's all closed up again. It'll be someone else's bright idea in a month or two.

She's here. But she doesn't remember getting here.

That's too dramatic. She remembers deciding to come here. It's not like she woke up in the place. She was over in the supermarket and she decided she'd come here on her way home. Because she was after buying a little notebook, and a biro. Because she wanted to make a list of the things she'd need for Christmas. Different lists. The food she'd need, presents, things to be done. She'd start on the lists and look out the window. So it's not as if she's losing her mind or anything. Going mad. She's been daydreaming. And that's nothing new.

She was miles away when she noticed the girl at the counter. The nice Italian young one. Smiling at her.

There's nothing wrong.

There's a mad one she sees on the Dart some nights. She wears colours that hurt Paula's eyes. Pink and orange DayGlo. Her eye shadow is always a half-inch to the left or right of her eyes. It's always red or purple. She wears stripy, odd socks. Pink ear-muffs, all year. And she whispers along to her Walkman. Paula sat near enough to hear her once. WE WILL BE TRUE TO THEE TILL DEATH. She was singing a fuckin' hymn. She must be well into her thirties. Listening to hymns on her pink Walkman. She's mad and she doesn't know it. She doesn't see what Paula and the others see.

Is Paula like that? Like, today. She's the woman they see every couple of days. The women in the supermarket, the girl here, people along the way. The woman Paula looked at in the bathroom mirror before she left — is that who they see too? Or do they see a mad one? The woman with the SuperValu bags. She's not wearing eye shadow or pink ear-muffs. If she had a Walkman she'd listen to Van Morrison or Deep Purple. Or the White Stripes.

She's tired.

She has the notebook on the table. She has her new pen. Jesus, it's some sort of sparkly thing. She thought it was just a biro when she bought it. But it's a madwoman's biro. She draws a line — pink.

She might as well use it. She has nothing else.

She's waiting on her coffee.

She hasn't seen the pizza fella since, the one she took a shine to in the summer. He seems to be gone. And she can't ask. Not today anyway, after what's just happened.

She was just suddenly there. Awake — she hadn't a clue. With a bag in each hand, standing at the counter.

She remembers being in the supermarket, at the till. She thinks she remembers taking things out of her basket. The feel of the chicken, cold from the fridge. Afraid her fingers would burst the plastic covering. She thinks that was today. But she thinks that every time she picks up a chicken in a supermarket. She's always afraid the blood will come through the plastic. She can feel the cold in the fingers of her left hand, picking it out of the basket.

And then she was here. The woman behind the counter was smiling at her — the usual way. Waiting for Paula to ask for her coffee and maybe a cake. The usual.

What did she look like? What do they see when they look at her?

She mutters to herself a bit at home, in the kitchen, wandering around.

Enough. She's grand.

She opens the notebook. She writes the names down the page. With her madwoman's pen. She can hardly read the pink ink. She definitely needs her eyes tested. Carmel and Denise need glasses for reading.

She writes the names. Jack, Nicola, Leanne.

She stops.

She tears out the page. The page says it all, the order she's written the names in — Jack, Nicola, Leanne. She puts the page in her jacket pocket.

She'll get a handbag too, when she's buying the coat. She might as well, go the whole hog. She heard a woman this morning, on Marian Finnucane. I just love a nice bag, Marian. I'm addicted to them. Fuckin' eejit. Spending thousands on handbags.

She starts again. The grandkids' names. John Paul's first. Then Nicola's two. Then Jack — he's still a kid. Then Leanne. Nicola. John Paul. Carmel. Denise. Nieces, nephews. The big, happy family. She can't remember them all. Denise's second lad. The one who did well in his Leaving. All sorts of honours. What's his bloody name? She knew it yesterday. Is that why she's suddenly keen on lists, because it's all slipping away?

She just wants to be organised. She wants to know what she has to do. How far she can get with the money she'll have.

Here's the coffee.

Kieran.

The girl puts it on the table, and the little jug of milk.

— Thanks very much.

— Are welcome.

Kieran.

She writes it down. It's a big list. It's taken two pages. And now she remembers, she left out two. Tony. That's Nicola's fella. And John Paul's partner. No-Arse.

The girl has a name and it's Carol. Except she calls herself Star. It's tattooed on the knuckles of her right hand. She did it herself. Paula will never need reading glasses to see those letters.

Are reading glasses expensive? Depends on the glasses. She supposes. She'll ask Carmel. She'll text her. *Glses exps?* She'll get the reply. *Spare pr. Wnt?*

Thank God for selection boxes. That's what most of these kids will be getting. And thank God for Rita Kavanagh, three doors up from her. It's 23 November and Rita has been up to Newry twice already, doing her Christmas shopping. Paula met Rita getting out of her car last week and the car was stuffed with bags, mostly filled with selection boxes. The whole back of the car was full of chocolate.

— I'm after saving a fortune, Paula, she told her. — It's a great day out. You should come with us. There's a convoy of us going up to Enniskillen next week. Jesus, the crack.

Paula's never been to the North. She suggested it to Jack last summer, a day in the train to Belfast. A big breakfast on the train, shopping for a few hours, maybe that tour of the black spots she heard about on the radio, and back to Dublin on the train. She'd have liked that, the day out with Jack, and the walk home through the estate with the Belfast shopping bags. But he wouldn't go. She didn't ask Nicola, because Nicola would have spent too much. And she never thought of asking Leanne.

That's a lie. She didn't want a long day with Leanne. Especially the journey home. Jesus, Ma, you'd need a drink after all that walking around.

She isn't going to Enniskillen. But Rita has promised to get her as much stuff as she wants.

— We're being robbed down here, Paula. And I'll tell you another nice thing about up there. The girls in all the shops and cafés and that. They're Irish. It's great. They know what you're talking about.

Those girls must be great if they know what Rita Kavanagh is talking about. Five minutes in the car with Rita would drive Paula fuckin' demented. She'd be writing on the car window with her mad one's pen. Let Me Out! But Rita's going to get her all the selection boxes.

She puts lines through the grown-up nieces and nephews. It'd be mad getting them anything. Carmel and Denise won't be getting anything for her older ones. Just Jack. Maybe Leanne.

She hates Christmas. She always has — or since she was a few years married and she realised she was poor and she was always going to be. She hadn't liked it much before then either. It always seemed a bit much for just one day. It was always a bit of a strain. She remembers going through the supermarket with a trolley full of six-packs and mixers and the rest. She couldn't make the trolley go straight. Jack was in the carrier part. She was afraid the whole thing was going to topple over. Leanne was pulling on the other side of it, asking for every biscuit and family pack they passed. And she actually — did she? — she smacked Leanne, until she let go of the trolley. She tried to smile through the whole thing, piling the stuff onto the conveyor. She threw a few bars of chocolate onto the pile, to make it look more normal, the expensive black chocolate kids don't even like, and Jack was trying to climb out and Leanne was snuffling and refusing to look at her. A chicken instead of a turkey and four bottles of vodka on the table. That was Christmas.

There were good ones too. But they were always a surprise.

Do Carmel and Denise know about Leanne?

Carmel knows everything. Denise knows nothing. They're a strange pair.

She told them about John Paul. It was hard to start but she doesn't think she was too embarrassed or ashamed. Heroin was so foreign. It had nothing to do with her. She'd thought that then. He'd walked into the house and he'd walked straight back out with the television. And that was how she'd started to tell

Carmel and Denise. It was so mad. Her own son. He was only sixteen. She hadn't seen him in weeks. She opened the door, he pushed right past her. Don't say Hello or anything. She watched him walk down the path, down the street. She didn't follow. As for the telly, she couldn't have cared less. It was only later, when Jack wanted to watch his cartoons, she realised what a pain in the neck not having a telly was.

— He's a heroin addict.

They'd probably known already. A lot of families had one — more than one. It was like an alien invasion. Nothing to do with them, but coming up the path. Junkies even look a bit like aliens. Like someone made a human but left out something — blood, colouring, something vital. It was devastating but safe. An accident. Nothing to do with her.

She looks at the coffee. She puts down the pink pen. She picks up the cup. She tastes the coffee. She hears the little voice inside her — this is me drinking a nice cup of coffee. She puts the cup down — this is me putting the cup down. She picks up the pink pen. She'll show it to Leanne when she gets home. Will you look what I bought today by accident.

She hasn't spoken a real word to Leanne in weeks.

Leanne hasn't spoken to her.

She picks up the menu. She has to hold it quite close to her eyes. There's a bit in small print at the bottom that she can't read at all, about vegetarians. It's in that slanting italic print. Even looking at it — it seems to shimmer — it makes her feel a bit sick.

The list.

She feels something coming. Something big and bad. She's dragging it to her.

The list.

She hasn't a clue what to get Leanne. Does Leanne still like music? She has no idea. Barbie was always a safe bet in the old days. Leanne and Nicola's room was full of Barbies, all of them sitting up and staring at Paula whenever she went into the room. She could still get her one, for the laugh. Melt the ice. Boozer Barbie — little bottles, one little shoe with a broken heel. Smashed-Ankle Barbie. The little medical card, the little tracksuit.

That's what's waiting for Paula at home. Smashed-Ankle Barbie herself. Leanne on the couch, in a dirty tracksuit, firing bullets at the telly with the remote control. She's been there for three weeks. It's no wonder Paula's going mad. Not one friend has come near Leanne. It's as if there's never been a previous life. Even work — Paula doesn't know if Leanne's job will be waiting for her when her foot is mended. She's afraid to ask too often.

Leanne called Paula. She was crying, not able to make proper words. She was in hospital, or on her way — something.

— What hospital, Leanne?

She didn't know; she wouldn't tell her.

— What hospital, love? I'll come and get you.

Leanne just cried. Paula was in the hall now, putting on her jacket, looking for the money to get her a taxi — where? — and back. She had enough. She'd been paid the day before.

— What hospital, Leanne?

— I'm sohhh-ry.

Paula tried to hear beyond Leanne's tears and gasps. A friend's voice, an ambulance fella — a word or hint that might tell her where to go. She ran out of the house. She headed for the main road. It was raining. She couldn't zip up the jacket and keep the phone to her ear.

— Mammy?

— Yes, love?

— Ma?

— I'm here, Leanne.

— Where?

— Coming to get you, don't worry. Where are you?

Eventually — Jesus — she got the name out of Leanne and she told her she'd be there in a minute. She turned off the phone and looked out for a taxi. She saw one coming. She put up her hand. The taxi slowed and did a U-turn.

— Where to, love?

— Beaumont.

— The hossy?

— Yeah.

— Are you alright?

— I'm grand, yeah. It's my daughter.

She was there quickly. The taxi driver was nice. He talked about his own kids and the dashes to hospital.

— I went to Temple Street twice in the one day. With two different children.

— God.

— I had a season ticket for that place.

— What was wrong with them?

She could tell that he loved his kids.

— Well, the eldest gashed his leg on a nail. That was in the morning. And the other lad started vomiting and he wouldn't stop. During the meningitis scare; are you with me? Straight back in.

— Was he alright?

— Ah, he was grand. They kept him in for the night just. As a precautionary measure. Put him on a drip. That's a horrible thing to see.

She texted Leanne. *On way.*

She was alone when Paula got there. She was calmer, but strange and far away. The young one who had wanted her mammy was gone. Paula never really found out what had happened. She sat with her. She held her hand. Leanne's hard, cracked hand. She watched women alone. She tried to smile at them. She watched men guard their women. She saw arms around shoulders. But who was she to judge? What did she know? An arm around her shoulders would have been nice. The pizza man's arm. Charlo's arm.

She sat all night while Leanne slept, and woke, and slept. It was a long time since Paula had been one of the women alone or John Paul had been one of the unconscious young lads. But the place was still the same. A war zone — worse now, when she was sober. She'd been hearing people on the radio, on Joe Duffy, giving out about people having to lie on trolleys for days because there were no beds. Now she saw it when she went to the toilet. All along the corridor, women, old men, people who might have been injured at work earlier that day, the day before, on trolleys. In rows, like a weird queue for the bus. There was a smell of smoke in the jacks, dirty toilet paper on the floor.

She took Leanne home three days after, in another taxi. She helped her up to her room and she helped her down again. She brought her food and treats and gave her the remote when she dropped it. She said Thanks at first. Then that stopped. Getting her to talk was hopeless.

Then she made the mistake.

— I'm just going down to the shops, Leanne. Can I get you anything?

The face lit up. She sat up on the couch. She smiled — grinned; the little girl who'd danced around the kitchen, trying to distract her father, trying to charm him away from her mother's broken body.

— Bottle of something would be nice, she said.

Paula tried to laugh it away.

— You're joking.

Still, the grin. Can I have an ice-cream, Ma? The little head bobbing. Can I? Can I?

— For fuck sake, Leanne.

The child's big eyes.

— Don't ask me, Leanne. Please.

She walked out of the room.

Leanne did it herself. She got up the next day and went to the off-licence. She used only one crutch. The other one was lying in the hall. Paula watched her struggle down the street. No coat or jacket on her. Using the neighbours' walls and gates. It was like she was climbing a cliff. Paula couldn't go with her. She couldn't go after her.

She went to work.

No one has come near Leanne, or phoned, as far as Paula knows. There are no names written on her cast.

It's not fuckin' fair.

She can't go home. She can't face the sight of her on the couch, the sound of the telly sliding from channel to channel, the bits of broken noise that do her head in. She'll go straight to work, with the shopping bags. She'll wander around town a bit. She can go to Smyth's, have a look at the toys for the grandkids. There's plenty she can be doing.

She's losing her fuckin' mind. She can feel it. She can put her hands on the cracks.

The list.

Jack.

She writes the word. She prints it. COMPUTER.

It's bought, hiding in Nicola's attic. In its big box.

She takes the last of her coffee. She holds it in her mouth. She knocks it back.

She found the extra hours. She worked. She went into the AIB and opened her own account. She chose a branch that wasn't the closest to home. It's about two miles away. The money that goes in stays in, unless she's prepared to walk. She isn't going to waste it. She wastes nothing. She's a rock of sense. She doesn't have a bank card yet. She didn't want one. She didn't want to touch the money until it was there, the exact amount. She didn't want to relax.

She trusts herself. She'll get herself a bank card after Christmas.

Does she, trust herself?

Not today.

It's not about money. It's about being careful. She has to be careful. For the rest of her life. It's killing her. She can feel it. Every word, every little decision. Chipping away. She wants to put her head on the table here. She wants to just give up. Not give up — but take a break. Not have to ignore Leanne. Not have to worry about Jack. To sit down and feel comfortable. To sleep. And wake up like she's rested.

She can't go on.

Why should she? Who's thanking her?

She's feeling sorry for herself. Fuckin' right she is. The blinkers she has to wear. She can't look left or right. Straight ahead, but never too far ahead. And no loitering — keep going, keep moving.

She's out of the café. She's heading for the Dart.

Leanne is coming at her. Going sideways on her crutch. She's hanging over the road. White-faced from the cold. And coming straight at Paula.

She stabs the path with the crutch. She was told not to put weight on the ankle. Paula was there. She heard the doctor tell her. But she's moving as if she has to keep the good foot off the ground. Like she's punishing herself.

— Leanne.

Leanne sees her and stops. Starts again, and stops. Paula makes sure she's not in her way. The street is empty. There's no one looking. She cares about that. It surprises her.

Leanne is skin and bone. Paula sees that, out of the house, out in the open. Leanne is dying.

— Where are you off to?

Leanne shrugs. She rubs her nose.

— Come home, love.

Leanne's knuckles are cracked and red.

— Will you come home?

She wants to reach out — she's put down her bags.

Leanne moves away. She doesn't look at Paula.

Paula picks up her bags. She can hear the crutch on the path. She goes home.

She pushes the door. She looks into Leanne's room. She goes in. She stays near the door. She stands there.

It's the Boyzone poster that does it. She sees it — it's been there, it must be ten years — and she's bending down, picking up the dirty clothes. Knickers, socks, a bra gone grey, she sweeps them all up in her arms. She throws them out, onto the landing.

She attacks the bed, gets the cover off the duvet. She bought the duvet three weeks ago, when Leanne came home from the hospital. She bought three of them.

The sheet — she pulls. It's worn, she can see the rubber sheet through it. She yanks it off. She hears it rip but she doesn't care. She feels it. It's damp, and stained. She'll throw it out.

She leans over the bed — she gets up on it and opens the window. The cold climbs around her.

She'll get new sheets today.

She gathers up the clothes on the landing, and the duvet cover and pillowcase. She looks into Jack's room. She throws the duvet over his bed. She flattens it out. She picks up one of his socks. She goes into her own room. She pulls back the curtains. She opens her window. She feels the cold come from behind her. The toilet door slams. There's fresh air running through the place. She takes her own jeans off the floor, a pair of socks, heels worn to nothing. She'll throw them out too.

She goes down the stairs. The cold air follows her. She'll put in a wash. Then she's going to make soup. She'll fill the house with the smell of soup. It'll smack Jack when he comes in from school. It'll get Leanne too, when she comes back.

She feels good. She feels calm. She feels hungry.

The washing machine is ancient. The door is going to come off soon. But not today. She has it shut without much of a fight. She's doing the whites first. They'll look good on the line, flapping away — she's always liked that sound — or draped on the chairs in the kitchen. The temperature numbers are worn off the dial. But the dial still turns. It clicks like a safe lock. She listens. She hears the water flow in. That's grand.

How long will she wait for Leanne? She'll have to go to work.

She'll stick with the plan. She'll make the soup. She might mop the floor. It's getting quite cold. She'll give it a minute, then go up and close the windows.

She has vegetables. Carrots, onions, enough potatoes. Two tins of tomatoes. Most of a bag of lentils. God knows how long they've been in the press. She takes them down. Something falls out, onto the floor. The seeds she was thinking of planting last spring. She picks up the packet. She shakes it. She feels the seeds. They seem quite big through the paper. Nasturtium — Empress of India. They look lovely on the cover. How would they be in the soup? She throws the packet to the back of the press. It hits the wall and falls behind the self-raising flour. She shuts the press door.

Leanne loves lentils. She loved lentils. The way they changed colour when they'd been cooked and the way they got fatter. She loved how they broke apart in her mouth.

— Nearly like biscuits.

There was once, Paula spread the cooked lentils on a slice of bread for her. An invention of their own. Just the two of them. After she threw out Charlo. Before he died, she thinks. When she wasn't drinking. She washed the little sieve — it's still in the cutlery drawer, in with the mess. She let Leanne scoop the lentils out of the pot.

— It's like fishing, Ma.

She emptied the sieve onto the bread. And they folded the bread.

— Quick. Before it bursts the bread.

Leanne's face. Bread and lentils.

— Is it too hot for you?

Leanne shook her head. Her mouth was packed, too full for chewing. Her eyes were huge and glowing.

Paula gets out the big pot. She gives it a wipe. She hasn't used it in ages. She fills it at the tap. She brings

100

it to the cooker. Jesus, it's heavy. She gets the gas going under it. She finds the lid. She gives it a wipe. She covers the pot. She washes the breadboard. She cuts the onions. They've never made her cry. She washes the carrots; they don't need peeling. She chops them. She finds the can opener. She runs the hot water. She fills the sink. She throws in the can opener. There's years of old goo on it. She'll leave it there for a while. She drops the spuds into the water. The washing machine is rattling.

She runs up the stairs — this is me running. She closes the windows — I'm shutting the windows. She finds Jack's other sock. She goes back down. She looks through the door glass. She opens the door. She looks down the street. There's no sign of Leanne. There's no sign of anyone. Most of the houses are empty all day.

The water's starting to bubble when she gets back to the kitchen. She gets the lid off the pot. She holds the lid with a tea-towel. She can feel the heat through the cloth. She gets the breadboard. It's plastic, not heavy. She holds it over the pot. She slides in the carrots and onions. She herds them all in using her knife. Nothing misses the pot. She's sure there's something she should do with the onions first but she can't remember.

She gets the opener from the water. She scrubs it and dries it. She opens the tomato cans. She's not sure about the mix, tomatoes and water. It's a long time since she made her own soup. She decides. There's too much water in the pot. She ladles some out, into a bowl. She empties the bowl. She does it again.

She peels the potatoes. She has too many. She peels them anyway; she's on a roll. She could go on peeling all day. She chops some of the spuds and slides them into the pot. And the tomatoes; she empties the tins. She holds them just over the water. The steam bites at her knuckles. She holds the bag over the pot and the lentils flow out slowly. She watches them float, and sink. She gets the wooden spoon. She washes it. She gives it a shake. She stirs the mixture. It'll start working soon. The house will fill with the smell.

She puts the last of the peeled spuds in a smaller pot. She fills the pot with cold water from the tap, to the top of the highest spud. She opens the fridge — there's plenty of space — and slides in the pot. They'll do for later, maybe tomorrow.

Jack will be home soon. The soup won't be ready. He can have some when he comes home again later.

Leanne. She has to concentrate on Leanne. The soup's for Leanne. The bedclothes, the wash — for Leanne.

She goes through the house again. She's looking for bottles. Leanne's gone looking for drink but there might still be some hidden. Paula hid her own for years. She thought she did. But Nicola took her around the house, another time when Paula wasn't drinking, and showed her every secret place. The back of the hot press, behind the toilet, under the polish and brushes.

She lifts Leanne's mattress. She looks in her wardrobe. She climbs right in. It's a flimsy, child's thing, not real wood. She feels it bending under her weight. She pulls back the wardrobe. She looks under the bed. She opens the window. She puts her hand along, under the ledge. She closes the window. Leanne isn't a mother. She has nothing to hide from children. Paula's wasting her time. There are no bottles here.

The room is a tip. There are cans on the floor. She taps each with her foot. They're all empty. There are cigarette butts, in a line on the sill, right over the bed. She's been smoking in bed. Drunk and tired, out of her face. Paula thinks it — Jesus Christ, she's as stupid as me.

She goes to the hot press. She gets down a sheet and a spare duvet cover. She can't go to work with the bed unmade. It would be cruel, like a scar, the rubber sheet exposed. She finds an old blanket behind the towels. She'll put it over the rubber sheet. It must be cold with only the sheet over it.

Why is she only thinking of that now?

Take it easy. Leanne's not a child.

Yes, she is. Paula will wash the blanket every day if she has to. She'll happily do it. She goes down to the kitchen. She fills the basin with hot water. There's just enough left. She brings it slowly upstairs. She washes the rubber sheet. She wipes it dry.

The new sheet isn't ironed. Paula hasn't ironed her own sheets since — she hasn't a clue. It's a waste of time. She's not changing her mind now. She pulls the sheet tight at the corners. She flattens it nicely. She's sweating. She gets the duvet into the cover. She knows all the tricks. She does this four times a week, in other people's houses. She irons *their* sheets. Eighteen different beds. Doubles, singles and bunks, bottom and top. Now she's doing Leanne's bed. She goes back to the hot press. She gets out two spare pillowcases. She goes into her own room. She takes one of the pillows off her bed. She brings it into Leanne's room. Leanne will have two pillows, to sink her head into. She's less likely to choke with two pillows; the thought smacks Paula's face. She closes her eyes.

The back of her mind, she sees — she remembers. She gets down and looks under the bed. A teddy, way back at the wall. It must have slipped down. God love her, she still has her bear. Traffic. That's the bear's name.

— Why Traffic, Leanne?

Leanne shrugged. Her chin rested on the new teddy's head. It was a present from Paula's mother.

— Just like it, she said.

— That's grand. Howyeh, Traffic. Sure now?

— I can call him what I want.

— Is it a him?

— 'Course.

She pulls the bed away from the wall. A second of terror — a syringe, pills — they'll fall to the floor. But there's nothing, just dust and the bear. She picks him up. She sniffs him — just dust. She climbs onto the bed. She opens the window. She holds him out. She leans out and she beats the bear, she batters the head off him. She closes the window. She puts the bear on the top pillow.

What's going to happen?

She hears the door. She goes out to the landing. Her heart is hopping — she's sweating.

It's Jack.

She calls down to him.

— Hiyeh, Jack.

— Hi.

The deep voice. She loves it. There's a squeak in it sometimes, like he hasn't got used to it yet.

She picks up the beer cans. She should hoover the room. She will if she has the time. She stands there. Her back is at her — it's been at her for years. Old injuries, the Charlo damage; she tries to keep them in the past. The scar on her chin, the pain in her back, the way she has to turn her head when she's listening to someone, because she can't hear too well with her left ear — they're the old Paula. The pain in her thumb is new. It's aching a bit, the left — Paula's left-handed. It's not too bad. She looks around. She'd love to paint the walls.

She goes down the stairs like a kid. Jack's making a sandwich.

— The soup's not ready yet, she says.

— What? Yeah.

It's years since she made soup. He probably doesn't remember.

— I just thought I'd make some.

He's cutting some cheese.

— D'you want a hand?

— I'm fine.

— I got some fresh bread.

— I know; yeah. I have it.

— Just in case you're using the old stuff.

— No.

— Lovely smell now, she says.

— What? he says. — Yeah.

She gets the tea-towel. She takes the lid off the pot. She lowers the gas. She watches the soup calm down. She slides the lid back across the pot. She leaves it open a small bit.

— You can have some when you get home later.

— Cool.

— I'll be at work.

— Yeah; grand.

His back is to her. He's eating his sandwich.

— Jack?

— Yeah?

— You've noticed Leanne.

His mouth is full. He's at the fridge. He takes out the milk.

— She's not well, says Paula.

He drinks from the carton.

— She's not herself.

He shakes the carton and drinks again, holds his head back.

— Would you not use a cup?

There are no glasses in the house. She threw them all out when she stopped drinking. It made sense at the time. It's ten months ago. She can be more exact.

He puts the carton back in the fridge.

— About Leanne, she says.

— I've to change me books, he says.

He moves towards the door. He picks his schoolbag up off the floor. It's falling apart but he didn't want a new one when she offered.

— Jack.

— What?

He stops. He looks at her.

— I'm trying to say something to you.

He waits.

— Sit down or something.

He doesn't sit. It isn't aggression. He's embarrassed, worried.

— Look it, she says. — She's not well. She has a problem. With her drinking. You've noticed.

He nods.

— Well, so, she has a problem. Like me.

She watches him redden. He's going to cry. She doesn't want that. But maybe she does. She'd love to hug him. She could hold his head. It would get rid of so much.

He stays where he is. He studies his bag. He messes with the strap.

— I don't drink any more. You know that. Don't you?

He nods.

— It's nearly a year.

He swings the bag onto his shoulder. She hears it slap his back. It nearly pushes him forward.

— But Leanne's in the middle of it. She's a mess, Jack. And I'm going to do something about it. And there might be blood and guts. I just wanted to tell you. Okay?

He nods.

— It'll be grand, she says. — But it might be — I don't know. Messy.

He nods, looks down.

— I'll never drink again, Jack, she says. — I shouldn't say that, I suppose.

He's leaning over, staring at his shoes — his skate shoes. He bought them himself.

— But, well. I know I said it before.

He shakes his head.

— Well, I meant to. But maybe I knew I wasn't ready and that I'd let you down. If I said it. So I didn't. But I know it now.

A few hours ago, she was giving up. She's a gas fuckin' woman.

He's still staring down. His arm goes across his face, under his nose.

— Go on, she says. — I've said enough.

He turns. He hesitates. He goes. She hears him on the stairs. She checks on the soup. It's looking good. She stirs it a bit. She pulls the spoon along the bottom of the pot. There's nothing stuck. She wipes her eyes. She puts the lid back on the pot.

She hears Jack on the stairs. He calls from the hall.

— Seeyeh.

— Seeyeh later, Jack. Have some of the soup when you come home.

— Yeah; seeyeh.

She hears the door. She hears the gas hiss under the pot as the outside air rushes in. She feels the cold. He shuts the door. She wipes her eyes.

Should she look for Leanne, or what? She needs to move. No. It would be a mistake.

She has to wait. But she has to go to work.

She checks the gas.

She's hungry.

She goes out to the hall. She opens the press under the stairs. She takes out the hoover. The flex is stuck in there. She pulls it — it's stuck. She pulls. She hears something fall in the dark of the press. There's no bulb in there. There hasn't been for years. The flex comes out this time. She gathers it up. It used to go right into the hoover, when you put your foot on the button at the side. The kids loved doing it. She picks up the hoover. She brings it upstairs to Leanne's room.

Paula's in bed now. It's later. She misses her second pillow. She feels too flat, too close to the mattress.

She gets out of the bed. It's cold. She closes the door over before she turns on the light. She hadn't shut it when she was going to bed. She wants to hear.

She gets her hoodie from the floor. It's an old one of Jack's, too small for him now. It's black and plain, with TONY HAWK across the front in yellow. It's nice, but she mightn't wear it again. People smile when they see it. An oul' one wearing a skateboarder's hoodie. She bought it for Jack three years ago. He loved it.

She folds it up. She puts it under her pillow. She opens the top drawer of her press. She tries to stop it groaning. She holds it tight, up off the hinge thing. Her thumb is still sore, still there. It's how she imagines arthritis. She takes out another jumper. It's a soft one and probably expensive — Nicola gave it to her, something she'd bought for herself, then didn't want. So Paula doesn't feel too bad about not wanting it either. She doesn't like the colour. She doesn't even know the colour. She folds it and puts it on top of the hoodie, under her pillow.

She finds the tub of skin cream beside the bed, where she dropped it. The tub is nearly empty; E45. It's Leanne's, for her dry skin. Although she hasn't been using it. Leanne's skin is red raw in places, like it used to be when she was a little one. Her neck, her wrists — it's horrible.

Paula gets the lid off the tub. She puts two fingers into the cream. She puts the fingers to her head, just over her forehead, the small patch where it still hurts. She rubs the cream in gently through her hair, to the skin. The coolness is nice. The cream softens the little hills and clots of blood. It isn't too bad. And it doesn't look bad; she's seen that already. She puts the lid back on the cream. She drops the tub beside the bed. She moves it with her foot, where she'll be able to reach it.

She turns off the light. She opens the door a bit more. She gets back into bed. She rubs her legs. She rubs her arms. She pulls the duvet up over her chin. The pillow's a bit better with the jumpers tucked under it.

She listens.

Leanne is in her room. She might be asleep. She probably is.

She came home before Paula went to work. Paula heard the key in the lock. She had her jacket on. She was already late. She took off her jacket. She threw it on a chair — she was in the kitchen. She took the lid off the soup. She dropped it — she caught it. She gave the soup a stir. She turned on the gas. She hummed. She heard herself and stopped.

Leanne didn't come into the kitchen.

— Is that you, Leanne?

She'd gone straight to the couch — she must have. Paula went out to the hall. Leanne was there. Leaning against the wall. She was still, but wheezing. And sweating across her grey skin.

Her daughter.

Could you force yourself to love your own child?

Holding her off-licence bag.

Paula grabbed Leanne. She got her arms around her. Her knuckles rubbed against the wall.

— Leanne, love.

She held her, and smelt her. She pressed her hand against Leanne's head and tried to get it — gently — to her shoulder. Leanne didn't stop her. But it was awkward. She was stiff. Paula rubbed her back. The feel of her tracksuit top was horrible, like carpet with a hardened spill in it.

She held her.

That was all.

She'd missed her Dart. The light was going; winter afternoon. The door glass was darkening. Jack would be coming in soon.

— Would you like a drop of soup?

— What?

— Soup.

— Soup?

— Can you not smell it? said Paula.

— Is that what it is?

— Yeah. I made it.

— Oh, said Leanne. — I thought it was just something burning.

She was still Leanne.

— Yeh bitch, said Paula.

She still held her. Leanne's arms didn't move.

Paula decided. She wouldn't go to work. She took down her arms. She looked at Leanne.

— Come on, she said. — Have some soup.

The hall was the wrong place. It was too like a cell. They needed the kitchen. Room to back off. There was no heat in the hall. Paula hated it.

She grabbed Leanne's sleeve. She tried to make it playful.

— Come in here.

Leanne limped in behind her. She'd left the crutch in the hall. Where was the other one? It wasn't in the house.

Paula grabbed a chair.

— Sit down there.

She made the move as Leanne sat down. She grabbed the bag. Leanne pulled it back. The brown paper ripped. Paula had the bottle before it hit the lino. Smirnoff. Three cans fell out with it, and a big bottle of Coke. They hit the floor flat and rolled. Leanne's hands were on the bottle but Paula held the neck. It was easier for her to pull. She was stronger too — that was shocking.

She was on her knees beside the chair. She had the bottle out of Leanne's grip. She started to stand up. She put the bottle on the ground beside her.

Leanne leaned out. Paula put herself in front of the bottle. But Leanne went for Paula's hair. Paula felt the fingers before she saw Leanne's scratched wrist right over her eyes, felt the weight of Leanne's hand and arm. She felt the fingers pull tight across her scalp. She grabbed Leanne's wrist.

— No!

She feels her scalp now. There's no hard, black blood there, demanding an excuse. I walked into a door; sorry. The cream seems to have lifted it away. She'll see in the morning. She pulls a finger over the place on her head. She's fine.

Leanne had her hair. She was pulling it hard. She was trying to get at the bottle with her other hand. Paula thought she'd have to give it to her. She held Leanne's wrist, right over her eyes. Her own thumb pressed into her forehead.

But it stopped. Leanne's hands were gone and Paula fell back. She sat on the floor. She was gasping. The bottle was beside her.

Leanne sat there. She was shaking, hiding behind her hair. It needed a wash.

Paula stood up. She put the bottle on the counter.

She went to the soup. She found the ladle. She kept an eye on Leanne. She had a bowl ready, the nicest bowl. There are five bowls in the house. This one was yellow, with blue around the rim. It was the last one of six. She'd had it for years. She remembered buying them, in the basement of Roche's Stores. Plates, cups, saucers, bowls. In a box with a plastic window that showed you the top plate. Springtime Classic. Charlo carried it home.

She lowered the ladle into the bowl. She poured carefully. She dipped the ladle again and dredged the bottom of the pot. She lifted the ladle and made sure she had loads of lentils. She poured the lentils into the bowl. When the bowl became the last one, Leanne decided that it was her favourite. It was her special bowl and it was left where she could always reach it. That was how it went, for years.

Would she remember it? Paula didn't know. She didn't care that much. The bowl wasn't the point. The soup wasn't even the point. The woman bringing the soup to Leanne, holding the bowl in front of her, not shaking — the woman was the point. She was always there for me. Paula heard some poor junkie talking on the radio a few days before, talking about her mother. She was always there for me. That was Paula.

She put the bowl on the table and she went back for a spoon. She had soup spoons. She'd bought them another time, when she'd had a few quid. She searched through the cutlery and got out a soup spoon. She got two. She'd have some herself. She was starving.

She put the spoon beside Leanne's bowl.

— There.

She was fine. It hadn't really happened, the fight. Leanne had stopped herself. That was the important thing.

She watched Leanne pick up the spoon. She went back to the soup. She filled a bowl for herself. Cracked bowl, no blue border.

— D'you want some bread, Leanne?

— What? Oh. Yeah.

— It'll be nice. It's nice and fresh.

She put three slices on a plate and brought it over to the table.

— Butter?

— No. Thanks.

She went back to her bowl. She tasted the soup.

— God, it's lovely. If I say so myself.

— Yeah.

Leanne gathered her hair in her fingers and put it behind her ear. She held it there while she went at the soup.

Paula put her hand to her head. She looked at her fingers. There was no blood. She was sore but it wasn't too bad. She remembered her domestic science teacher, a mad oul' bitch called Miss Travers. She said it one day. We don't drink soup, girls. We eat it. Well, Paula drank hers now. She lowered it like a vodka and Coke, with carrots. And it was fuckin' lovely.

She put the vodka bottle up in the press. She got up on her toes and pushed it well back.

Then she pretended to go to work. She'd done enough, for now. That was what she told herself. Leanne got the message. And she'd see her room cleaned when she went up. Fresh bedclothes. The extra pillow.

She put on her jacket, said her goodbyes and she left.

She went into town. She went one extra stop on the Dart. She got off at Pearse instead of Tara, in case anyone she knew saw her. That waster, Hristo, or one of the others from work. She'd phoned in sick before she'd left the house. She'd tried to make herself sound croaky. It hadn't been too hard.

She walked down Nassau Street. The blood and the little cuts were hidden by her hair. She thought they were. She put her hand to her head. She kept doing it. Her hair seemed good and thick. She could feel little clots under it, just in a small patch.

She went into Trinity. She hadn't been there in years. She wasn't sure she'd ever been there. Jack would have fitted in among the students she passed. He looked no different. He dressed the same. Even Leanne — when she was on the mend. Leanne could be a mature student. Paula knew a girl — a woman — who'd done that, gone to college, after her own kids had finished with school. It wasn't Trinity but it was a real college. The place in Glasnevin with the Helix — she thought it was there. Leanne was bright. Leanne was the brainiest of her kids.

She came out the arch, through the little gangs of students, onto College Green. She went up to Grafton Street. It took her ages to get past the queues at the bus stops, along the Trinity wall. The crowds coming from the opposite direction — she had to stop and shift, and start, and wait. Grafton Street was a solid wall of kids. Girls in black hoodies like Paula's, and fat jeans — she didn't know what the style was called. Girls with their tummy buttons pierced, their bellies hanging out. Paula was in better shape than most of them. She'd get her own belly pierced. She'd bring it home to the kids.

She'd fall back on the couch and pull up her top. She was always there for me.

She went towards the top of Grafton Street. The shops were shut or closing. The bookshop near the top of the street was shut. That was a pity. She'd have liked a book. She was in the mood and she had enough money. She'd like to have held a new book.

Around the Green and then she'd go home. She thought she was doing it right, staying away for a while like this. Leanne had to decide.

There were people getting off the Luas. It looked gorgeous. She'd go on it one of these days. She'd go to Tallaght, on the one that went from Connolly. Off the Dart, straight onto the Luas. She'd make a day of it. She'd never been out to Tallaght. She'd have a look at the Square. She could bring the grandkids, Nicola's children. They'd love it, the day on the Luas with their granny. They run to her when they see her. They're still that lovely age.

She's still awake in bed now, nowhere near tired. But she doesn't mind. Jack can get himself up in the morning. But she knows. He'll be worried. He'll be wondering is she drinking. Is that why she isn't up? She'll just get up. It's easier.

She lifts her head a bit. She listens. She drops her head back to the pillow. She closes her eyes.

She came home from town. Leanne was on the couch and Jack was beside her. They were watching something — photographs of a woman, Before and After pictures. Then she saw the actual woman, screaming, being hugged by a younger, better-looking, woman.

— What's that?

— *The Swan*, said Leanne.

— What?

The bottle was on the floor beside Leanne's bad leg, with the Coke and a cup. Half empty. Half full. Would she have a limp for the rest of her life? There was a plastic bottle of pills standing beside the bottle.

— *The Swan*, Leanne told her again. — Have you not heard of it?

— No.

Paula sat down on the side of the couch. Leanne's head was close to her hip.

— What is it?

— Women get plastic surgery and you see them before and after.

— Ah no, said Paula. — And during?

— Yeah. A bit.

— For fuck sake.

— No, it's great. You get to know their stories and that. They've had tragic lives, some of them.

Paula laughed. She leaned back and hit her head off the wall.

— Serves you right, said Leanne. — See her?

— Which?

— Her. The presenter. The gorgeous bitch. She's Irish.

— Is she?

— Yeah. Amanda.

— Good girl, Amanda. And is that one the same girl in the photos?

— Yeah, said Leanne.

She sounded a bit proud, as if she'd just proved something. The Smirnoff bottle was at Paula's feet. She leaned down. She picked it up. She sat back up. She held the bottle by the neck. She didn't hide it.

— Can they do all that with surgery? said Paula.

— Yeah, said Leanne. — Big difference, yeah?

Paula would remember this. She knew. Her kids on the couch, herself, the bottle. Two alcoholic women and a teenaged boy, watching women being sliced apart and reassembled. And it was great.

She stood up.

— What's her story? she said.

She nodded at the telly, at the brand new woman. She was still screaming. I'm gorgeous, I'm gorgeous.

— She had very low self-esteem, said Leanne.

— Is that right? said Paula. — Does she still have it, d'you think?

— She looks happy.

— Well, if her self-esteem is as big as her tits there, she'll be grand.

— Ah, lay off.

Paula went to the door. She didn't hide the bottle. Leanne didn't say anything.

It didn't mean anything. These things were easy, these deals and promises. Never again. Paula had said it so often. She'd said it while she was picking up a glass. It meant fuck-all. The smiles, the hugs. They were the

119

sentimental shite that addicts love. She was always there for me.

She went to the sink. She turned on the taps. She ran the hot and cold water, full blast, so the smell and the taste wouldn't lift up and grab her. She got the top off the bottle. She poured.

Hme?

She texted John Paul earlier, to make sure she didn't waste her time. She'd done that once, before she got the mobile. She'd gone right across the city but they weren't home.

It's the last Sunday before Christmas. Two buses and a bit of a walk.

Hme?
Yes.
3.00?
Okay.

She's going out with the presents. Six days before Christmas. That's as near as she'll get. The new granny.

She has two of Rita Kavanagh's selection boxes. She has a Dougal, the dog from *The Magic Roundabout*, for Sapphire; a nice, soft one. There's a film of *The Magic Roundabout* coming out soon. Maybe she'll get to bring Sapphire to see it. That would be nice, just the two of them, maybe. Sapphire is four. Find out their birthdays. Write them down. She has a Tamagotchi for Marcus. Rita Kavanagh told her that it was what all the kids wanted this year. She'd been looking for a Tamagotchi for her own granddaughter.

120

— I've been through Newry and Enniskillen, she said. — Ballymena, even feckin' Belfast.

But she couldn't get one.

Then Paula saw Tamagotchis, dozens of them, in a little shop on Talbot Street that looked like it might be closing down soon. There was that run-down look about it. She bought three of them, one for Marcus and two more for Nicola's pair. She was halfway down the street — she was on her way to work — when she stopped and checked her money and went back and got a pink one for Rita.

She's doing her best. She's trying to like it. She's trying to mean it when she wishes people a Happy Christmas. She even tries to beat them to it.

She's exhausted. She's nervous.

Jack wouldn't come with her.

— Your niece and nephew, she said.

That was cheap but she'd wanted the company. She doesn't like going to places she doesn't really know. It makes her jittery. John Paul's flat is in Rialto. He hadn't offered to pick her up and bring her.

Jack didn't even respond to that. He walked out of the kitchen — that was his answer.

She might miss her stop; she has to be careful. It's hard to tell on the South Circular Road. It looks kind of the same every time she looks out the bus window, especially on a pissy day like this.

They dashed at her, the last time she visited. They had the SuperValu bag out of her grip and they were grabbing at the goodies before she was even in the door.

— What's in it, missis?

She laughed.

— She's your granny, said — what was Paula supposed to call her?

Star.

Their mother. John Paul's partner.

— Oh yeah, said Marcus.

— Is she? said Sapphire. — Are you?

— Yes, said Paula.

They've been to her house since, five times. John Paul brought them. Star stayed at home. The last time, Leanne was on the couch, asleep. Little Marcus hit her with the crutch. She didn't wake up. Jack looked at them all, nodded and went out. John Paul put on cartoons for the kids and left them on the floor, with Leanne on the couch behind them. They didn't stay there. Paula could hear them upstairs, all over the place — she heard something break; she thought she did. They charged into the kitchen, charged out, back up the stairs. While Paula and John Paul tried to talk to each other.

She's off the bus. She knows the way now. She holds the bag close to her chest. Her hand holds it shut. She doesn't want the rain wrecking the wrapping paper.

John Paul's not a talker. He doesn't chat. He's in control; he can never let go. It's a powerful thing. But it's frightening. He manages every part of himself, like a sheepdog at the sheep. A loose hand on the table gets pulled back in. His lips never curl. He doesn't sigh. Every word is examined before it's let out. He's worked very hard. Wherever he got this strength, he didn't get it

122

from his father. There are parts of John Paul that are Charlo, but Charlo was never in control. He could never have stopped and turned.

Paula did.

John Paul did. But, God. She even asked him.

— Are you religious, John Paul?

— No.

He said no more.

She was a bit surprised. It would have made sense. He's like some kind of a preacher, from an old film. A man in black. A preacher who doesn't say much.

There's none of the child in John Paul. There's nothing about him that brings a rush. He was a jumpy kid, always flying. Looking everywhere but taking nothing in. Adorable, because he was heading the wrong way. People patted John Paul, when they could catch him. He was a stupid kind of kid and she'd loved him more for that. She'd laughed. She'd shaken her head. She sat beside him as his stomach was pumped. She was drunk, and hating herself; they were some double act that night. He was fourteen. She learnt nothing. He was addicted to heroin; he was gone from the house before she started looking for signs. He was months gone before she really lost him. She moved through fat, yellow fog. Dead husband, dead son. Then this man rang the bell. Alright?

She thinks this is the corner. Then they're down a bit to the left.

It isn't that John Paul has become a hard, solid man. She doesn't think he goes to a gym.

— Have you been in jail, John Paul?

— No.

He doesn't have the powerful arms, pulling at his T-shirt. He always wears a black T-shirt. He's not as well-built as his father. A little different, a little less, and he'd be scrawny. But he holds himself up; he pulls himself out of his size. She's wondered if he's involved in anything bad. She can't help it. There's so much that makes no sense. Does he collect money? Protection? Is he even a bouncer?

— What do you do, John Paul?

— Work?

— Yeah.

— Drive a van.

— Oh.

— Mine, he said. — I've an ad in the *Herald*.

— Oh.

— People moving. Want anything moved. I do it.

John Paul never shrugs.

She rings the bell. She hears it inside. The flat is half a house. The bottom half. She hears a door. She hears feet. There's no glass in this door. She'd like one like it. The door opens.

He smiles. He decides to smile. She's being unfair; she's a bitch. She's watching a miracle. She should be down on her fuckin' knees.

He stands back.

— Come in.

The kids are behind him, beside him, trying to get through. He uses his legs to block their way.

— Let her in, let her in. She's soaked.

He adores them. She can hear it. They're in and out of his legs. Sapphire whacks his arse, like that's what it's there for.

Suddenly, Paula wants to cry. She catches herself. She laughs.

— It's the granny-woman!

That's Sapphire again. Paula is the old woman who isn't her granny, but is.

The hall isn't theirs. They share with upstairs. There are two bikes and a buggy, and a hoover. Her leg hits a pedal as she gets past one of the bikes. The front wheel bends towards the wall but the bike stays up. There are marks, a line of them, all along the wallpaper, right to the back of the hall, where handlebars have scratched and stained. The hoover looks better than hers.

She feels hands on the SuperValu bag. She laughs but she holds tight and pulls it back. She follows them in, straight into the living room.

And Star.

Paula will never like her. She doesn't know how much it matters. The letters on her knuckles, they scare Paula. She's skinny and fat in the same body. Her legs are skinny, withered-looking. Paula has seen that when Star is sitting down. It happens to a lot of women, and men too, who drink for years. Their legs become like the legs on a wading bird, a stork or something. It didn't happen to Paula. And Star doesn't seem to have a proper arse. But she has a bit of a gut that hangs over the elastic of her pants. There's the red mark from the elastic whenever she moves; the pants are always sliding off her. She hitches them up. She's not an attractive woman.

But that's not it, although Paula would love to see someone glowing and gorgeous for John Paul. She's vain about her children. They're all handsome — or have been. Star frightens Paula, and it's not just the tattoos. She has another one, a little tear, under her right eye. And another just over her arse, where her arse should be, a triangular shape, kind of pointing down. It's what Carmel calls a fuck-me-here tattoo. Half the young ones in Dublin have them. Nicola has one. It looks nice on her. She has the figure for it. It's not just the tattoos.

She's there now, smiling. Star doesn't like smiling but she's trying. Her teeth are bad. Bits of the front ones are eaten away.

Paula is smiling. They don't like each other and they know it.

— Did you come on the Luas? says Star.
— Does the Luas go by here? says Paula.
— Yeah. Rialto.
— Or Fatima, says Marcus.
— I didn't know.
— Yeah; it's great, says Star.

The kids are hopping around Paula. They're trying to look into the bag. Sapphire pulls at the wrapping paper.

— Can we open it now, can we? Granny-woman!
— Lay off, says Star. — They're desperate, she says to Paula.
— They're lovely, says Paula.

Star doesn't look like a mother you'd run to. She doesn't look like a mother at all. Maybe that's it. Paula looks at Star and she sees herself. She's not good enough.

— I'll go back that way, says Paula. — That'll be nice.

— You can get the Dart from Connolly then, says Star.

— It's not running at the weekends, Paula tells her. — They're extending the platforms or something.

— It is, says John Paul. — It's running for December. For Christmas.

— Oh, says Paula. — That's great.

She feels stupid, and hopeless. She came all this way on the buses. She waited in the rain. And she could have come in luxury — Dart and Luas. She uses the Dart all week. How could she have missed that it was running on the Christmas weekends? One step off her path and she can't cope. She wants to tell them how hard she works. She wants to show them her lists, and the lines through all the things she's done.

Star looks like a junkie. That's it.

Paula doesn't trust her.

— Sit down, says John Paul.

Paula takes off her jacket. She looks for somewhere to put it. It's wet but not too bad. No one takes it from her. She hangs it on the door handle. No one else is sitting. The kids are moving in on the bag again. They'll win if it comes to a tug-of-war. Why doesn't she just let go?

Star grabs them and drags them into the kitchen. They grunt and struggle; she really has to pull. Paula can hear her wheezing. She closes the door over, not quite shut.

It's just her and John Paul now. There's a small sofa. It's the kids' bed too. Sapphire told her the last time Paula was here. There's a tartan rug thrown over it. There's an armchair, black leather. It's nice. There are two straight-backed kitchen chairs, against the wall. She feels like an eejit. Why can't she just sit? She doesn't know how to behave. She's never been good in other people's houses; she's never liked visiting. But this is ridiculous. This is her son.

John Paul moves. He sits on the sofa. She sits in the armchair. She pushes back into it. It's a bit cold, the leather. She's not sure she'd want it. She still holds the SuperValu bag.

— It's not all good, says John Paul.

She looks at him. What's happening?

— The Luas, he says.

He looks at her. He doesn't sit back. His legs aren't crossed.

— The landlord wants us out, he says.

— Oh no.

— He wants to sell.

— Because of the Luas?

— Yeah, says John Paul. — The value of the houses around here.

— They've gone up?

— Yeah.

— Like at home, she says.

She doesn't own her house. The Corporation — they've changed the name — the City Council owns it. Charlo laughed, the time she'd said that maybe they should buy it.

— With what? he'd said. — You fuckin' eejit.

— It's mad, she says now.

— Might be no harm, says John Paul. — Might get somewhere bigger, yeah?

He looks at her. Is there something he wants? Is she being thick? If she was any good she could offer him help. Is that what he's looking for? For her to give him the money, take out the chequebook and a pen that clicks. But it couldn't be that. He's looking for nothing.

What is it she has against him? It's there, the urge to sneer. She doesn't know why. She really doesn't.

— Will you look around here? she says.

— Maybe, he says.

It'd be nice to have him nearer home. She could have the kids around and spoil them. She could see John Paul more often. She could get used to him.

The door to the kitchen is given a shove. Marcus comes in. Sapphire comes after him. She's been crying. Her face is blotched. Her eyes are tiny and black. Did that skinny bitch hit her? She looks undernourished.

— Ah, she says. — What happened you, pet?

She shifts in the chair, to make room for Sapphire. But Sapphire stays back. She rubs her eyes. She pulls her damp hair away from her face. She points at the SuperValu bag.

— Mammy wo-won't let me open them, she says.

129

She turns to the kitchen door. She sees Star coming in. She stamps her foot.

— I *want* to!

It floods into Paula — it's lovely. Sapphire looks a bit like Leanne looked, when Leanne had the hump, when she was working her way to getting exactly what she wanted.

— She's like Leanne, she says to John Paul.

He leans out and picks up Sapphire. Her face is cross but she's happy to be lifted. He bounces her gently, just barely lifting his knee.

— She's her own woman, he says.

— She is, says Paula.

The blotches are gone. She's happy there. But she's still staring at the bag. Paula nearly laughs. She wants to give in. But she doesn't want to interfere. They have their own way of doing things.

But the Star one there. She has that look. That hungry, mean look. John Paul's the one holding it all together.

She's going to be sick.

— Alright?

It's John Paul.

She feels the hot wave flow across her face. That's how it feels — a wave. A sick wave that takes everything out of her. For a second or two. Just oily, white heat. She'll faint.

But then it's grand. She's fine. She can breathe.

But it's worse. She knows. She shouldn't be here. She can't cope. It's too much.

They look at her. The four of them.

She smiles. She can feel her face again. She can feel the leather around her. She holds out the bag to Star.

— It's just a few things.

Star takes the bag.

— Thanks.

There's nothing in the bag for Star. Paula can't believe that now. Not even a selection box. She wants to take the bag and run. But there's nothing in it for John Paul either. She couldn't think of anything to get him. She really couldn't. She doesn't know him.

— For the kids, just, she says.

— That's cool, says Star. — But yis aren't to open them till Christmas.

— It's Christmas now.

— Christmas Day.

— Ah, Mammy.

Paula watches Star go to the window. She walks like a much heavier woman. It's getting dark outside. It's dark in that corner. Star bends down and the Christmas tree is suddenly there. Star has plugged it in.

— Oh, look at that, says Paula.

They don't have a tree at home yet. She's only thought of that now. She sits back. She's feeling better. It's nice, not guarding the bag. She's glad she's here. She looks at Sapphire.

— What's in them? says Sapphire.

— Not telling, says Paula.

— Ah, says Sapphire.

Paula looks at Marcus. She winks at him. He stares at her. Who is she?

John Paul came to her. He rang the bell. He wants her there.

— D'you want a cup of tea?

It's Star.

Sapphire and the little fella are at the tree. He's trying to get around it. He's very small for his age. He's getting in behind the tree. She watches it shift and start to topple. He disappears behind the tree, and reappears on the other side. The tree's still standing. It's nicely done up.

Star is standing at the door to the kitchen. It's tiny in there; Paula saw it the last time. They need more space.

Paula looks at Star.

— Tea? says Star.

— Yeah, says Paula. — Lovely.

— I know what's in them, says Sapphire.

She's squatting down, examining the packages. She doesn't touch them. The tree's shaking again. Marcus is back behind it.

She'll get a tree tomorrow. She'll make Jack come with her, to help her carry it home.

— How's Leanne? says John Paul.

She stops herself; she doesn't answer too quickly. She's grand, she's great. None of that easy shite. He'd know, and so would she. She thinks about it. She lets him see her.

— She's up and down, she says.

— Hard, he says.

— Yeah.

— She staying away from it?

— No.

He's seen Leanne. He's seen her on the couch.

— It's not as bad, she says.

Why is she saying that?

— She's on and off. She's sometimes grand.

She hears something fall. She looks, and sees one of the decorations bouncing across the floor and rolling. Marcus crawls out from under the tree. Sapphire is still on her hunkers, staring at the parcels.

— Where do you hide their presents? she whispers to John Paul.

He nods at the door to the kitchen.

— Her ma.

— Grand, says Paula.

Her mother's an addict too. John Paul told her that, one of the first times they met. It's a hard thing to imagine, a granny who's a heroin addict. But John Paul got there before Paula; it was hard to imagine a granny who's an alcoholic. He wasn't being vicious. She even smiled.

Star comes in with the tea. She has it all on a tray, three mugs, and two bottles of 7-Up. She walks slowly, carefully, staring at the tray. Her mother's been clean for years. So John Paul told her. Her father's been dead since Star was a baby. Why can't Paula like her? She's carrying a tray with tea for Paula. There's biscuits on it as well. They're on a plate and all. She's only a kid. Paula sees that. She's not much older than Leanne.

She'll drag him down.

— Here, Star calls to the kids.

Paula smiles at them. They don't see. They grab at the bottles. Star holds the bottles up in the air.

— Manners.

Her skin is white. She's right beside Paula. Her top is lifted way up. White and kind of lifeless. It isn't a young one's skin.

— We can't give them Coke, she tells Paula, after she's handed over the bottles. — Sure we can't, Popey?

Her name for John Paul.

— They go mental, says John Paul. — Should be banned.

Star bends over the tray. The tray's on the floor. There's no table.

Popey.

She looks at him. All through those missing years, there was someone calling him Popey.

— Well, says Sapphire.

She's back over at the tree. She's staring at the presents.

— One of them's a —

She turns, to look at Paula. To judge.

— Selection box.

— Not telling, says Paula.

She winks at John Paul.

— She misses nothing, he says.

Paula wants him in her arms. Fuckin' God, it hurts.

Nicola's downstairs. Her voice has been there all day, right below Paula. She's taken over the house.

Paula's sick. The flu — whatever it is. She came home from work two days ago and it hit her, bang. She's loving it.

134

She's too sick to read. She has the radio on but she doesn't have to pay attention. She was listening earlier, to Joe Duffy; people who'd been at the Tsunami disaster, who'd witnessed the whole thing. There was a woman still out there, somewhere, talking about how she was sitting on a balcony, having her breakfast, when she saw the wave coming at her. It destroyed everything, except the building she was in. And a man talked about trying to get home, and his kids swimming in the hotel pool, while there were bodies in the streets outside. She listened, in and out of it. She didn't like it, that she didn't care. Because she did; she does care. It's terrible. But she's sick.

It's just music now. She knows the song but she can't think of the name. It's Barry White — she thinks it's Barry White. Or it's Billy Joel. She'll find out from the DJ when it's over. It must be Ronan Collins. It's that time of day, she thinks — late afternoon.

It's 2005. She's not sure of the date, but it's the second week of the new year. But the people on the radio keep going on about it. Resolutions, joining a gym, finding more time for yourself. All that shite.

She's hot again. Nicola brought her a face-cloth, wet with cold water. She put it across Paula's forehead. It was a shock, then gorgeous. Where's it gone? She could bring it to the bathroom and wet it again, lie back and put it on her forehead.

She'll wait. She pulls the duvet down a bit. There's another song. One of those half-opera things, a duet in Italian or Spanish or something. She missed the name

of the last singer. Barry White died. A few years ago —
last year?

She smells food. She won't eat. Feed a cold, starve a
fever. That's what Carmel said, and Denise. And
Nicola.

Earlier — maybe yesterday; she's not sure — it was
dark and Nicola was sitting on the side of the bed. She
knew it was Nicola. Something about the way she was
sitting. The angle of her back. Paula said nothing. She
wasn't wide awake. She just watched Nicola. She could
feel her weight. It was pulling down the duvet at her
leg, like it was tucked in, a bit too tight. It was nice,
though. It was lovely. Being looked after.

It wasn't Nicola. She looked up, at the door;
something had distracted her. It was Leanne sitting
there. She looked so lovely, so finished.

Paula slept. She woke. The room was empty. She
slept, and woke again. Nicola was there. It was
definitely Nicola. She was putting the face-cloth on
Paula's forehead.

— Jesus, Nicola, the fuckin' cold.

— It'll bring your temperature down.

— I don't want it down.

— Shut up.

She was awake then, while the cloth was cold and
wet. Then she was gone again — she's not sure about
this. She woke. Leanne was there, sitting on a chair.
She was talking quietly, on her mobile. Paula didn't
move. Her head was buzzing; there was an ache, the
beginning of an ache. Leanne didn't say much. Yeah.

No way. Cool. A girl, Paula guessed. Leanne was chatting to another girl.

She slept; she must have. There was potato in her mouth, muck. Her mouth was dry — she wanted to shout. There were fingers at her, fingers hurting her, between her legs. She wanted to scream; she couldn't move. The fingers were hard, they tried to cut straight through her. She screamed — she couldn't. There were fingers in her mouth, pulling out clumps of white dryness. Her mouth was full of it.

Leanne was rubbing her shoulder.

She was awake. Definitely awake. Her mouth was dry, horrible. Her body was soaking. She could even feel the slickness on her ankles.

Leanne's face was close to hers. Her chin was on the duvet.

— Okay? said Leanne.

Then there was water, a cup. She sat up. The cup was at her lip. Water in her mouth — the dryness broke away. Drops fell from the cup and burnt her neck. Then it was nice. She didn't want to cry.

— Okay?

— Thanks, love. Jesus, though.

The sheet was hard under her. It was curled and lumpy and she was caught in the duvet. The hard fingers were still there, just beyond her.

— You were dreaming.

Leanne's face was back, close to hers.

— It wasn't dreaming.

— I was here, said Leanne. — You're grand.

— Yeah.

She sat up a bit more to get out of the tangle. To get away from the fingers.

— Yeah, she said again.

— Can you get out for a sec?

— Why?

— I'll straighten the sheets for you.

The air attacked her as she stood beside the bed. She rubbed her arms. She watched Leanne patting the sheet flat.

— God, it's wet.

— I didn't —?

— Sweat.

Leanne pulled the sheet off the bed. The duvet was on the floor. Paula bent down. She felt her head follow her. She took the duvet in her hands. It was heavy. She got it around her shoulders. She still shivered but she felt the circles under her skin getting smaller. Leanne came back with a sheet. The landing light was on outside. Leanne was limping. She stopped and lifted her hands. She disappeared behind the sheet. The sheet was the room. Then it rose, lifted. Then she saw Leanne looking up at the sheet, holding it, waiting for it to drop.

That was yesterday. She's lost a bit of weight. She went out to the toilet a while ago. She stood on the scales. Her Christmas present from Denise. What sort of a fuckin' present is that?

— I got it for the colour, said Denise.

Paula has lost four pounds, in only a couple of days. According to her slate-grey scales. She leans sideways, lifts her T-shirt. Her arse looks the same. It's red, from

138

where she's been lying. That'd be lovely now, bedsores. She's thinking too much. She must be getting better.

Someone's laughing. It could be next door. That sometimes happens. Paula's often thought there's someone in the house, but it's someone next door coming down their own stairs. She doesn't know the neighbours, either side. She's only seen them a few times. The crowd on the other side of her bedroom wall, they've only been there a few months. She's not sure how many. They're all young. Leanne thinks they're Russian. Jack says they're Polish. Three tall girls. Leanne says they're prostitutes or lap-dancers. Jack says one of them works for Google.

— How d'you know? she asked him.

— She told me, he said.

She watched the colour rise up over his face.

— What's Google?

He showed her. They went up to his room. She sat on the side of his bed. He sat at his desk. He had to go over the bed, around Paula, to get to it. The desk came from Nicola's husband, Tony. That's what Tony does, supplies office equipment. There was a scratch across the top; a customer refused to accept delivery. So it's Jack's. The computer's right on top of the scratch.

He went on-line. She watched him. It looked easy enough. Then he typed in something — she leaned closer to the screen — www.google.ie.

— It's a search engine, he said. — A bit like a library. He didn't look at her.

— What do you want to know about? he said.

— Jesus, Jack. Where would I start?

He hated when she spoke like that. She was supposed to be his mother.

— You choose, she said.

— No, he said. — You do.

It was nice, the way he said it. But she couldn't think of anything.

— Look, he said.

He typed in Thin Lizzy.

Her favourite group. He clicked the Google Search button. The screen was blank for a second, then a new page appeared.

— See? he said.

He pointed.

— There are 317,000 different sites.

— All about Thin Lizzy?

— Most of them, he said. — A lot of them would be just CD prices and catalogue stuff. But look at this one.

She watched him click thinlizzyfan.com.

— This is brilliant, she said.

— Yeah, he said. — Sometimes. A lot of it's just shit.

— Look at this though, Jack.

It was a photograph of Phil Lynott playing chess. She'd never seen this one before. It was a long time since she'd seen any photo of Phil Lynott. It appeared gradually, scrolled down. He looked great. Philip Parris Lynott. August 20, 1949 — January 4, 1986.

— Jesus, said Paula. — He's been dead for nearly twenty years.

— Yeah.

There was a cartoon flame under the photograph, flickering like the Olympic torch. And the words, Eternal Flame.

— There was no one like him, she said.

— D'you want to see anything else? said Jack.

— Put me in it, she said.

— What?

— Type in my name, she said. — Just to see.

— Okay, he said.

She watched him type. He was fast. She watched her name grow in the box. She watched him click the button. The page disappeared. It was blank for a second, then the new page was there.

She wanted to get away. She couldn't sit there.

Jack was laughing. He pointed.

— 575,000 hits, he said. — More than Thin Lizzy.

She stood up to see better.

— What're they about? she asked. — They're not about me.

She couldn't make sense of the list.

— I think they're about a woman who writes baby books, said Jack.

— Called Paula Spencer?

— Yeah.

— All of them?

— I think so, he said.

He clicked again, at other pages. She saw her name again, in heavy black. She was all down the page. She sat down. It was safe now; she knew what it was. She sat back. But she couldn't read. She had to get her eyes close to the screen.

— *Parenting Guide to Pregnancy and Childbirth*, she read. — I don't remember writing that one.

She put her hand on Jack's shoulder. He stayed still. He didn't try to escape.

— *The Happiest Toddler on the Block*, she read. — Can you get more, Jack?

He did the clicky thing. The screen was blank, then she saw a book cover. A smiling kid, American-looking, gleaming, confident. And she read the full title of the book.

— *The New Way to Stop the Daily Battle of Wills and Raise a Secure and Well-Behaved One-to-Four-Year-Old*. For fuck sake.

There was a Paula Spencer out there who thought she could do all that.

— I actually did meet another woman called Paula Spencer once, she said.

— Yeah?

— Yeah.

— Cool.

— At a funeral. She was my cousin or something.

— Whose funeral?

— I can't remember. One of my uncles, I think. I'm not sure. Your granny would know. I could ask her.

She saw another name. She pointed.

— Let's see that one.

"The Mom Next Door".

— That's me, Jack. The mom next door.

— Hi, Mom, said Jack.

— Hi, sweetie. Want some pie?

— Shove it up your arse, Mom.

They laughed. She put her arm around his neck. She couldn't feel an objection. He didn't stiffen or shudder. She let go and sat back a little bit.

There was a photo of a woman, this other Paula.

— That must be her.

She looked okay but kind of mad, her eyes wide-big, like the skin around them had been pulled back. Maybe it had. There was a photo of her children. And that was it. She looked like one of them. She looked like a child, kind of a withered girl, grinning. Trying too hard to please.

— Seen enough? said Jack.

— Yeah, she said. — It's brilliant though, isn't it? The Net and that?

— It's grand; yeah.

There's no more noise from next door. She heard them in bed one night. She heard the bed, when she was falling asleep. She didn't know what it was — it was something far off, barely intruding — and then she did know. A couple making love. She'd recognised the sound, the rhythm of the bed. She'd been pleased with herself, the mystery solved.

More laughing from downstairs. It sounds like a man. It isn't Jack. He doesn't have it yet, that deep sound. It could be Tony, Nicola's husband. But he isn't really a laugher. It annoys her, not knowing. She must be getting better.

The News is on the radio. It's after five o'clock. She can't hear it properly. That's fine. She'll turn it up when she hears the Angelus at six. She'll get the headlines. It's what she does. She stays informed. Sinn Féin are acting the maggot. There's a child gone missing in Cork.

She remembers the other Paula Spencer, the one she met at the funeral. She was a good bit older than Paula, but younger, probably, than Paula is now. It was years ago. It was the only thing they had in common. The name. It *was* a good one, though. They'd both married men called Spencer. She wore a headscarf in the church, the other Paula. They all went back to the house — whose house? — and Paula's mother introduced them to each other. They'd laughed. They were both drinking tea. She remembers holding the saucer. She wouldn't drink anything stronger in front of her mother, or her father.

It clicks — her Uncle Eamon. He was the one who'd died. Her father's brother. She won't have to ask her mother. That'll save her half an hour. Her mother's memory only works when she wants it to.

The door's opening. She hadn't heard the stairs. She tries to sink without moving. She pretends she's waking. It's Jack. She sees the silhouette.

— Alright?

It's John Paul.

That's twice she gotten them wrong. Nicola was Leanne and now Jack becomes John Paul. They're knitting together, her children; they're coming back to her. That's what it feels like.

— John Paul, she says.

— Feeling any better?

— I'm grand, she says. — Much better. Was that you I heard laughing?

144

— Don't think so, he says.

— I heard someone laughing.

He says nothing.

She sits up. She doesn't make a meal of it. It's not Nicola or Leanne. She doesn't want John Paul leaning over, punching her pillows. She's sitting right up before she thinks about it. He's a man. He's a stranger.

— There, she says. — That's better. Who told you?

— What?

— About me.

— No one. I mean, downstairs. They told me. At the door, like.

— I didn't hear the bell.

— I didn't ring it.

He hasn't moved.

Now he does. He closes the door over a bit. He talks as he does it.

— I know, he says. — You don't like the bell.

She's stunned.

— God, she says.

It's true. She used to hate the sound of the doorbell. It lifted her off the floor, every time it rang. It was always the Guards or some butty of Charlo's — bad news. It was reality, the end, trying to get in at her, taking away her children.

— That's long ago, she says.

She still can't see him properly, now the door's closed over. It's dark at the curtains. It's night-time. But the shape, his silhouette, it could never be Jack.

He moves. Slowly.

— One of the kids saw me.

He touches the bed. He sits.

— Nicola's. She was looking out the window.

His weight pulls the mattress down.

— What're their names? he says.

— Who?

But she knows who he means as she says it.

— Vanessa's six. And Gillian. She's nearly four.

— Must've been Vanessa, he says. — Strange.

— Not knowing their names?

— Yeah.

— You know them now.

She cries. She tries to stop, not start —

— Sorry.

He says nothing. He doesn't move.

She wishes he'd go, he'd get the fuck out of her room. She shouldn't have woken up, or pretended to. She feels exposed. The guilt rips through her — it never lets up.

— You're alright, he says. — Must get them together with my gang.

Nicola and Star. Jesus.

— That'd be nice, she says. — I'd like that.

— Yeah.

She wipes her eyes and her nose. She uses the duvet. She doesn't care.

— I'd really like that, John Paul.

He stands up slowly. She feels the weight go off the bed before she sees him move.

— We'll see, he says. — You know yourself.

She doesn't.

— Nicola's a wagon.

146

— She's great, says Paula.
— I know.
— She's been great to me.
— Yeah.
He moves to the door.
— Good luck, he says.
He's good. She knows that.
— Bye, love, she says.
Too late, it's out — *love*.
But he's still there.
— Thanks for coming, she says.
— No problem.
He opens the door. She doesn't want the light.
— There wasn't a reason why you wanted to see me, was there? she says.
— Leanne.
— What about Leanne?
— Came to see her.
— Oh. Grand. Great. Bye.
He closes the door.

Things are happening because she's out of the way. If she gets up now and goes downstairs, she'll wreck it. They're all down there because she's up here. She's at her own fuckin' funeral. They're having her wake downstairs.

She poisons everything good that happens. She was sick and they came to help out. They've been lovely. They're all downstairs. Her family.

What's he doing with Leanne?

Helping her, you fuckin' clown.

— What did he want?

She's awake again and Nicola's in the room. She's ready to go home. She has her jacket buttoned, and that lovely scarf with the red in it that makes Nicola's face look radiant. She doesn't know what time it is. She's really been asleep.

Her mouth is dry again. It's the worst feeling. Waking up old.

— What did he want? Nicola had said.

— John Paul? says Paula.

— Yeah.

— Well, she says.

She tries to sit up. She can't manage it.

— Here.

Nicola leans over, helps her up. Paula's not messing. She's heavy with sleep; she wants to fall back. She's not hot now, though.

— He came to see Leanne, she says.

— Did he? says Nicola.

— Yeah. He did. Is there any water left in that glass, love?

— I'll get you some fresh. Did he ask you for anything?

— Ah Nicola. No. No, he didn't.

She grabs Nicola's hand when she leans down for the glass beside the bed. She doesn't grab. She puts her hand on Nicola's hand.

— He's not like that now, she says.

— Maybe, says Nicola.

Paula pats the hand. It's a lovely hand. Paula can't see it properly, but she knows. The fingers are long and her nails are always perfect, never a scratch or a cracked

148

nail. Nicola has never let work or age get into her hands. That's the most amazing thing about Nicola, Paula thinks. Or what it stands for — they stand for, her hands. Nicola is in control. Nicola can manage. Nicola is much, much more than she's supposed to be. Paula adores her.

— He's changed, she says. — He has.

He's a lot like you, she wants to say.

— Just, be careful, says Nicola.

Nicola's right. Paula must be careful. About John Paul, about Leanne, about Nicola and Jack, about herself and everything. Nicola knows all about taking care. She's been looking after them all for years. They hate her for it. They hate her and they hold her beautiful hand. She's had her problems and they haven't cared. They don't want to know. She's been their mother, and mothers can't have problems.

Paula wants to be Nicola's mother.

She understands why John Paul's arrival worries Nicola. Nicola knows. One cracked nail and it's over.

She'll get up tomorrow.

Rita is getting something out of her car. Paula can see her, leaning right in. Her arse fills most of the open door.

Paula keeps walking.

— You're better, Paula.

Paula stops. She smiles. Rita's standing beside the car.

— I am, yeah, Rita. I'm grand.

— Your Jack was telling me you weren't well.

Poor Jack.

— It was just the flu, she says.

— It's everywhere, says Rita.

They stand there. It's cold. Rita's wearing a purple fleece thing.

She speaks.

— Wasn't that desperate about that poor boy in Cork?

— Dreadful, says Paula.

The missing boy has been found, murdered.

— The poor parents, says Rita.

Paula nods

— Desperate.

They say nothing for a while.

Rita sighs.

— We're lucky, Paula, she says.

This morning, Paula agrees with her.

Rita nods at her front door.

— The kettle's on.

Paula follows her, past the car, into the hall. Over the white carpet — Paula's sure she can hear it breathing. She follows Rita into the kitchen.

— We'll crack open a tin of biscuits, says Rita. — I've a few tins of those Fox's Assortment left over.

Paula puts down her SuperValu bag. She takes off her jacket. She watches Rita tear the tape off the lid of the biscuit tin.

— Jesus, says Rita. — They're fierce generous with the tape.

Paula can't help it; she's excited.

150

— I could hold onto them till next Christmas, I suppose, says Rita.

She pulls the lid off the tin.

— Too late now, says you.

She puts the tin in front of Paula.

— The guest goes first, she says.

Paula hesitates.

— Go on.

— I'm making me mind up, Rita. Take it easy.

Rita's not the worst. She knew Charlo. She's seen Paula with her arm in a sling, with stitches in her lip. She's seen Leanne struggling down the street. She's watched Paula go through it all and she still smiles at her. And Paula's seen her share. She saw Rita's son getting himself into trouble. She saw the squad car. She saw him being walked out to the car, his hands cuffed, two Guards holding his arms. That's Raymond. He's the same age as Nicola. Paula can ask about him, how he's getting on. She knows that the girl who calls Rita Mammy is actually Rita's daughter's child. Her name is Shelley, a lovely kid. She's a few years younger than Jack. It's no big deal. Everyone knows, including Shelley. But Paula *knew*. Paula and Rita can look straight at each other. She admits it. She likes Rita. The biscuits help.

Leanne's in the kitchen when Paula gets home. Her cheeks are still red from the shower and her hair is wet. She's making a sandwich for herself.

— Want a bit? she says.

— No; you're grand.

The cast is off her foot but she's limping. She's going back to work next Monday. So she says.

She's up and down. And Paula's up and down with her, dipping and rising as she watches and waits. She tries not to be. She knows it's no help. She's thinking of phoning John Paul. She's not sure if she should.

Leanne's still drinking. That's the thing. It hasn't been the happy ending. But it's not the long binge on the couch. Leanne saw that; she disgusted herself. She's back to normal. There's space between the binges. But the spaces are hard to measure. There's no such thing as a casual remark. It'll be better when Leanne goes back to work. Leanne has always worked. She'll be getting up, going to bed early. They'll be able to talk to each other during the week.

That's the plan.

She's in Rita's again. It's two days later. She's had three biscuits from the tin. That's her limit. She's not sure why — it's not her tin. Two chocolate ones and a plain. They're in the front room, sitting back. The gas fire's on. It looks like real coal; it really does. Paula could stare at it for ever.

— I wouldn't move from here, Paula, says Rita.

— No, says Paula.

— Paddy talks about it, says Rita. — He'd like something a bit bigger. But I say to him, what would we do with the extra space?

Fill it, says Paula, to herself.

She looks around. The fire, the flat-screen telly, the three-in-one. Rita isn't boasting, or she doesn't know she is. She's just content — Paula thinks. And that's fine. Good luck to her. She begrudges Rita nothing. And anyway, Paula's fridge is bigger than Rita's.

Rita has no sisters.

— None, she says, when Paula asks her. — I'd have liked one or two.

— You can have mine, says Paula.

— Ah, now.

Paula had three sisters but Wendy died in a motorbike crash. She was the passenger, behind her boyfriend. They went into a wall in Wicklow, somewhere near Glendalough. That was years ago. She was six years younger than Paula.

— Who have you got? says Rita. — There's Carmel. And who's the other one?

— Denise.

— That's right, says Rita. — Well, I have to say now, you can keep Carmel.

They laugh.

— She'd be a bit too much for me, says Rita.

— Ah, she's not too bad, says Paula.

It dawned on Paula, when she was sick. Carmel and Nicola are very alike. She'd never put them together before. She was sick and afraid to go to bed. She heard Carmel's voice on the phone and she heard Nicola talking to her little ones as they walked up to her door. And she knew. She could be sick now. Carmel and Nicola were there. They were coming to the rescue.

Paula loves them for that, and resents and sometimes hates them for it.

Has she ever hated Nicola?

She's alone now, at home. Leanne's out — where? — and Jack's at school. She's on the couch, so she can look out the window at the sky above the roofs across the road. She decided to sit here more often, after sitting in Rita's front room. The telly's off. She has her coffee. She'll be getting up soon, off to work.

Hate's something you don't come back from. That's the way she sees it. You don't slip in and out of it. It builds up. You cross some sort of a line. It's permanent. She's never hated Nicola.

But there's Charlo. She hated him. Her body is a map of his abuse. She just has to look at the bones in her right hand, or feel her shoulder when she knows it's going to rain.

But it seems like a different world, and different people — all that happened then. It's the same house. She still hates the hall. She thinks back — she doesn't have to — she sees herself, lying on the kitchen floor, or lying on the floor here, under the window, the telly on loud, a baby crying — Leanne — and it's not her. It is, but she's different. She could get up and go over to the exact spot where she lay after Charlo had given her a hiding. She could lie down and put her legs and arms in the right places, as if her outline had been chalked on the carpet. She could do that now, and she'd feel nothing.

Maybe it's age. And it's definitely the drink. She's not sure. Maybe it's the way the brain works to protect itself. It invents a new woman who can look back and wonder, instead of look back and howl. Maybe it happens to everyone. But it's definitely the drink, or life without it. It's a different world. She's not sure she likes it that much. But she's a new-old woman, learning how to live.

What a load of shite. She's the same woman. And she knows. She hated the man who put her on the floor, who kicked her as she tried to roll away. She hated him; it's still hot in her gut. She hated him. She still hates him, the bastard, the fuckin' cunt. But she loved him too. If he walked in now she'd love him. He'd save her life, just walking in. He'd lift her out of this existence.

She's never hated Nicola. Or Carmel. They've annoyed her and they've made her feel useless and so guilty she's wanted to maim herself, to push the guilt in under her skin so no one can see it or smell it. But she knows. Without them she'd be dead. She's glad she's not dead and it's a good while since she felt different. She's not stupid; she'll feel that way again. But she'll know. She'll recognise it. She'll be able to deal with it.

That's the plan.

She wants a drink. Now. She can feel it, here, still fresh. She sits because she tells herself to. She'd rather be busy. She's better off moving. It's harder to feel it when she has things to do. She'd like to relax. She'd like to learn to. But relaxation's a bit of a trap. She sits back and it sits beside her. The need, the thirst — it's there, here.

She has to move. She goes into the kitchen. She empties the kettle. She fills it again. She sees herself doing it. She watches herself.

She's so alone.

Where's Leanne?

But her sisters. Carmel is older than Paula and Denise is younger, but they've always been the pals, Carmel and Denise. The allies, rivals, the sistery stuff. They bypassed Paula.

It goes back. She cut herself off. The drink did that. And there was Charlo.

Her sisters drink like fish. Paula's shocked when she watches them. They lower the stuff. Especially Denise. It used to be Carmel who was first to refill her glass. But the last time she was with them, in Denise's house, Denise was pissed when Paula arrived. Paula would swear she was.

But she's not sure. Everyone's an alco these days. Everyone who's pale or too red, or limping, or scruffy, or too well made-up. She sniffs, everywhere she goes. She comes home from work on the Dart on Thursday nights, on Fridays, surrounded by gin fumes, Guinness fumes. She's the only solid citizen on the train. It's how she copes. If you can't join them, beat them. She quite likes it, feeling superior. She sits on the Dart and tut-tut-tuts.

Her sisters.

Where's bloody Leanne?

She'll have to go to work. She goes to the hall and gets her jacket — Jack's. She goes back into the kitchen. She drinks the last of her tea. She sips it standing up.

Her sisters. They're all in Carmel's kitchen. Paula goes there straight from work. Denise is after joining a gym. She tells them this as she leans over to get the wine bottle. Denise and Carmel drink wine these days.

— Why? says Carmel.

— Why what? says Denise.

— Why have you joined a gym?

— To get fit, says Denise.

— What age are you? says Carmel.

— What's that got to do with it?

— You're, what? Forty-eight?

— Forty-seven.

— So? says Paula.

— What's the point? says Carmel. — She was never fit.

— I used to run, says Denise.

— You stopped that when you were twelve.

— Thirteen.

Denise doesn't smile. It's not funny yet. But Paula thinks it's hilarious.

— So, says Carmel. — Thirty-four years later you've decided to get fit. Are you not a bit late? I don't like this one much, by the way, she says, nodding at her glass.

That's allowed because the wine came out of her own bottle. She hasn't opened Denise's yet. Paula brought a large bottle of Ballygowan. She had to bring something. And she brought as well — she feels a bit of a wagon for doing it — three peeled carrots, in a plastic bag.

— One each? Carmel had said.

— Not really, said Paula. — They're kind of for me.

— They look interesting, said Carmel. — What are they called?

— Fuck off, Carmel.

— Carrots. Isn't that it? I've a bag of them in the fridge over there. I knew I'd seen them before.

Now Carmel is still at Denise.

— Well? she says. — You are a bit late, Denise. Aren't you?

— You're never too late, says Denise.

That's real Denise; she can be hopeless.

— Sure, Jesus, Denise, you'll be dead before you're fit. Even if you go to the gym every day. If you live in the fuckin' place. Which one is it anyway?

— Lay off her, says Paula.

— Let's be fuckin' realistic here, says Carmel.

Paula watches her. Carmel mightn't think much of the wine but she's fairly knocking it back. Tut-tut.

— Get real, ladies, says Carmel. — We're finished.

— Speak for yourself.

— Our get-fit days are over. We're falling apart.

And she holds up her glass.

— Cheers.

She looks at Paula.

— And you with your fuckin' carrots. Between the pair of yis; Jesus.

She nods at Denise.

— Have you met Ms Midlife?

— You're just jealous, says Denise.

That's another real Denise line.

— Of what?

That's a real Carmel one.

Denise looks at the kitchen door, making sure it's closed. She moves her chair an inch closer to the table. She looks at the door again. The house is empty. It's just the three of them.

158

When Denise speaks she's not looking at Paula or Carmel.

— Just because I've met someone, she says.

Paula watches Denise redden before she really understands what she's just heard. Denise's face — excitement, fear.

Jesus Christ, she's having a fling.

Paula looks at Carmel. It's news to Carmel too.

— What's this? says Carmel.

Denise shrugs.

Paula's stunned. She hasn't felt this way — slow, stupid, outside the meaning — since she stopped drinking.

Her sister is having an affair.

Denise still hasn't spoken. Neither has Carmel.

Her sister, whose husband isn't dead, is having an affair.

She looks at Denise. Denise is coming down from the shrug. Her hand goes for her glass. She's shaking a bit.

Paula decides to get in before Carmel. It'll be easier for Denise.

— You're seeing someone?

Denise nods. She gulps. She hides behind the glass. Then she puts it down on the table. She still holds it.

— A fella? says Carmel.

Paula can't help it; she laughs. But it's not fair. Carmel makes it sound so silly. Fella. Denise is running around with some sixteen-year-old. They're snogging behind the chipper. He has his hand up her jumper.

It's cruel.

But Denise is wise this time. She just nods.

Carmel looks at Paula. Paula can tell. Carmel needs to know if Paula knew about this before her. She'd love to cheat — Yes! I did! I fuckin' introduced them! She'd love to break Carmel's heart.

She shrugs.

Carmel looks at Denise.

— So, she says.

Denise giggles. She does. It's the only word to describe the noise that comes out of Denise. Paula could kill her; she's not sure why. She'd love to be Denise right now and she wouldn't be fuckin' giggling.

Carmel sighs.

— Tongues and all, yeah? she says.

Paula doesn't laugh this time. She looks at Denise.

— Tongues and all, says Denise.

And the tongues have just gone across her eyes. That's what it looks like to Paula. Or a hand, fingers have gone down Denise's back. She sits up — she arches, the bitch — in the kitchen chair. She looks as if she's going to lick her lips.

— Well, says Carmel. —We'd better hear it. Tell your Auntie Carmel.

— Where do I start? says Denise.

For fuck sake.

— Your eyes met, says Carmel.

— Sneer away, says Denise.

Paula hasn't seen Denise like this before. She's dangling it all in front of Carmel. Carmel bites; she always has. And Denise doesn't care.

— In the gym? says Carmel.

160

Denise shakes her head.

— Wrong, she says.

— Look it, Denise, says Carmel. — We're not going to spend the rest of the night guessing.

— Parent-teacher meeting, says Denise.

— There's romance, says Carmel.

But Paula thinks it's lovely.

— He sat — , Denise starts.

She sits up, nearly acting it out.

— We were sitting beside each other.

All those years, Paula didn't go to those parent-teacher meetings. She'd been too afraid to go. Afraid of what she'd hear, of how she looked. Too busy; otherwise engaged. She'll go to the next one.

— A teacher?

— No! says Denise. — A parent. A father, like. A dad.

— We know what a father is, Denise.

— There was a queue at the English teacher's desk and I'd seen all the other ones. The other teachers, like. And Anthony's very good in school —

Anthony's her youngest, a few years younger than Jack. A nice kid, but a bit thick — Paula thinks.

— So I didn't mind waiting. I knew that whatever she — his teacher — was going to say about him would be good and I'd go home on a high.

— And you did, says Carmel.

— I didn't go home at all, says Denise.

She giggles again.

— Well, I did.

— You're not a complete slut, so, says Carmel.

— Yes, I am, says Denise.

What the fuck is happening here?

Denise sits up again; she keeps sliding. And Paula sits up. And — Paula watches her — so does Carmel. There's a man in the room.

— But I was bit late, says Denise. — Home. But not that late. We went for a drink, just.

Anthony doesn't go to the local school, the same school as Jack. They sent him to the Christian Brothers, even though there aren't any Brothers left in the school. They're all dead or in jail. Paula remembers Denise saying about it being better suited to Anthony's abilities. Paula knows the school. She goes past it every Wednesday, on the bus, on her way to her Wednesday house. She tries to remember, to see, the nearest pub to the school. She tries to see its inside. The lounge. A corner. A lounge girl, the tray.

— How'd it happen? she asks.

Denise looks at her, surprised, disappointed it's Paula asking and not Carmel. Then she realises that Paula is serious.

— Well, says Denise. — He said —

— D'you come here often? says Carmel.

Denise looks caught, confused — ashamed.

— He didn't, did he?

Denise nods.

— Yeah. But it wasn't — . It was the way he said it. He was funny.

— It's a great line.

— Feck off, Carmel.

— He was being ironic, says Paula.

162

— Yeah, says Denise. — And it really was funny. And anyway, we just got talking.

— What about?

— I'm not sure.

— Yes, you are.

— Our boys.

— Lovely.

— Just at the start. Anyway, what else would we have talked about?

— Football, the Peace Process, Charles and Camilla.

— I didn't go there for it to happen, Carmel, says Denise. — It just —

— You weren't on the prowl, no?

— No.

— How long was the queue?

— Long enough, says Denise.

Good girl.

— He was just —

She looks at Paula.

— Nice.

Paula nods.

— We just chatted. And he was in front of me —

— Nice one.

— And he went to the seat at the teacher's desk and I must say now —

But she doesn't say now. She doesn't say anything. She holds her glass. Paula thinks she's going to smash it, her fingers are so stiff. Paula's going to lean over and take it from her. But Denise breathes out.

— I liked the look of him, she says.

— The look of him, says Carmel.

— Yeah.

— What? His —

— Don't cheapen it, Carmel, says Denise. — Use your fuckin' imagination.

And Paula sees it; they all sit up again. The synchronised fuckin' sisters.

— And he had his few minutes with the teacher. Miss Murray. She's very nice. And he got up and I sat in the place where he'd been.

— Nice.

— And Miss Murray said her bit. He's doing really well. She says he'll sail through his Junior Cert.

— Good, says Paula.

— Yeah. And I said thank you very much. I was thrilled, you know yourself.

Paula nods.

— And I got up and I was finished then. I'd seen them all. And all the teachers were in the one big room, at tables. The assembly hall, I think they call it. And I was going to the door. And there he was.

— At the door.

— Yeah.

— Blocking your way.

— Yeah. No. Just there. I could've walked past him. I was going to. I mean. I was on my way home. But I —

She stops. She puts both her hands on the table. She moves her glass.

— Something, she says. — I slowed down, I suppose. I didn't stop. But I slowed down a bit. I didn't decide to. Not exactly.

She isn't drunk at all. Paula can see that.

164

— But I did slow down. So I'd go by him slowly. He smiled. Like, a goodbye smile, you know. See you next time. Who'd be a parent? You know, like?

Paula nods.

— And I smiled back. And he opened his mouth, like he was going to say something. And I said, What? And I stopped. And he said, Sorry? Like that, you know. And we laughed.

— Ah.

— And I was blushing; Jesus.

She's blushing now. Paula wants to hug her. And kill her.

— And he said would we go for a drink. But, like. Hesitantly. Like, only if you want, if you have the time. He wasn't used to it. You could tell.

— Used to what? says Carmel.

— Going for drinks with women. Asking them.

— That's nice.

— Well, it was.

— You're his first slut, so.

The timing's perfect. The oven goes ping. It's the bell, the timer. They laugh. Paula leans across and pats Denise's hand.

Carmel stands up.

— Here we go.

She puts her face down to Denise's.

— Finger food.

And that sets them off again. Denise takes her glasses off; they're steaming. She wipes her eyes. She smiles at Paula.

— She's a wagon.

Carmel bends down, opens the oven door.

— Jesus.

The heat — Paula can see it — sails out, up, past Carmel's face. Carmel steps back. The smoke alarm goes off. It's on the ceiling, over the oven. Paula doesn't have a smoke alarm at home.

— Give us the brush, there, says Carmel.

It's a horrible noise. Paula wouldn't have it. She'd rather burn to death.

— That's the only bad thing about this alarm, says Carmel. — It fuckin' works.

Paula finds the brush. It's beside the back door.

— Open the door while you're there, says Carmel. — Get some air in.

Paula does. The cold air goes past and around her. The alarm is still going. It's a good brush. A blue handle, electric blue. And grey bristles, but not the usual shape.

— Hurry!

Carmel takes the brush. She holds it by the working end. She stretches, and stabs at the alarm with the handle. Paula looks. There's a button on the side of the alarm. It's like a little spaceship stuck to the ceiling. The handle hits the button. One last yip — the noise stops.

— Oh, thank God.

The brush falls out of Carmel's hand. Paula catches it, before it hits the table. She's pleased; it was easy. She could do it again.

— Now, says Carmel.

She bends down again.

— These look grand; I wasn't sure.

She pulls out the oven tray. She puts it on top of the hot plates; they're all off.

Carmel stands back.

Paula shuts the back door.

Carmel takes a fag from the packet on the counter and she lights up. And Paula realises. Denise is off them. She hasn't smoked all night. She's a forty-a-day woman — was. It must be serious, whatever's happening to her.

Carmel exhales. She nods at the oven tray.

— I got these in the new Tesco's, she says. — The Darndale Opera House.

— Is it any good? says Paula.

— It's open twenty-four hours a day, says Carmel.

— Jesus.

— Things taste better if you buy them at five in the morning.

Paula's starving. She loves the look of the prawns wrapped in pastry, like little spring rolls, and the miniature quiches and the little sausages wrapped in bits of rasher.

— And they all take the same time to cook? says Paula.

— That's right, says Carmel.

— That's brilliant, isn't it?

— Dips and all, says Carmel. — There's nothing to it. Just throw them on the tray and take the lids off the dips.

She throws her cigarette into the sink. Paula hears the hiss.

— Mind you, says Carmel. — They always look much better on the packet.

— These look lovely, but.

— We'll see. Sit down.

Carmel puts on oven gloves. They're tartan. They're clean. She shakes the oven tray.

— Grand.

Paula looks at Denise. She looks a bit impatient. She wants to get on with her story. Maybe she's just hungry. Paula smiles at her.

Adultery, though. It's a good one. And Denise. It's a surprise. She'd kind of expect it of Carmel. She'll probably find someone now; she won't be outdone by Denise.

That's not fair.

Yes, it is. Stand back and watch.

She hears the scrape. Carmel is hoisting the food onto a couple of plates, with a spatula.

Denise smiles at Paula.

— Can I borrow some of your water?

— What's wrong with the tap? says Carmel. — The alco here needs her bubbles.

She's standing beside Paula now, and Paula whacks her on the leg.

— Fire away, she tells Denise.

Carmel puts the first white plate onto the table.

— Don't dare touch them yet.

Denise pours some of the Ballygowan into her wine glass. She's over the hump, Paula guesses. Now she's just thirsty. Paula's thirsty all the time. She lowers the water, day and night. She brings a plastic bottle with her, with tap water, whenever she thinks of it; when she remembers. And it's the thing that's there when the situation is tricky, with Leanne, or John Paul or even Nicola. When the talk is awkward, the past or the present — it's the roaring thirst. The dry throat that actually takes over her whole body. And it's not alcohol; that's not what she needs — that's a different one. It's just water — dehydration. But it's nearly the same need. She can't cope until she feels the water crawling down through her, and up to the place behind her forehead, the pain there, and the joints right below her ears. Like oil. Calming her, softening the dry edges. It's even had an impact on her skin. She looks at the back of her hand. It's not as dry; there are no open cracks. It's the skin of a hard-working woman. She's seen a lot worse.

Leanne's hands are desperate. Scratched raw, especially the wrists. Paula hates to see those scratches, self-inflicted — all her life. They remind her of the little girl, holding onto Paula, clinging, getting between Paula and Charlo. Protecting her. Leave my mammy alone. The skinny little wrists, the little red fingers, the nails bitten to blood and nothing.

But Leanne's creaming her hands again. She carries a tube of E45. Paula bought it for her. And she's going back to work. I'm proud of you. Paula can't say that. She'd wear the words out; they'd mean nothing. Leanne puts on eye shadow. She puts on a skirt. She puts her key in the door without falling over. I'm so, so proud of you.

Paula's having a great time but she wants to be at home. It's where she should be. She doesn't know if Leanne's at home. She can't phone. She can't do anything. It's depressing, if she lets it be. It'll never end. If Denise's man had been talking to Paula — Who'd be a parent, eh? — she'd have put her head on his shoulder and started to bawl.

Carmel puts the second plate on the table, and smaller plates for each of them.

Paula stretches her hand. She rubs the lower knuckle of her thumb. She doesn't think it's swollen. It doesn't look it. On the bad days, the soreness goes to her wrist, to her elbow. Like a disease, spreading. She doesn't want to know.

She loads her plate, two of each thing. She loves this stuff. She can taste it. She promises herself — she did before, but she forgot — she'll get some of this for a Friday night, herself and Jack. Leanne. And a video. Jack says that videos are on their way out. There'll soon be none to rent or buy. So that's another thing on her list, between Coat and Year Off — Maybe Australia. A DVD player.

It's back to business.

— So, says Carmel. — Where were we?

— In the pub, says Paula.

— It's not really a pub, says Denise. — Hotel.

— Already? says Carmel. — You were quick off the fuckin' mark.

— No, says Denise. — The bar, Carmel; stop messing. It's in a hotel.

Paula knows the one. She hasn't been in it.

170

— Go on, says Carmel.

— We just chatted.

— Is he married? says Paula.

— Yeah, of course. He was at the parent-teacher meeting.

— He's not separated, no? Divorced?

— No. But he's not happy, Paula.

— Ah, God love him, says Carmel. — Are you happy, Paula?

— No.

— I'm not either. Are you happy, Denise?

And fair play to Denise.

— I'm very happy, Carmel. I was in bed with a complete stranger a couple of hours ago. Why wouldn't I be happy?

Carmel's mobile goes off — the text buzz — while they're laughing.

— Just to be clear, says Paula.

She'd like to touch Denise right now. Just to prove to herself that she's real. To see if she could feel what's happening to her.

— Is the complete stranger the same fella you met at the parent-teacher meeting?

— Ah, yeah, says Denise.

But it needn't be; it doesn't matter. That's what Denise is parading in front of them.

Carmel's jabbing at the mobile. She holds it in one hand and presses the keys with a finger of the other. She brings the screen closer to her face. Then she stabs the Send button.

— So, she says. — Denise?

— Yes, Carmel?

Carmel's mobile buzzes again. It rattles on the table. She picks it up, brings it closer. She puts it back down.

— So. After you chatted.

— We said goodbye, just. He has a nice voice. Oh, and we swapped mobile numbers.

— What's his name?

— Thomas.

— Is that what you put in your phone book?

— Yeah, says Denise.

She sits up.

— But I changed it after. In case.

— It fell into the wrong hands.

— Right; yeah.

— What did you change it to?

— School.

It wouldn't have been Paula's choice. She could do much better than that. But then, she wouldn't have to hide the name. She'd have it, in lights, on her roof.

Carmel shakes her head.

— What if Harry has to phone the school and he decides to use your phone?

Harry is Denise's husband.

Denise shrugs. It's very dramatic. A girl, to another girl. A lucky girl to a plain one.

— He'll find out, she says.

— Did he phone you the next time? says Paula. — Your fella.

She bites into a little quiche. They're nice, but too filling. Too — a word Paula got from the radio — toxic.

They're still nice, though.

— Well, says Denise. — I'm not actually finished with the first time.

— S, l, u, t.

— We left at the same time. To the car park. Together, like. There was no reason not to.

She looks at Paula.

— I was kind of hoping we'd be seen. Just to prove there was nothing. To myself, like.

Paula nods. She understands. She knows all about fooling yourself.

— And we were parked near each other. And I was looking at his car.

— What is it?

— Honda Civic.

— Nice.

— Yeah. Grey. But he's changed it since.

— How long have you —?

— Three months, says Denise.

— Jesus, Denise. Why didn't you tell us?

Denise shrugs.

— I'm not sure.

That's fair enough, Paula thinks. I'm not sure. It's what Paula thinks a lot these days.

— Oh, I knew all along, says Carmel.

It's another surprise. Carmel doesn't seem to care too much, all this going on without her approval. Maybe her sisters aren't as easily read as Paula thought. Maybe you have to be drunk to think you can understand other people, and yourself.

— So, anyway, she says. — What happened?

— What? says Denise.

— The car park.

— Oh, says Denise. — Yeah. Well. He put his hand on my shoulder and he kissed me.

Carmel turns to Paula.

— Have you tried the little sausages, Paula?

— Delicious.

— And it was great, says Denise.

She looks a bit annoyed now — the interruptions.

— What then? says Carmel.

— Well —

— Let me guess, says Carmel. — It was love.

— Lay off, Carmel.

— You gave up the smokes there and then.

— No.

— And you joined the gym on your way home. So Thomas wouldn't lose his hands in the cheeks of your arse.

She's hilarious. But there's an edge there now, in Carmel's voice. She's swinging away; she's had enough. The text message seems to have knocked her, whatever it was.

— Ha ha, says Denise.

She sits up. Carmel sits up.

Paula's annoyed. She wants to know what happened then, but she mightn't find out now.

— What about Harry? says Carmel.

— What about him? says Denise.

The bitch. Harry's a bit of a dose but they've been married for twenty-five years. They suit each other. Paula's always thought that. He's reliable, kind, safe as a fuckin' house. They were made for each other.

174

The bitch, Denise. She hasn't a clue.

— Does he know?

Denise shrugs.

— No.

— Sure?

— Yeah. I don't — nearly sure. I don't care.

— Yes, you do.

— I don't. I don't care.

Carmel stands up. She goes to the kettle.

— What's wrong with poor Harry?

Poor Harry. Carmel can't stand poor Harry.

— Nothing, says Denise.

She looks at Paula.

— He's old.

— For fuck sake.

— In his head, I mean, says Denise. — He's old.

— What age is he? says Carmel. — Fifty what?

The water drums the sink. Paula hears the kettle fill, the hiss, gush, water on water.

— Three, says Denise.

— Fifty-three's too old, is it?

— I told you. It's his head. He's boring. We never went anywhere.

— Went? Are you leaving him?

— Go; lay off. And no, I'm not leaving him. I don't know.

— And what age is the other fella?

— Fifty-one.

— A fuckin' toyboy.

The kettle hits the counter like a hammer. Paula hears Carmel switch it on.

— He's great, says Denise, to Paula. — He's different.

— Where were you? says Paula.

Denise looks at her.

— What?

— Earlier. You said. The complete stranger and that.

— Oh. Bewley's.

— Did he ride you on one of the tables?

That's Carmel.

The Bewley's cafés closed down months ago.

— The hotel, says Denise. — Bewley's Hotel.

Paula nods.

— Newland's Cross, says Denise.

Paula doesn't know where that is. She's heard of it, on the radio; the young one with the traffic news, in the mornings. But she hasn't been there. It could be south or west. She doesn't know.

— What do you do? she says. — Not — I mean, that's your own business. But I mean, do you just go in and book a room?

— Jesus, Paula, says Carmel.

— I want to know, says Paula.

— Why?

Because it's a brilliant thing to do and I've never fuckin' done it.

— I just do, she says.

She looks at Denise.

— Over the phone, says Denise. — That's the way I do it.

— For the night? Or a few hours?

— Oh, the night.

— Waste of money, says Carmel. — Tea or coffee? Come on.

— Nothing for me, says Denise.

— The same, says Paula. — I'm grand.

— For fuck sake, says Carmel.

—I couldn't just ask for a couple of hours, says Denise. — I don't know if you can, anyway. I'd be too embarrassed.

Paula nods.

Carmel sits. She picks up her mobile. She looks at it.

— Are you going to tell Harry? says Paula.

She'll ask the questions. It might keep Carmel off Denise; there's something going on there.

—I don't know, says Denise. — I'm not in love with him or anything.

— Harry?

— No. Thomas.

— Oh.

— He's great and all.

Paula nods. She feels it. She's racing against Carmel. She doesn't look at her.

— It's an adventure, says Denise.

— Yeah, says Paula.

Fuck you and your adventure.

— Nothing serious, so? she says.

— Oh, it's serious, says Denise. —You can't do this and not be serious, Paula. D'you know what I mean?

And Paula looks at Carmel.

Carmel is crying.

— What's wrong?

— Oh, nothing, says Carmel. — Sorry for interrupting you.

— What's wrong?

— Honest, Paula, says Carmel.

She rubs the back of her hand across her eyes. She sighs, and rubs her eyes again.

— Honest to God now. I'd much rather listen to Denise than listen to myself just now.

She looks at Denise.

— You're right, you know. It's an adventure. I could do with one. Where's the corkscrew?

She's not crying now. She's Carmel again. She picks up the corkscrew.

— What's happened? says Paula.

It's her turn. She can listen, maybe say something. She can help. She puts her hand on Carmel's shoulder.

— Hang on, says Carmel. — Let me get the cork out here and then you can hug me.

Carmel again. Hard, sarcastic, loving; the tough nut with the heart of gold. She'll need no help from Paula.

— I wasn't going to hug you.

She's Paula again. There'll be no change. She's the one who needs the help. She doesn't give it. That's not what Paula does.

Carmel fills her glass. Paula loves the sound. It would be lovely on a tape or CD.

— So, says Carmel. — Poor Harry.

Jack's in the kitchen when Paula gets home.

— Not in bed, Jack?

Why does she say these stupid things? But it's after midnight. It's not stupid at all. She's asking him, gently, why he isn't in bed yet. Exactly what she should be asking, and exactly how.

Jack doesn't answer. He's eating a bowl of cornflakes.

They have the milk. They have the cornflakes, one of the huge boxes, nearly full. And it's two days to payday.

— Nothing wrong, no?

— No, says Jack.

She looks at him. She believes him.

— Just hungry, he says.

There's nothing wrong with one of her children. There's no need for concern or worry. He's healthy — it's there, in his skin. He's content — look at the way he's holding his spoon. He's hopping his foot. There's a song going on in his head as he eats. She'd love to ask him which one it is.

He's self-aware. He's bright. He's gorgeous.

She looks at Jack. She doesn't feel guilt. She'll never have to beg forgiveness.

She'll lose him. He'll crumble away on her.

Jesus, it's terrible.

She remembers. She has asked him to forgive her. More than once. More than twice. They all come tumbling, all the times, one over another. Drunk and sober.

It's fuckin' terrible. And it's funny. She sees that.

— Is Leanne in?

— Don't know.

— Fine.

She looks at the clock. She's in the kitchen. A minute left. She waits.

It's ten-past four.

She picks up the éclair. She licks the cream out of it.

She watches herself. It's fuckin' stupid.

But.

She bites into the chocolate, and the pastry that's been softened by the cream.

Jack's not home yet. Leanne's at work. Paula will be leaving, herself, in a bit.

She's a year off the drink. Exactly a year.

She looks at the clock.

A year and a minute.

She likes to start in the kitchen. Especially in the winter. She's not supposed to. Dympna told her to start at the top of the house and work her way down. But she doesn't. Dympna plays golf or something when Paula's in the house. Paula has her own key.

— Dympna?

Paula stands in the hall. She closes the door.

— Dympna?

She listens. She hears nothing. She's alone.

The kitchen is warm. The radio's on. Marian Finnucane. She's interviewing some women when Paula comes in and starts listening. They're the McCartney women, the sisters of the man who was murdered by the IRA in Belfast a few weeks ago. There's a note on the table. Hi Paula. Any chance of defrosting fridge? Many thanks. D. The money is under the note. Seventy euro. Paula puts it away, into her pocket. She puts on the kettle. She unplugs the fridge. It's an old one, much smaller than her own. She empties it. She puts everything on the table. It's not too bad. There's not much in it. Nothing gooey or half-alive. There are a few old vegetables in the bottom. Old carrots, spuds with hair. She drags the bin over and throws them in. There's a compost heap out the back but it's cold out there and it's warm in here.

They've three coffee plungers. Four-cup, two-cup, one-cup. In a row, on the counter, against the wall tiles. The handles all point the same way, a bit like the cranes she sees every day from the window of the Dart. She takes the one-cup. She pours in some of the hot water from the kettle. She rolls it around in the plunger. She has all the moves. She pours out the water. There's a black plastic scoop in the coffee jar. She gives herself two scoops, into the plunger. She fills it with the water. She puts the plunger itself on the top, like a lid. The smell takes over the room. The outside cold is out of her nose.

The McCartney women are great. She hadn't noticed their brother's murder when it happened. There are so many murders. A murder in Limerick, a murder in Cork. Every day, it seems like. A murder in Dublin — she'll listen, to see if she knows the place where it happened. She heard Charlo's name on one of those news reports, when he murdered a woman and then got himself shot by the Guards. She's been through it. She used to listen out for John Paul's name. A young boy out there, with junkies, gangsters, unfortunates. Found dead. By the river, down a lane. She'd relax, she'd move again when they started on the sports results or the weather. But a murder in Belfast.

The first part of the word — Bel — she's not listening any more. Only the really awful murders get through, like that child in Cork or the girl, Rachel, in north Dublin, whose husband was arrested and let go. She's not sure what happened there. And that just proves it. Five miles from her house, she doesn't know what happened.

She didn't see Leanne this morning. She'd had to get out of the house early, to do a job, a one-off, in Sutton. A family moving back in, after the builders had moved out. Paula cleaned their new extension. She washed the floors and walls. It was cushy enough, just cement dust. She left when the removals truck arrived.

She can still feel the cement in her mouth. She pats her shoulder. She watches the dust. She's taken it out of one house, and dumped it in another. Cleaning the same dust twice in one morning. It's mad.

She has to know where Leanne is. All the time. She's on her own here, but she's never alone. And it's not just Leanne. Her children are all around her, all their different ages and faces. She has four, divided into thousands. There are so many Leannes. She sees and feels hundreds of her, every day — it's no exaggeration. The little girl clutching Paula's leg. The teenager painting nail varnish onto bleeding skin. The baby crying while her mammy tries to crawl under the cot. The wreck on the couch. The young woman hobbling to work. The little girl who never sits still, who makes everyone laugh. The little girl who wets the bed. The teenager who wets the bed. The woman who wets the bed. They're all there, all day. The young woman she'll see tomorrow morning. The skinny monster she might see tomorrow morning. The girl who hugs her. The woman who hit her. Jesus.

And John Paul. The little boy in his communion gear, counting his money. The boy with the flu, with a pair of cold, wet underpants on his forehead, to cool him out of the fever, water trickling into his eyes; the two of them laughing about it. The boy on the hospital trolley. The boy at the table, doing his homework. The baby, just born, lowered to her breast — We've a boy here, Mrs Spencer. The boy who didn't come home. The hole there, the cancer; the fuckin' little bastard. The junkie. The waster. The hope; the absence. The stranger at the door. The man. The father. The recovering addict. The boy who flew around, shouting and roaring. The man who stays still. The boy she couldn't ever stop hugging. The man she hasn't touched.

It's fuckin' exhausting.

There are other Nicolas. There are other Jacks. All there, too. Climbing all over her, prodding and patting and biting.

She knows nothing about Leanne. She used to. She's sure she did. The happy ache, watching her move and think and eat, and all of it. Two years ago. Less. It was there, the love. She could lean in closer. Even when there was drink on the breath. It was harmless; she was growing up.

What happened?

What happens?

The McCartney murder won't go away. Paula knows all about it now. She's seen pictures of the pub where it started. She's seen the lane beside the pub where he was killed. He was from the Short Strand area, in Belfast. She hears the name. She's not sure if she knew it before. It sounds like North Strand, in Dublin. That makes it seem familiar. She's seen pictures of Robert McCartney's kids. She's seen his partner. She's there with the sisters, with Marian Finnucane.

There's hardly anything in the freezer. A couple of bits of — it looks like salmon, in a plastic bag; salmon steaks. She's never had salmon that way, only smoked. She's had that a few times, at weddings. She's not mad about fish. It's good for you but she doesn't like it. She remembers her mother gutting mackerel. She'd haul the guts out with her finger. It frightened Paula. That was why she watched. She thought her mother was amazing. Paula will never do it. But she might give salmon steaks a go. She rubs ice off the plastic. These steaks look solid and meaty. She could like them, she thinks. She's seen them in the supermarket. She knows where to find them.

There's a pizza and half a bag of garden peas. And fish fingers, way at the back. They don't put up much of a fight. It's just the ice she has to hack. Paula's fridge at home defrosts automatically. She'll tell Dympna about it the next time she sees her.

She presses down the coffee plunger. Her thumb aches, all the bones on that side of her hand. But she kind of likes this one. She can worry it without going back through the years. The pain is new, like the duvets and Jack's computer. She earned it. She knows that as she works. She can feel it charge and recede as she holds brush and mop handles, as she gets the lid off the disinfectant.

A thought drops through her. Richie Massey will be getting out of jail.

Richie Massey is the man who did the job with Charlo. Paula doesn't know him. She'd never heard of him until she began to find out what had happened that day. She's never even seen him, except on the telly, going into court. Even then, he had a jacket over his head.

She chooses a white mug.

What if he comes looking for her?

Another ring on the bell.

She pours. She gets the milk from where she left it on the table. It's a lovely table, very light wood. Blond, she thinks it's called. It's the centre of the kitchen. You can't help looking at it all the time. There's always stuff lying on it. Bills, schoolbooks, toys. She likes the mess. They must just shove the stuff out of the way when they're eating. Dympna never leaves the breakfast things for Paula. They're always in the dishwasher.

Richard "Richie" Massey. That's the way his name was given in the *Herald* and the other papers. He'll be out soon; he'd have to be. He didn't kill anyone, he wasn't armed — it's twelve years ago. But there's no reason why he'd come after Paula. Charlo wasn't living at home when it happened. He'd been gone for more than a year. And it's not like they've been sharing a cell. Drop in on the missis, Richie. Make sure she's behaving herself. There's no story there at all. Charlo died immediately. Tell her I love her, Richie.

She sniffs the milk. It's grand. Dympna would be fuckin' stunned if she saw Paula sniffing her milk.

He might be out already. There's no real reason why she'd know. There's no one to tell her. He could walk past her today and she wouldn't recognise him.

She pours. Her hand is steady. Brown sugar. There's no other kind here. Paula doesn't use the brown at home. It hardens too quickly. It's like breaking cement.

She stirs. She sips. That's great.

She goes back to the freezer. She listens as she hacks. The women are talking about living in their part of Belfast. A Padre Pio is a bullet through the hand. Or the knee. She's not sure; it's been said before she fully takes it in. Probably the hand. Jesus though — enough.

But she doesn't turn off the radio. It would be too violent, turning off those voices. She leaves them on. She thinks, They'd listen to me. It's true. They probably would.

In another of her houses, they've a huge freezer, as well as the one that comes on top of the fridge. It's colossal, like a supermarket shelf stretched out on its back. She looks in it now and again. But she's never been asked to defrost it. She wouldn't anyway. It'd be too big a job, way beyond the call of duty. She always thinks of Christopher Lee when she lifts the lid. The cold lifts up, around her. It's like a tangle of bodies. Legs of lamb — she thinks. Huge slabs of darker meat. Deer, maybe — she's never had it. All packed in thick plastic. It's like forensic evidence, put there till the trial. It's too much, really. Paula wouldn't have it.

Charlo and Richie Massey went to a house in Malahide. The house belonged to a bank manager, Kevin Fleming, and his wife, Gwen.

Paula's been there, where the house is. She went out on the bus, just to see. To kind of — she doesn't know. She's never been really sure why she went. Mr Fleming was fifty-three when it happened. He's probably retired now, maybe married again. Living in Spain, or somewhere. That's why Paula went that time. To see that life went on, that her husband hadn't torn it away completely.

They pushed their way into the house, with a shotgun and balaclavas. It was eight o'clock in the morning. Richie Massey and Mr Fleming then went in Mr Fleming's car. They were going to Mr Fleming's bank while Charlo held Mrs Fleming, with the shotgun.

He shot her. He killed her.

The Guards were onto them. There was a roadblock waiting for Richie Massey. And they came over the back wall of the house, for Charlo. He shot her. He ran. He ran to the stolen car Richie Massey had parked across the green from the Flemings' house. He jumped in. He remembered — did he? Was he that thick? It dawned on him. He couldn't drive. He tried to get out of the car. Holding the shotgun. Aiming it. They shot him.

She sits at the table. She takes out her notebook. Soap, washing liquid.

She sees her children in a list. Jack, Nicola, Leanne, John Paul. In that order, down the page. It's wrong. It's reasonable, but it's wrong. What she wants to do is change the list. The names in the same order, but across the page. That's how she wants it. Like a horse race, about to begin. Starter's orders. But there'll be no winner, because the race won't start.

Can she do that?

Yes.

No.

Yes — she doesn't know. She wants to. More than anything. That's true.

But today. That's where it's hard. Where it's horrible. She dragged them all through shite, for years, all four of them. So there's a kind of equality there. But today she can point at Jack and she can say, That's my son. And she can point at Nicola and say, Over there. That's my daughter. You should see her children. See the car? It came with her job. She passed the test the first time. Paula could go on for hours. You wouldn't think it, would you? She's my daughter.

Paula gave birth to Nicola. She's her mother's daughter. It's thrilling. Despite the circumstances, the drink, the beatings, a big part of Paula survived — there, every time she sees Nicola. And Jack. It's not just love. It *is* love. She loves them; she loves herself. She made them.

She was walking past a kids' clothes shop, a few weeks ago. In one of the shopping centres. She went with Rita Kavanagh. She didn't buy anything. She'd no money. Thirteen euro, sixty cent was what she had. They were walking past, and they stopped. They pointed at what they liked, what they'd like to get for their grandchildren. But what hit Paula was the name of the shop, Pride and Joy. Those words, together. It was exactly what she felt when she saw Jack or Nicola.

They didn't go into the shop. Rita knows the story. They were just there to look.

— It's the first thing I noticed, Rita said that day. — The first sign that the country was changing.

— What was that? said Paula.

— The clothes shops for kids, said Rita.

Paula nodded.

— They were the proof, said Rita. — People had more money than they needed. It's great.

Paula nodded. She agreed.

— I noticed them before all the new cars, said Rita. — And the talk about house prices. Even all the cranes.

— Jesus, Rita, said Paula. — All I noticed was the price of vodka going up.

She can say that to Rita. She can joke and be serious.

The kitchen's done. She's turned off the radio. Marian Finnucane is over. Pat Kenny was talking to Des Cahill, about the sports. Two men trying to outdo each other. It's too early in the day for that.

She'll finish her list, then get going on the bedrooms. Butter, plain flour, eggs. She's making pancakes for tomorrow's tea. Tomorrow's tea. She's thinking ahead. Chicken pieces — for Jack's sandwiches. Bananas, apples, carrots. Salmon steaks — she'll have a look at them. Mince — for Leanne. She loves spaghetti bolognaise. Spaghetti, tin toms, onions.

Can she point at Leanne and say, That's my daughter? Or at John Paul. That's my son.

Pride and joy. Shame and fear.

She has to put the biro down. She rubs her hand. It's hurting her. She thinks of her mother's hands and swollen legs.

She loves her children.

That's easy to think. Easy to believe and say. Of course, she does. She loves them.

But she has to be able to point. That's my daughter. That's my son. There has to be pride.

Who'd want to point at Paula and shout, That's my mother? There's no reason why any of her kids would do that. She has no right to expect it.

She doesn't expect it. It's the world that goes on in her head. The conversations she has, the situations she makes up. It's in her head she needs to say, That's my daughter. To someone she might not know, who might not even exist. She needs to feel the honesty, when she's alone. It's herself she has to fight against, not Leanne or John Paul. They're innocent. Leanne doesn't have to pass any tests. She doesn't have to do anything. Leanne is Leanne. That's what Paula has to accept and love. The Leanne she'll meet later today. Or the Leanne who might not come home. Leanne tomorrow morning. That's my daughter.

Maybe Leanne has John Paul's strength. Whatever it is that John Paul has. He's been talking to Leanne; she knows that. Two years ago — last year — she'd have thought he was supplying her with heroin or something. She doesn't know him.

190

She's changed all the beds. She's put the first wash into the machine. Dympna's well ahead of her there. Her washing machine is much better than Paula's. But that's not saying much. Paula's should be on top of the dump, in County Meath or wherever they throw those things. Dympna's is a space-age job. It's almost silent. And the powder doesn't congeal in the tray. Dympna's dryer is the real thing though, even better than the washing machine. It knows when the clothes are dry. It keeps going until they are. And it's always right. Paula has tried to catch it out. She threw in a wet pillowcase, just when the other bedclothes were dry. The machine kept going, the pillowcase was dry when it stopped and Paula took it out and ironed it.

That's my daughter. That's my son.

They're fighting, and losing. They're fighting and winning. Like Paula.

Leanne loves bolognaise. The salmon can wait. Paula will do bolognaise for tonight. She'll leave it for Leanne. She'll leave a note with it.

Love, Mammy.

Love, Paula.

X, Mammy.

X x, Paula.

Xxxxxxx, P.

Something like that. Just a little note. Dinner's in the pot. I'll eat with you, if you can wait till I get home. If not, fire away.

Xxxxx, P.

Leanne sitting at the kitchen table. Ruling her page with a red biro. Only a red biro would do. She wouldn't make do with a blue one or a pencil. Paula had to give her the money to get one. About twenty pence back then. The line was perfectly straight. Behind all the giddiness, the restlessness, that was Leanne. Slogging away. Working hard. Concentrating. It was funny and lovely. And brilliant. That was Leanne.

That's Leanne.

That's my daughter.

— Mammy says you don't drink.
   — Does she?
   — Yeah.
   — Did she tell you that?
   — No. I heard her.
   — Did you?
   — Yeah.
   — Who was she talking to, pet?
   — My daddy.
   — Grand.
   — Do you not?
   — Do I not drink?
   — Yeah.
   — No. I don't.
   — How do you not die?
   — Oh. I drink. I drink plenty of things.
   — What?
   — Water and coffee and —
   — Coke?
   — Sometimes.
   — I seen you drinking Coke.
   — I'm sure you did, love. Do you like this one?

— It's alright. I don't like the colour.

— I thought all girls loved pink.

— Not all pink. It's alright. It's a bit not nice. Gillian's.

— What?

— You drank her Coke.

— This one then? It's nicer.

— No. Why did you drink it?

— What?

— Gillian's Coke.

— At the party?

— Yeah. Gillian's party.

— I drank Gillian's Coke at Gillian's party. I shouldn't have, should I?

— No. You didn't ask.

— I just took a little bit. There was loads more left.

— You didn't ask.

— I'm really sorry.

— It wasn't mine.

— Will I say sorry to Gillian?

— Yeah.

— Was she upset when I drank it?

— No. She didn't know.

— Ah well —

— I seen you.

— Fair enough. I must have been thirsty. Grannies are, sometimes.

— Why did Mammy say that?

— Well —

— I know.

— I knew you would, Vanessa.

— You don't drink beer and that.

— That's right.

— It's called alcohol.

— That's right.

— I knew.

— Of course, you did. What about this? It's nice, isn't it?

— Yeah.

— Do you want it?

— No.

— Why not?

— Don't like it.

— Okay. Your choice. Some people shouldn't drink beer and alcohol.

— Why not?

— Because it's bad for them. They become addicted to it. D'you know what that means?

— Yeah.

— Of course, you do.

— You can't do without it.

— That's right.

— You become ob-sessed.

— Oh, very good.

— Like chocolate.

— A bit like that.

— Yeah. Some people are addicted to chocolate.

— That's right.

— And sex.

— What?

— I seen that. A man in a programme.

— What?

— They said he was addicted to sex.

— Oh. Before you ask, Vanessa. I'm not.

— Addicted to sex?

— No.

— Sex is stupid.

— Bang on. But I am addicted to alcohol. That's what your mammy meant.

— I know.

— I love you, Vanessa, d'you know that?

— They all do.

— They're alright. It's a nice feeling, I'd say, is it?

— It's alright.

— Tell us. Do you know everything?

— Yeah.

— Everything?

— Yeah. Nearly.

— Look it. I want to buy you something. It's getting late. Choose something.

— These.

— Socks?

— They're brilliant.

— They're only socks.

— I like them.

— Okay.

— That's stupid.

— What is?

— What you said.

— What did I say?

— They're only socks.

— Why is that stupid?

— Socks aren't supposed to be anything.

— Except socks.
— Yeah.
— You'll go far, love.
— Where?
— Oh, anywhere you want.
— Australia?
— Yeah.
— I don't want to go there.
— Wherever.
— Granny? Will Gillian come as well?
— If you want.
— And Mammy?
— If you want.
— And Daddy?
— *If* you want.
— And Hairy Bear?
— *If* you want.
— And Mister Pig?
— *If* you want.
— And you?
— If you want.

She leans against the wall. It's cold.

She's waiting for her bus.

The house was empty. The minute she opened the door, she knew there was something wrong. The door didn't drag across the rug.

There was no rug. There was nothing. Everything was gone. Everything.

She'd kept going. Down to the kitchen.

This is Paula's Tuesday house, in Clontarf.

There wasn't a trace of anything. The emptiness was spotless. The thought hit Paula. They'd had cleaners in, to clean up after them. The fuckers.

Gone.

It's that time of day. The buses seem to hide. She wants to get home.

It's cold.

They didn't owe her anything. It's not that. The money had been on the kitchen table for her last week. She hardly knew them. She hardly ever saw them. She was American, the wife; that bouncy type of way about her. She'd never seen the husband. But she'd ironed his shirts and sorted his socks.

Three years. Near enough.

There's no For Sale sign. There's no sign of anything.

She has the key.

She could move in.

She feels like she's been sacked. It's not fair.

It's a good story though. She'll enjoy telling it. She won't add anything. It's weird enough.

She needs the money. Sixty euro a week, always on the table.

There's no table there now.

For fuck sake.

She still has the key, and the alarm code.

She gets away from the wall. She looks up the road. She can see as far as the wooden bridge. No bus.

She walks back to the house. It's not far. Just around the corner. She walks up the drive. It feels strange, now that she knows the house is empty. Like she's doing something she shouldn't be doing. Her feet on the gravel. She gets to the door. She takes out the keys. She puts them through the letterbox. She hears them hit the floor.

Leanne's asleep. She's quiet. She's not snoring. She's on her side. Her head is on the pillow.

Paula leans over, a little more. She kisses Leanne's temple. She feels the warmth, and the slight wetness. The sweat she'd had when she was a little girl, after running or dancing. Not drops, just a glow.

She straightens up. Her back is at her. She goes across to her own room.

She looks at Nicola. She doesn't look great.

She does. She looks lovely. But behind it, the face she wears when she's out in the world, she looks very tired. There are small wrinkles at her eyes.

Paula's the mother of a child with wrinkles.

— Did you get my message? says Nicola.

She has that voice — you're going to disappoint me. Paula could do without it.

— No, she says. — I forgot the mobile this morning. It's up beside the bed.

Nicola sighs.

Paula knows. She's expected to say Sorry. But she's not going to. It's only a fuckin' phone, and she has wrinkles of her own.

— What did it say? she asks.

— I just wanted to know if you'd be here.

Nicola hangs her bag from the back of the chair.

— Well, there's no need for me to leg it upstairs, so.

— No.

Nicola sits down.

— Are you alright, love?

The edge is gone out of Paula. It's a long time since she looked down at Nicola's head. It's a long time since Nicola let her.

— I'm fine, she says.

— You don't look fine.

Nicola looks at Paula. She looks up at her.

— You look tired, says Paula.

— I'm always tired.

— I know, says Paula. — The kids, your job.

Nicola shrugs.

— It's life, she says.

— You're right, says Paula.

She pulls back a chair, so she can face Nicola. She sits.

— Anything else?

Nicola shakes her head, once.

— No.

She doesn't look away. She looks straight back at Paula — go no further.

Paula smiles.

She's not to be trusted. Nicola looks after Paula, not the other way round.

She puts her hand on Nicola's. Her hand is cool, beautiful. She squeezes gently.

She wakes up. She's out of bed. She's downstairs. She's picking up the kettle. It's a ton — she feels it in her wrist. It's not even that, the pain in her thumb, her hand, beginning to eat further along her arm.

It's not that.

It's —

She doesn't know.

She doesn't sit. She has to move.

It's a day to skip. But that's no cure — go back to bed, go back to sleep, wake up feeling better. It's on her already.

It's drink-pain. Half-seven in the morning. A drink would help. Just the one.

That's the worst part. The honesty of it. A drink would help. There's no arguing. Thirteen months, two days — she can feel the certainty.

Leanne wakes up.

— What're you doing? Ma?

She's looking under Leanne's bed. She's stretching, hoping her fingers will touch a bottle, a can.

— Ma?

Her fingers expect it.

She hears the creak. She doesn't look or stop. Leanne's getting out of the bed. She has to step over Paula.

— What are you doing there?

She feels the hands on her shoulders. She shrugs them off. She pushes an elbow back. She pushes her other hand further under the bed. Her face is pressed into the side of the mattress.

— Mammy?

She feels something. It goes from her fingers. She's pushed it away. She stretches further. It hurts. Her face cuts into the bed frame. She has it. A can. She has it.

She has it.

She pushes back, against Leanne's legs. She makes space for herself. She puts the can to her mouth. She knows, but she does it.

It's empty.

She can taste it, dried, on the lip of the can. She can taste — it's nothing. Nothing there to lick.

She pushes back, into Leanne. She wants to hurt her, to knock her over. Get her throat, get at her eyes.

— Have you anything else?

— No.

— Fuckin' liar.

— I don't.

She grabs Leanne's legs. She feels them bend, Leanne's weight falling on her. She's shouting. No words — she's grunting. Leanne falls over her head. She's stuck between the bed and Paula, half on Paula's lap. She's hissing, gasping. She's terrified. The bitch. The selfish —

Light.

A change; the angle.

The door has moved.

It's Jack.

She tries to stand. Paula's stuck. Leanne is on her lap. Her feet under her arse — they're twisted, and numb.

It screams through her now.

Jack —

It's always there but sometimes — now — the shame is enough to kill her.

She hits Leanne. She thumps her; she feels it in her hand.

— Get off me!

He's outside, on the landing. He might be — he is. She pushes.

The shame.

She pushes Leanne off her lap. There's no weight in Leanne. She isn't fighting back. Paula doesn't care. She has to get up. And downstairs. She can start again. Put on the kettle. Start the day.

She feels wet on her hand. She feels teeth.

Leanne bites her. Nips her. Like a pup they once had, before Jack was born. Like a warning.

The teeth are gone. Leanne is coughing. Paula can't see her. She's right under the bed.

Paula puts her hands on the bed and pushes back. She gets her feet from under her. She watches Leanne crawl out. She can't see her face.

She leans to the side. She can see out to the landing. Jack isn't there. There's no shadow or breath.

— Jack?

God, God, let him be asleep. He's such a deep sleeper. If a drink was put in front of her now she wouldn't want it. She wouldn't take it.

She's over it. She's grand. She's embarrassed — Leanne is sitting up — she's mortified. But she's grand. Her breath, she's puffing — she's sweating — her forehead is soaking, her neck. Just give her a second chance.

They're knee to knee, like two little sisters, playing on the bedroom floor. It's ridiculous.

— Sorry.

— Okay.

— Sorry.

She means it. She thinks she does. She'll get up in a sec. She'll look into Jack's room. He'll be asleep. She'll go back downstairs. She'll put his waffles in the toaster. She'll make her coffee. She'll make tea for Leanne.

The can is beside them on the floor. A can of Dutch Gold. The shine is off the tin. She can see a dent. It's been empty a long time.

— Are you drinking again? says Leanne.

Again.

Paula hates that fuckin' word.

— No, she says.

— But —?

Leanne nods at the can.

— You got there before me, love, says Paula. — Thanks.

If that sounds malicious she couldn't care less. She knows what's happening.

Her mammy's protector. Leave my mammy alone.

Can a child ever stop? Paula can't face it. It's so fuckin' horrible. The shame; sweet Jesus.

Leanne will stop drinking now. She won't touch another drop, so she can look after her mammy. She has Paula where she wants her. Where she knows her.

The house isn't big enough for two alcoholic women. One needs to look at the other, from a height, from a depth. They both need the love that's given to those who hate themselves. Jesus, it's poison. It's only beginning.

She breathes in. She breathes out.

Is this the way she'll save Leanne? Find a bottle and put it to her mouth. Pull back her head. And Leanne will be saved.

— Leanne, she says.

— What?

— I'm not going back.

Leanne says nothing.

— You woke up in time, says Paula.

— It was empty, an'anyway.

— I'd've kept looking. I'd have gone out.

— There's nowhere open at this hour.

— You know what I mean, love.

— Yeah.

— It's not going to happen.

She wants to see Jack.

She stays where she is. She makes sure her knees are touching Leanne's.

— Mad, wha'.

Leanne nods.

— I'm grand, says Paula.

Leanne nods.

— Thanks, says Paula.

Her legs are killing her. She hasn't sat like this in years.

— I'm fine, she says. — Do you believe me?

What happens now?

Leanne nods, two sharp nods.

Will Leanne go on the rampage? Jesus, the shame. It swims through her all day. A shark. Waiting for blood. Relaxed and smug, never hungry for long.

— I have to get up, says Paula. — My arse is killing me. Jack must think we're mad.

— Nothing new there, says Leanne.

It hurts. It's not meant to, but it does. Jack knows. Jack *knows*. Jack has grown up knowing. Jack smells her breath, every day. Every morning, every lunchtime. Jack checks. Always on his best behaviour, always at the ready.

— Anyway, says Paula.

She gets ready to stand.

— Jesus.

She can't get up. One of her legs is dead. She's so confused, she doesn't know which one. She laughs; it's not funny. She puts out her hand.

— Give us a hand.

She feels Leanne's hand. She feels the pull, the strength, the rough skin.

She's on her feet. She shakes the leg. The left. She laughs.

— Yoga, Leanne.

— What about it?

— What's it like?

— How would I know?

— Would you be into it?

— Don't know, says Leanne. — Maybe.

— There might be classes, says Paula. — Will I find out?

Leanne shrugs.

— I suppose so; yeah.

— Mad, isn't it? says Paula.

Leanne nods.

— One minute I want a drink. The next, I want to go to fuckin' India.

— I'm sure there are classes nearer than that.

— Will I put the kettle on for you?

— Yeah; thanks.

— This is mad, says Paula. — I can't cope with it. Pretending. I'm sorry I hit you. I'm sorry.

Leanne gets it right. She says nothing.

— Can we talk about it later? says Paula.

Leanne nods.

— Okay; yeah. Will I stay at home?

— No.

— Okay.

— I'm grand.

Jesus. She's grand. Nothing to it.

— See you downstairs.

— Okay; yeah.

Jack isn't asleep. He isn't in bed. He isn't in his room.

He heard it all. He must have. She can still feel Leanne's skin in her hand.

She hears a footstep. He's in the kitchen.

— Hiya, Jack.

— Hi.

He's having his cornflakes standing up. He doesn't look at her. The elbows of his jumper are nearly gone. She can see the white of his shirt.

— D'you want your waffles?

— I'm grand, he says.

Jesus Christ, they're all fuckin' grand.

— Won't take a minute, she says.

Please, please God.

— Okay.

He's in no hurry to escape. He mustn't have heard. The day has started. She'll run to work. She'll run all the way.

But there's no work. It's Tuesday. That empty house in Clontarf; it's not hers to go to. She doesn't have a new one yet.

She takes the waffles from the freezer. There are eight left in the box, and three more days to payday. She's two waffles ahead. She'll leave them to Jack in her will.

She drops them into the toaster. One of them sticks to her finger, the cold. She has to shake it off. She puts the finger into her mouth. She presses down the toaster's lever.

— There, she says. — What sort of a day have you, Jack?

He shrugs. She takes back one of the spare waffles and puts it aside for Leanne. To my loving daughter, Leanne, I also leave a waffle. There'll be no fighting at the funeral.

— The usual, says Jack. — Nothing much.

— Same ol' shite, she says.

She's trying too hard.

He smiles. He shrugs.

— Did I tell you about that house being empty, when I went there a few weeks ago? she says.

— Yeah.

— Did I?

— Yeah.

— Mad.

— Yeah.

— Can you imagine it? Coming home from work or something. And finding the house empty.

Of course, he can. He probably expects it, every day of his life.

— Maybe you'd like it that way, she says.

He smiles — he shrugs.

— You'd cope, she says.

Why is she doing this? Leave him alone.

— Did you hear Leanne and myself up there?

Leanne and myself. Not Myself and Leanne. She's blaming Leanne.

— It was my fault, she says.

He says nothing.

— It was stupid, she says. — It was nothing.

She hears Leanne on the stairs.

— It's grand, she says.

The toaster pops. Jack's looking at his bowl.

— Okay?

He nods; he doesn't look.

— I'm fine, she says. — Okay?

— Okay.

It's horrible, cornering him like this. But it's the only — it's the right way. She's sure of that. No hiding.

— It's hard, she says.

He nods. He still isn't looking.

She puts the waffles on a plate.

— But I'm grand, she says.

Leanne walks in.

She's forgotten the kettle, Leanne's tea.

208

It's hard.

Leanne looks twitchy. She's pulling at her top, pulling her hair. She's never still.

Paula says nothing. She gets the kettle and brings it to the tap. She empties the old water, fills it with new. She brings it back and turns it on.

— Did you hear about that woman? she asks the two of them.

— What woman? says Leanne.

— In America, says Paula. — It was on the News.

— What about her?

— She's on a life-support machine.

— I know how she feels.

Jack laughs.

What a strange fuckin' day. It's swinging all over the place.

— And she's been like that for fifteen years.

— Jesus.

— Yeah, says Paula. — Anyway. D'you want a waffle, Leanne?

— No; thanks.

— Sure?

— Don't like them.

— Did you hear about it, Jack?

— Yeah, he says. — We did it in Religion.

— What do you think?

Leanne rescues Jack.

— What does he think about what?

— Well, her husband wants the machine turned off.

— Yeah.

— But her parents want her kept on it.

— After fifteen years?

— Yeah, I know. But it must be hard. Anyway, it's gone to the courts and everything.

— And what happened?

— Well, the Congress or something, the Senate, passed an emergency law and I'm not sure what that's about. But it's real American. You know. All over the telly. People with placards, screaming and roaring.

— It'd be the same here, says Leanne.

— Would it?

— Yeah. The Pro-Lifers and that. They're mad cunts.

— Ah, Leanne.

— Well, they are.

— What do you think, Jack?

He looks at the clock. He's afraid of being wrong. He doesn't want to upset her. It's why he's such a good kid. He's afraid to be anything else. He's grown up minding Paula. He's her slave. She knows it now.

— Well, says Paula. — All I'll say, if it happens to me I want you to turn off the machine.

— Where's the fuckin' plug?

That's Leanne.

Paula laughs. They're all laughing, all able to look at one another. It's mad. It's the best moment of her life. It probably is. She looks at Jack and Leanne, still laughing. She can wipe her eyes. It's all fuckin' mad.

Her mother's hands are twisted and savage. It's the same at every corner of her body. She's shaking. She never stops shaking. And she's shrunk. She's a small woman now, much smaller than she used to be. She sleeps in a bed downstairs. She hasn't gone upstairs in more than a year. She never goes out. She can't. She won't.

But it's not her body. It's the whinge. It was never there before. Paula can't stand it. This is the first time she's seen her since just after Christmas.

Her mother is furious, but not at Paula — not just at Paula. She's spitting at everything. Young people, old people, the country, the world. Her daughters, her sons. She smacks the huge, red knuckle of her wrist. She wants to hurt herself.

There are clear moments, like now. They're longer than moments. They're long enough to fool Paula. She wonders if her mother is playing with them. Fooling them all.

— That's a lovely-looking day out there, says her mother.

She's looking out the window.

— Yeah, says Paula. — It's a real spring day.

Whatever that is.

— The flowers coming up.

— That's right, says Paula.

— It's my favourite, says her mother. — I was never mad about the summers. But spring. I often thought it would have been great to live somewhere where it was really cold in the winter. Russia or Canada. Just to wait for the spring. The heat and the flowers. Wouldn't that be nice, Paula?

— Yeah, says Paula. — It would. The winter, though.

— Oh, I know, says her mother. — But that mightn't be too bad either.

Her hands are forgotten, the pain, the rubbing. They're on her lap. She's not an old woman. Not these days. She was only a kid when she was having her own kids.

— The snow and that, she says. — That would be lovely too. Chestnuts. Isn't it chestnuts they eat?

— Yeah, I think so.

— Did you ever eat a chestnut, Carmel?

There's nothing in her face. She's talking to Carmel; she's talking to Paula.

— No, says Paula. — I don't think I'd like them.

— No, says her mother. — It's hard to imagine. Conkers. Do boys still play with conkers?

She looks at the window again. She moves her head slightly, as if she's listening to children outside. Paula can't hear anything.

— No, says Paula. — I don't think so.

— Your Jack. He doesn't?

— He'd be too old.

— Would he?

— Yeah.

— I never see him, of course. Did you come in your car?

— I don't have a car.

— I thought you had a car.

— No.

— Who has the car?

Fuckin' everyone.

— That's probably Carmel.

— Yes. Carmel.

She doesn't look, to check who she's talking to.

— And Denise.

— Yes.

Your daughter, Mammy. She goes to hotels in her car and fucks men.

— And Wendy.

— Wendy's dead, Mammy.

— I know that. I know well she's dead.

The hands are moving again.

— She was the best of you.

Paula nods. She doesn't disagree.

The window's gone. Her mother isn't looking at it any more.

— Would you be interested in going outside, Mammy?

She's too late. She knows.

— For a few minutes, just? she says.

— They put their rubbish in the bin, says her mother.

— Who?

— The foreigners.

— What foreigners?

She doesn't know why she's asking. It keeps the flak off her. The foreigners can take their share for a while. She looks at her mother's legs. They're full of hard weight, right down past her ankles.

— They eat goats and all, says her mother.

— I'm sure they don't, says Paula.

— Her husband beat her.

It's like a slap. When Paula arrived with black eyes or splinted fingers, her mother never commented. Not once. All those years.

— You fuckin' oul' cow, says Paula.

— Beat her to a pulp, says her mother.

Paula's not sure if she spoke out loud. Her mother didn't notice, if she did. She's rubbing that knuckle. It's raw. She looks around, to see if her skin cream is near. What is it about the people close to Paula? They're all cracking open. They all have to baste themselves.

She can't see any. The place is filthy. Carmel comes over on Mondays, and Denise on the Thursdays, but they're fighting a losing battle — if they're fighting at all.

She looks, and her mother is looking at her.

— You're looking lovely, she says.

— Thanks very much, says Paula.

— You haven't had it easy.

— Ah. I'm fine.

— Good.

Her hands are on her lap again. That's her mother now, the woman sitting there.

— I always liked Charles.

— No, you didn't.

— Ah, I did.

— You didn't, Mammy. You were frightened of him.

— I don't remember that. Being frightened.

— We were all frightened of him, Mammy.

— Were we?

— Yes. Will I make us more tea?

— I'm frightened all the time, says her mother.

— D'you want more tea?

— I'll only have to go to the toilet.

She wants her mother, but not this version. She's here; she wishes to fuck she wasn't.

But she's here.

— What has you frightened? she asks.

And she knows. She sounds exactly like her mother used to. What has you frightened? What made you do that? But she looks at her now, and that's her mother. She loved her. She loves her. That's true.

— I'm afraid I'll fall, says her mother.

— You won't if you're careful, says Paula.

— It's not being careful, says her mother.

She hits her leg, hard.

— I'd love to be careful. I can't bloody well *move*.

She groans. It's not pain.

— I liked getting old, she says. — Up until —

She rubs her leg where she hit it. She can hardly manage that. The side of her hand rasps against her skirt. The skirt isn't clean.

— It was lovely, she says.

Her hand is on the table now. It looks like something dead, a fish, thrown there.

Paula remembers her mother's hands. She remembers watching her work. Peeling apples, wringing clothes. Taking her rings off before she put her hands in the sink. Cutting bread, combing hair with the lice-comb. Paula remembers the feel of the comb, of her mother's hand on her neck. She remembers the newspaper on the floor, right under her face, the little tappy sound when anything landed on the paper. She remembers her mother laughing when Paula read the headline that was below her.

— Bishop Deplores Seaside Behaviour.

— The poor bishop, her mother said.

In this kitchen.

Paula looks down at the chair she's sitting on. It's the same chair. In the same place. It must be forty years ago. Even longer.

She'll ask her mother if she remembers it, the headline that made her laugh.

But she won't.

She'll visit more often.

— I can't manage the bin, says her mother. — With my hands.

— Never mind the bin, says Paula.

She hates herself as she listens. Her mother wants to talk about bins. So, let her.

— And they put the goats into it if I don't get it out on time. The bits they don't eat.

— That's terrible, says Paula.

— The girls are useless.

Paula nods.

She has one speaker on the floor, at the door, and the other at the window, as far from the sink as she can get it. She pushes the wire on the floor closer to the wall. She'll get tacks or something, to keep the wire in place. The player itself is where the bread-bin was.

The bread-bin is out in the hall. She'll put it up in the attic. It's an old tin one. She never used it. Jack used to put his little toys into it. He'd drag a chair to the counter and climb up with the toys, cars and Lego things, one at a time. He'd refuse help — always.

216

— It's my work to do.

It was like a fort, or a stage. She'd sit and watch him for hours, and listen to his little serious voice.

She's looking at her new stereo — €199. She got it in Power City. Rita Kavanagh drove her up. She took her time choosing it. She touched everything. She pressed buttons, watched doors pop up, slide open.

She went for the slider. Panasonic. A name she knows. A CD player and radio. It's silver. The speakers are wood, a nice light colour. They look great, like furniture.

She takes the plastic off her new CD. It's hard work, the packaging. It's fuckin' ridiculous.

There were bargain CDs in Power City. But they were all old stuff — Smokie, the Carpenters. That's not what Paula wants. Not yet. Rita bought five of them.

— You have to.

But Paula had already bought her first CD. She's had it for weeks.

She has the plastic off it. She needs to let her nails grow. They're nearly as bad as Leanne's. Anyway, she has it open. She loves the red and black circles on the disc. She takes it out. It resists a bit. The teeth things in the centre of the box are holding it tight. She presses the teeth down with her finger and the disc lifts. It's ridiculous, really. It's not the first time she's handled a CD. But it feels that way. Maybe it's just ownership. She bought this disc. She bought the player. She worked for these things. For herself. For the house. Jack will play his discs in the kitchen, if he wants. And Leanne — if she wants. Leanne doesn't play music. She has a blaster in her room. Paula got it for her, years ago — a birthday present. She was fourteen, and mad into Boyzone. She doesn't know if the blaster still works. She hasn't seen any CDs up there.

She presses a button, CD 1. There's a short whirr, and the holder slides out and stops. She lowers the disc onto it. It slides back in.

She's not even sure if she'll like it.

She presses Play. She barely has to touch it.

It was just, when she saw the cover, the four lads, not much younger than herself, but sitting together like teenagers, lads she'd like to see Jack with, if she was walking back from the shops or something. There was just something about the photograph, the sunshine, their shoes. But mostly, it was the four of them together, friends, pals at their age — nearly her age. She thought it was lovely.

How to Dismantle an Atomic Bomb.

She knows nothing about them. U2 — she's never liked the name. They come from her part of the city, but she missed them. She was being hammered, battered to the floor, while they were becoming famous. Nicola and John Paul weren't into them. Or Leanne, or Jack — she thinks.

She wants it loud. She wants to ignore the fact that her left ear isn't good. There's a dial for the volume. She turns it, clockwise, with just one finger, the way she's seen women in films turning cars, just one finger on the steering wheel. She's always loved the way they can do that.

And it's at her. The music.

218

She's grinning.

LIGHTS — GO DOWN. IT'S DARK.

It's exactly what she wanted.

THE JUNGLE IS YOUR HEAD.

It's modern. It reminds her of nothing. It's not an oul' one crying into her glass. It's Paula Spencer, looking ahead.

HELLO HELLO —

She'll fill the house with it. This is what will welcome the kids when they come home from school and work.

I'M AT A PLACE CALLED VERTIGO.

It's everywhere in the kitchen, with her.

THE GIRL WITH CRIM-SON NAILS.

She can spin in it.

HAS JESUS ROUND HER NECK.

That's how she feels. She could nearly spin. She knows, she'd go on her arse. But it's the way she feels, the way this music makes her feel. She's been brave. She's jumped right in.

She turns on the water. She bends down. She drinks straight from the tap.

They're alone. It's Friday night. Leanne is just in. She's eating. She has the plate on her lap.

Paula watches her.

She has the telly on, Sky News. The sound is down. She's been watching the pictures from Rome. She'd love to be there.

Leanne's putting away the food. Two sausages, two rashers, fried potatoes, beans. She'd phoned earlier.

She'd had to work late, because someone had messed up an order. She was on her way home.

They're both trying hard.

Paula's only in, herself. She's home about an hour. She was getting stuck into a sausage sandwich when Leanne phoned.

— Have you eaten? said Paula.

— No.

— I'll do you something.

— Great.

— It'll be ready when you get here.

— Can't wait.

That's Leanne. That's the way she's always been.

Then there's the terror. Things change so quickly. Ten minutes is a long time. The phone is easy. Paula doesn't trust it.

But it's grand. Leanne came straight home. She wasn't hobbling. She's eating. They're talking.

Paula sacked someone tonight.

— Why?

— I had to, says Paula.

— Why?

— He was useless, says Paula.

— Can you sack people for that? says Leanne.

— Well, says Paula. — Yeah. You can.

— They're all useless where I am, says Leanne.

Leanne works in a furniture distribution place.

— Including me, she says.

— Ah, Leanne.

— Don't worry, Mammy. I don't mean it.

— How're the fried spuds?

— Best ever.

— I had the potatoes left over.

— They're great.

— From last night. I didn't want to waste them.

— Jesus, Mammy. They're beginning to taste a bit fuckin' dry. So you sacked this fella.

— Yeah.

— Was he good-looking?

— Leanne.

— Was he?

— No.

— He was. I can tell.

— You *are* useless.

— Told you.

Leanne wipes her plate with a chunk of that Cuisine de France bread. Paula got it earlier, when it was still hot. She looks at the telly. The same words go across the bottom of the screen. Breaking Story — Pope has lost consciousness.

— Were you on your own? Leanne asks.

— How d'you mean?

— When you sacked him.

— Oh. Yeah.

She'd been a bit frightened. She'd reported him a few weeks ago to Lillian, the supervisor. Lillian thanked her and told her that it was up to Paula to give him the good news. But she did nothing for two weeks. She chickened out, three times. She was going to sack him last night, but the bollix wasn't there.

— He thought it was his charm, she says now.

— What was?

— He thought — the Hristo guy.

— Where's he from?

— Romania.

— Is he a gypsy?

— No.

— How do you know?

— Actually. I don't. But it doesn't matter.

— Go on; sorry.

— You asked me was he good-looking.

— Yeah.

— He thought he was.

— Yeah; go on.

— He thought he had me, says Paula. — Where he wanted me.

— Sounds good, says Leanne.

Paula smiles at her. How many times has Leanne made Paula smile?

— The poor oul' one, you know, says Paula. — Putty in his hands.

He'd smile, the times he came in.

— Like you should be delighted to see him.

— Yeah.

— We've one of them in work, says Leanne. — He's Irish but, God love him.

— It annoyed me, says Paula.

— So you sacked him.

— No.

— Yeah, yeah; maybe.

— No, Leanne. I didn't sack him because he was full of himself. He wasn't doing his job.

Leanne shrugs, the wagon. She nods at the telly.

222

— Is he going to die tonight?

— Yeah, says Paula. — So they're saying. It's sad.

— Yeah, says Leanne. — He's been Pope for ages, hasn't he?

— 1978.

— Jesus. I wonder how John Paul feels.

— Why?

— His name, Ma; duh.

— Oh. Yeah.

— You gave it to him, remember?

— Yeah, I do, actually. I can remember that one.

John Paul was born a few months after the Pope came to Ireland. She'd been big and sick when she watched it all on the telly.

— I'll text him, says Leanne.

— What?

— John Paul, says Leanne. — I'll text my condolences.

Paula feels suddenly annoyed. She feels rejected. She pulls it back; she tries to.

— You get on well, don't yis?

— Yeah, says Leanne.

She looks at Paula.

— He's great.

Paula nods.

— I've some ice-cream in the fridge, she says.

— Nice one, says Leanne.

She nods at the telly.

— We can change the channel while we're eating it, she says. — We can't be eating ice-cream while he's dying.

Jesus, thinks Paula, she's amazing; she's so sharp.

She goes into the kitchen.

She hears the telly. Leanne has the remote.

She puts the ice-cream on a plate, and into the microwave. She blasts it for ten seconds, so she can get the bread-knife through it. She gets down two bowls. She's in front of the stereo. It's lit, even though it's not on. It's like an altar or something, the tabernacle. She keeps looking at it. She can't help it. There's a CD on the counter. *Lullabies to Paralyze*. By Queens of the Stone Age. It's Jack's. He must have been playing it when he got home from school, when she was at work sacking Hristo. She's delighted. She's not sure why. Leanne, Jack. The ice-cream.

It's a home. That's the feeling.

She cuts two good pieces from the block. She picks them up, one at a time, on the side of the bread-knife and drops them into the bowls. She puts the rest of the block back into the freezer. She gets a couple of teaspoons. They'll make the ice-cream last longer. She picks up the bowls and goes back in to Leanne.

— No change?

— No.

— Nothing else on?

— No.

— There you go.

— Thanks.

Leanne takes one of the bowls, and a spoon. Paula gets back on the couch. She holds her bowl well out, so the ice-cream won't spill as she settles into a corner.

Her feet are touching Leanne's. Leanne doesn't move them. She hears Leanne's spoon tap and scrape the bowl.

— It's only vanilla, she says.

— I noticed, says Leanne.

— There's more if you want it, says Paula.

— No, this is grand.

Paula watches her lean out, put the bowl down on the floor. She comes back up and leans back into her corner. She shifts her feet, pulls them nearer to her. She does it softly. She's not pulling them away from Paula. She puts her hand to her foot. Paula sees a hole in one of Leanne's socks, at the big toe. Leanne pulls at the sock. She stretches it, and pulls it back under her foot — like she's putting the toe to bed, tucking it in. She's looking at the telly.

— I wonder what all the John Pauls are thinking, she says.

— How d'you mean? says Paula.

— Like, they were all named after him and now he's nearly dead. It must be a bit weird.

— I never thought of it, says Paula. — When I gave him the name. That hundreds of others were doing the same thing. Did you text our John Paul?

— Yeah.

— And?

— He didn't get back yet.

Leanne flicks quickly through three channels, then back to Sky News.

— Was it just you that gave him the name? she says.

— Was your daddy involved, says Paula. — Is that what you mean?

— Yeah.

— Well, it was my idea. That one. I think Charlo wanted to call him Charles. But, yeah, he was interested, if that's what you mean.

— Charles?

— I liked the name when it was Charlo. But not the full name, Charles. Or Charlie.

— Does it bring it back a bit?

— Looking at this?

She has to be careful.

— It's a bit strange alright, she says. — But it wasn't all bad. Not then. It got worse.

She looks at Leanne.

— How about you?

— I wasn't even born, sure.

— But thinking back. About your daddy.

— I don't.

— At all?

— No.

They both look at the telly. Leanne is the first to speak.

— I'm going to bed if he doesn't die soon.

— Me too.

Rita talks about retirement. There's not much that Paula can say back. She's only starting. She has to work. She used to drink to sleep. Now she wants to be exhausted. She has to drive herself to it. The real work starts when she opens her eyes in the morning. It never stops.

Her hand is killing her. She won't go to the doctor. He'd tell her to rest it. She'll live with the pain.

Rita says We a lot. We're looking into early retirement. We were looking at a carpet last week. Her husband, Paddy, is a nice enough fella. Paula's not sure what he does. He's away a lot. She's seen him getting into taxis in the early mornings, with one of those wheelie suitcases. He doesn't wear a suit. Jeans and a zip-up jacket.

— We were watching a thing on the telly last night, says Rita.

But Paula knows that Paddy wasn't in the house last night. She saw him going off in his taxi yesterday.

But maybe that's what it's about. It's the feeling of being together that matters, not whether or not they're actually sitting beside each other, cuddled up, whatever. They can still think We, even if they're miles apart. She doesn't know. There was only ever Charlo.

But maybe it's just sad. Clinging to something that's not there. She hopes not. She likes Rita.

She'd be in trouble if she didn't work. It isn't just about the money. She doesn't hate her work. She doesn't like it either. It keeps her going. The buses and trains, the hours.

The panic attacks, whatever they are, don't come if she's busy.

They do come. But not as often, not as badly. She can't go too mad if she has to go to work. She measures it out in steps. One day at a time, sweet Jesus. Whoever wrote that one hadn't a clue. A day is a fuckin' eternity.

227

Jack comes home with a note. He's in the house a good while, upstairs, before he gives it to her. He doesn't really give it to her. He puts it on the table.

— What's that about? she says.

— You've to sign it, he says.

— That's not an answer.

She's never spoken to Jack like that. She doesn't think she has. She doesn't look at him.

But she stops that. She looks. It's her guilt, not his. She looks at him.

— What's up? she says.

— I've been suspended.

He's looking at the table, at the note, or the letter — whatever it is.

— What? she says.

But she heard him. She wants to run to the school. She'll go at the throat of whatever bastard wrote that note.

She's been making more soup.

Fuck all that.

— Why?

He says nothing. She picks up the note and reads it.

— Jesus Christ.

She looks at Jack. She throws the note at the table. It slides off the table and lands on the floor. Jack bends down and picks it up.

— They just fill in the fuckin' gaps, she says.

She takes the page from Jack. She looks at it again.

— My name, your name, the date he wants to see me.

— She, says Jack.

She brings the page closer to her eyes.

— Is it even a proper signature?

— Don't know, says Jack.

— Who is it?

— Miss O'Keefe.

— Who's she?

— Year Head.

— Okay. I thought she was nice. I'm a great fuckin' judge of character.

— She's okay, says Jack.

— Does she not have the time to write a proper letter? Dear, fill in the blank, I am sorry to report that your son or daughter, fill in the blank. For fuck sake. It's serious. Why, Jack?

— Why is it serious?

— No. *Why*?

She looks back at the note.

— It isn't even on it, she says. — Why are you suspended?

— I said something about a teacher, says Jack.

— Ah, no. What?

— I said he couldn't teach properly.

— Ah, Jack.

— He's useless.

— We're all useless, she says. — I don't mean that. But —

She looks at the note, at the date for the meeting — the order to appear.

— That's tomorrow, yeah?

— Yeah.

— Okay. Why did she take it for granted that I'd be able to go? Did she ask you for a time?

— No.

— Why didn't she phone?

— Don't know.

— Did you use bad language?

— No.

— Sure?

She puts up her hands.

— No, no; sorry. I believe you.

She gets her mobile. It's on top of the stereo.

— I was supposed to meet John Paul.

It's annoying. It's more. She wants to cry. One son drags her away from the other.

That's not fair. It's not Jack's fault. It *is* Jack's fault. It took ages for her to phone John Paul, weeks. To work up the nerve, the courage — whatever it is. Just to ask him to meet for a chat. But he'll understand. He's a father himself.

She holds the phone. She changes her mind. She won't text him. She'll phone him. She'll talk to him properly later.

— So, she says. — Okay. Now. Let's get ready for this.

She looks at him.

— What did you say to — who was it anyway?

— O'Driscoll.

— Mister O'Driscoll.

— Yeah.

— What did you say to him?

— I didn't say anything to him, says Jack.

— No messing, Jack. Please. Tell me.

Jack looks at her.

— You know ratemyteachers.ie?

— What?

— It's a website, says Jack. — You can rate your teachers. Like, give them marks and that.

— And is that what you did?

— Yeah.

— What's it like?

He kind of shrugs.

— You grade the teacher, he says. — Helpfulness, clarity, popularity.

— Is it legal?

He's surprised, worried for a second — he's thinking. Then he settles.

— Yeah.

— Sure, Jack?

— It looks like a report.

— Except it's for the teacher, says Paula. — Instead of the kid, like.

— Yeah.

— So, she says. — I don't get it. What happened?

— I gave him his grades. 1, 1 and 1.

— And that's bad.

— Yeah. Out of 5.

— Why did you do this, anyway?

— I just did, he says. — They were talking about it. In school, like. And, you know. I did it for all my teachers. I gave them all grades.

— All bad marks?

— No, he says. — Mostly good. They're sound, most of them. It was on the News, about ratemyteachers. Something about the teachers' unions giving out about it. And Gozzer — you know him. John — you say he looks like that cheesy singer.

— Tom Jones.

— Yeah.

— He's lovely.

This irritates Jack. He's almost squirming.

— He looked it up and filled it in, like. And he told us about it, so I did the same. I just filled it in.

He looks at her now.

— There's nothing wrong with it.

— Did you sign it, Jack?

— No.

— So, says Paula. — I'm still a bit lost.

— You can put in a remark, says Jack. — For each teacher.

— Ah.

— So, I wrote that he was a useless teacher. He is.

— And did you sign that?

— No.

— It was all — what? — anonymous?

— Yeah.

She points at the note from school.

— What happened?

— The religion teacher, Miss Kelly —

— She's nice, says Paula.

She remembers a good-looking woman, in a black suit. Smiling, leaning across the desk to shake hands with Paula, at the parent–teacher meeting last month, the first one Paula had ever gone to.

— Isn't she? says Paula.

— She asked us about ratemyteachers and what we thought of it.

— She ratted on you.

— Yeah.

— The fuckin' wagon.

— Yeah.

— The cunt — sorry.

She sits up.

— So, let's get this sorted, she says. — You told her about what you'd written.

— Yeah.

— Did you write about her, by the way?

— Yeah.

He's really blushing now.

— Nothing dodgy?

— No. Just, she was great.

— I'd better see it.

— What?

— The ratemyteachers thing.

— Why?

— So I know exactly what it's about.

She stands up.

— And you're sure it's legal now, Jack?

— Yeah, he says. — Why wouldn't it be?

It's her turn to shrug.

— I don't know.

— The teachers just don't want it to happen. But it's okay. It's monitored and that. You're not allowed to swear or write anything too mental.

— Let's have a look at it.

— Okay.

They go up to Jack's room and, again, Paula loves the way Jack knows what he's doing, tapping away at the keyboard, like a bright kid in a bad film.

— That's the home page, he tells her.

— What's the home page?

— Kind of, the front. The contents.

— It looks nice, she says.

There's a group of students, some black ones and a gorgeous Chinese kid.

— Are they Irish? she says.

— Don't know, says Jack. — The idea came from America.

— It'll be an Irish picture soon enough, anyway, says Paula. — The way things are going. Are there any black kids in your class, Jack?

— One, he says.

— D'you like him?

— It's a girl, he says. — I don't really know her.

He's blushing again. She's standing behind him but she can see the colour in his neck.

She puts her hand on his shoulder. She leans nearer to the screen. She reads.

— Honest, Essential Critique. That's fair enough, isn't it?

— Yeah.

— Can you print this out for me, Jack?

— Don't have a printer.

— Oh. Yeah. Sorry.

Her defence is already in tatters.

— Doesn't matter, he says. — I'm buying one, myself.

— Are you?

— Yeah, he says. — I have half of the money.

— You're great, she says.

She squeezes his shoulder. He pulls it away. She takes her hand down. She has to keep learning. She never got this far with John Paul. He was gone when he was Jack's age.

She reads a bit more. A new world is upon us. Embrace it and thrive!

— That's a bit much.

She points at the words. She touches the screen.

He rubs the screen where she touched it. She wants to laugh; she wants to slap him.

— Let's see the evidence, Jack, she says.

He shifts the mouse. He clicks.

It's there. He scrolls down the list of teachers. There are little faces beside each name. Smiley faces and frowny faces. Most of them are smiley. He gets down to the end of the list.

— What's their problem? she says. — You all love them.

Jack shrugs.

— Show me the site for Mister O'Driscoll, says Paula.

— It's not a site.

— I'm trying my best, Jack.

— Okay.

He clicks. There's nothing there that makes much sense, at first. Jack touches the screen. She's tempted to wipe it with her sleeve.

— See? he says. — They're his marks. They're the comments, there.

— There's only four.

— Yeah.

— That's not many.

She reads the comments. She has to lean over.

— Sorry.

She reads out loud.

— We call him Dopey. No more info needed. Did you write that one?

— No.

He points at the third comment in the list.

— That one.

She leans down again. She reads.

— Useless.

She looks at Jack.

— It's not very nice, Jack.

— He is useless.

— Okay, she says. — Now I know.

She stands up straight.

— No, hang on.

She taps his shoulder.

— Show me Miss Kelly.

— Why?

— Go on. And the other teachers.

She hears no clicking.

— Evidence, Jack, she says. — You wrote nice things about the others, didn't you?

— Yeah; kind of.

— Come on, she says. — I'd better see it all. They'll have seen it, when I go in tomorrow.

He clicks. The screen goes white, and fills again. She leans down.

— Eight comments, she says. — She's popular. Which one is yours?

— They're all kind of the same.

— Which one?

He points.

— Legend. Babe. She certainly knows her popes. Jesus, Jack, you're a messer.

She wants to hug him.

— She certainly knows her popes?

— It's all she's been talking about for weeks, says Jack. — Because of the election for the new one and that.

He points at Legend.

— That means she's a really good teacher. It's in loads of the comments for other schools.

— And what about this one? says Paula.

She points at Babe. She doesn't touch the screen.

He doesn't answer.

— Do us a favour, she says. — Write out all the comments you made on a piece of paper for me. So I can show them that you think they're all great and — Jesus!

— What?

— No; it's grand, says Paula. — I've just had an idea. I think.

— What?

He's worried; she can see it.

— Can you change the comments there, if you want to?

She points at the screen.

— I'm not sure, he says. — I think so.

— See if you can, says Paula. — Then change them.

— Why?

— Take out Babe. It's not nice, Jack. It's not appropriate. And change the one about Mister O'Driscoll. Make it something — just nicer.

— But they've seen it already.

— It doesn't matter, Jack. Do it. Trust me.

Trust me. She believes it — here, now. Jack can trust her.

— Look it, she says. — Tomorrow, right? They'll have it all printed out. I'll pretend I haven't seen it. They'll expect that.

She keeps going. She doesn't look at him.

— I'll ask to see it on a computer, just to understand it properly. Is there a computer in the Year Head's office? What's her name again?

— O'Keefe.

— Miss O'Keefe, Jack.

— Yeah.

— Is there a computer?

— Yeah.

— Grand. I'll ask to see it. They'll see the comments, changed. I'll say I know nothing about the changes. They'll believe me again. So, you did it. On your own initiative. Sorry for your sins and all that.

She hops to the door.

— I'll leave you to it, she says.

The good days are always a surprise. She's a tactical genius. And Jack fancies his religion teacher.

She goes downstairs.

She takes her phone off the table. She finds his number.

— Yeah?

It's not John Paul.

— Star?

— He's not here, says Star.

Where is he? she wants to ask. And what're you doing with his mobile?

— How are you, Star? she says.

What did Star see on John Paul's screen when she was picking up the phone? What's the name in his phone book? Ma? Paula? Hopeless Fuckin' Alco Bitch?

— Alright, says Star.

— How are the little ones? says Paula.

— Good; yeah.

— Lovely, says Paula.

Star says nothing.

— So, says Paula. — He doesn't have the phone with him.

— No.

— Will he be home?

— Yeah.

— Will you tell him to give me a —

— Yeah.

— Grand. Bye, so.

— Yeah; bye.

— Nice talking to you, Star.

— Yeah.

The phone's dead. Paula puts it on the table. She stands up. She's not doing too badly. She called the woman Star — three times, she thinks. She's getting there. Star doesn't like her, and she doesn't like Star. It's up to her to change it, not Star. If Paula shifts, so will Star — or she might. That's enough.

Jack fancies his religion teacher.

She finds Leanne when she gets home from work. She's on the couch, passed out.

— Leanne, love.

Leanne's on her side, face hidden by hair. In the dark. The curtains are drawn — it's not dark out yet. The telly's on, the sound down.

She has to touch her — it's dreadful. What'll happen? What won't happen?

She calls Jack.

No answer.

She calls as she moves to Leanne. She calls again —

— Jack!

She gets Leanne's hair away from her face. She feels the sweat, the wet heat on her fingers as she pulls Leanne's hair back. Her face turns from the touch, deeper into the couch.

She's fine.

Jack hasn't answered. She can't hear him upstairs.

Leanne is stretching, waking. Paula sits down. She pushes gently for space on the couch.

— Move over there, she says.

She can feel her heart. She can hear it. She takes off her jacket and throws it over at the door. She puts her hand back on Leanne's head. She rubs her, caresses her, the way she used to. It's in her hand — the way she used to. From her temple to behind her ear, bringing her hair with her fingers. And again, and again. Leanne's awake, her eyes are open. She knows what Paula's doing.

— I fell asleep, says Leanne.

— Tired.

— Yeah.

— Me too.

Leanne moves. She's sitting up.

— Hungry? says Paula.

— No, says Leanne. — A bit.

— An omelette.

She has the eggs. She bought them today.

Leanne nods now.

— Yeah. Nice.

Paula stands up. She makes sure she doesn't groan. She's caught herself groaning when she bends down or stretches, especially at work. She hates hearing it, too late.

— I'm hungry myself, she says. — Is Jack in?

— Don't know, says Leanne. — I just kind of conked out.

Paula walks to the door. She picks up her jacket. She doesn't grunt.

— I'll just check, she says. — He might like one too. Back in a minute.

She goes to the stairs.

— Jack?

He isn't there.

He's at work — she remembers.

— He's in trouble at school, she says in to Leanne as she walks past the door, to the kitchen.

— What for?

— I'll tell you in a minute, she says.

She's in the kitchen. She hits the Pause button and listens again, where she left off this afternoon before she went to work. She hasn't listened to music this way since she was sixteen or seventeen. Getting into it. That was what it was called. Listening to the record, over and over. Are you into it yet?

She's getting into *Elephant*. By the White Stripes.

She gets the eggs from the fridge.

This — this now — is as good as her life has been. That's true. She'd love a drink. But it's true. Life, now, is good.

It'll all fall apart.

She doesn't believe that. Not today. Tomorrow might be the same. It might be good. There's no reason why it won't be. And five minutes ago Leanne was dead.

She gave up all cooking at one point. She's not sure for how long that was. When she gave up altogether. Months — she thinks. Leanne could probably tell her. Nicola definitely could. Then she started again.

It was the sight of them all one day. One Saturday morning. She walked into the sitting room. Nicola was trying to change Jack's nappy. Really, he was too old for it. He wouldn't stay still for her. There was a stain under him, on the carpet. Nicola was crying. She couldn't do it. She was sixteen. Jack had a bit of bread in his hand. Paula saw the mould on the crust and she nearly got sick. She got down beside Nicola. She slapped her out of the way — she can feel it now. You're useless. She said that. She slapped Nicola's leg. She saw

Jack's dirt on Nicola's jeans and hand. Her head — she remembers; she can feel the ache breathe in and out. And she saw Leanne. In the corner, pushed back against it, under the window. Big eyes, falling out of her face. Scratching her arms. Staring out, but not at Paula. She gave Nicola time to clean herself, then she sent her down to the shops for breakfast.

Cheese.

She'll ask Leanne if she wants cheese in her omelette.

She presses the Pause button. It's track 6. She picks up the cover; she brings it right up to her face. She reads the name. "I Want To Be the Boy To Warm Your Mother's Heart."

For fuck sake.

She goes into the hall.

She stops.

Leanne is talking.

She must be on the phone. Paula hadn't heard the ring tone, that stupid frog thing she hears all the time on the Dart.

She listens.

— Okay, says Leanne. Oh-kay.

Then Leanne's listening, to whoever — she must be. Then she speaks again. She's saying goodbye.

— Okay, girlfriend. Talk to you.

Then Paula hears her moving about on the couch, maybe pulling her legs up under her. She hears the mobile, she thinks, drop to the floor.

Girlfriend.

Something about it — Paula goes back into the kitchen.

She's not really crying. It's a burst of — it is — happiness.

Girlfriend. She's never heard it — the word — used like that. She has, in films. But not by someone real. And Leanne. She just sounded so —

The tears don't flow. It's over, really, before it starts. Like a sneeze, from the eyes. She puts her hands to her face.

She's fine now.

She opens her mouth, stretches her jaw. She feels the skin on her cheeks stretch too.

She wipes her eyes. She goes back out to the hall.

It's the first really nice day. They sit out in Carmel's garden. They were supposed to go to Denise's, but Carmel texted Paula. *My hse x C.*

Paula's been telling them about Jack, about her meeting at the school. He's been suspended for three days. She's still not sure why. Because he hurt their feelings. She doesn't really care. She has her story — I did this, and then I said that. The meeting went well. And the teachers weren't too bad; they were all quite nice. She stayed calm. She shook their hands. She's pleased with herself. She thinks she's entitled to be.

They're down near the back wall, in a block of sunlight that's slowly getting smaller. She can feel the sun on her face. She moves her head, eyes away from the sun. She can feel the wooden frame under the

244

canvas, under her temple. It's an old chair. The canvas smells a bit damp, but it's kind of nice.

— We'll go back in in a minute, says Carmel.

— It's lovely, says Paula.

No work tonight; it's Saturday. She can hear children, somewhere. She loves that noise, and the birds.

— We should have had a barbecue, says Denise.

— Too much effort, says Carmel. — And we'd never be left alone. It's the only thing sexier than a sexy woman. A sexy woman cooking fuckin' sausages.

Paula laughs. She feels a cloud get in front of the sun. She looks again at Denise's ankle, at the little silver chain that's hanging around it. There's something shocking about it, and blatant. And high-heels, in her sister's back garden.

Paula's jealous. Fuckin' right she is. She'd love to see that chain on her own ankle, a man's hand on it as —

She sits up.

She looks for her glass. It's beside the chair, empty, on its side.

— Fuck it.

Carmel is looking at her.

— There's more in the jug, she says. — I didn't forget about you.

The jug is on the tray, on the grass.

— Thanks, says Paula.

She's deep in the chair. She has to climb, edge out, over the lip of the chair. She passes Denise's ankle on her way to the water.

— Anyway, says Carmel.

Carmel's been quiet, Paula thinks. She hunches down and fills her glass. It's a tumbler, nice and heavy, with a pink pig on its side.

— I've a bit of news for yis, says Carmel.

Paula sits down, but she doesn't sit back in the chair. There's something up; there's something wrong. She doesn't want to be here.

She knows before Carmel says the word.

— Cancer.

— Oh Jesus.

— Who, Carmel? You?

— Yes, Denise.

She's amazing, Carmel. She smiles at Paula — their thick sister. Paula smiles back at her. She leans out and touches Carmel's knee. Carmel puts her hand on Paula's.

She's crying.

Paula doesn't cry.

— God, Carmel, says Denise.

Carmel nods; she shrugs. She drinks. She coughs.

— Lungs? says Paula.

Carmel shakes her head. She can't talk. She shakes her head again. Then she manages it.

— Breast, she says.

— Why were you coughing?

— There was something in my throat, Denise.

— Sorry, says Denise. — I'm being stupid.

— You're grand, says Carmel. — It should be the lungs, really. The years I've been smoking.

— How did it — ? says Paula. — I mean, what happened?

246

Denise has gone over to Carmel. She puts her arms around her. Paula hears Carmel cry. She can't see her now. Denise is in the way. She listens to them cry. She stands up. She has to. She feels too small sitting down. She's far away, and stupid. She puts her hand on Denise's back. Denise moves back, to let her in.

— For fuck sake, says Carmel.

She's shorter than the other two and she's sitting down.

— I'm being smothered by tits here, she says.

They laugh and give her room, and wipe their eyes and look at Carmel.

They sit down.

— Killed by breasts just before the breast cancer gets me, says Carmel.

— Ah, stop, says Denise.

— Will you have to have a — I can't think of the name, says Paula.

— Mastectomy, says Carmel. — And, yeah. I will.

— God. When?

— We're not sure yet.

— Is the waiting list long?

— We're in the VHI, says Carmel. — Plan E. The best.

Only Carmel could make a boast out of breast cancer.

— Yeah, she says. — Mastectomy. That's the word, Paula. I've been reading all about them. I can even spell it. And radiation. And chemotherapy.

She sighs.

— I can spell that one as well.

— How did you find out? says Paula.

— A lump, says Carmel. — Just, in the shower, you know.

— What did you do?

— Nothing, says Carmel. — I pretended it wasn't there. It was easy. We're covered in fuckin' lumps, aren't we, really? I hoped I'd wash it away. And it wasn't sore or anything. So —

— How long —?

— Months, says Carmel. — If I'm being honest. But it didn't seem long. But I kept at it, to see if it was gone. Like brushing your teeth when you have a toothache, you know. I couldn't ignore it.

Paula wants to examine her own breasts. They're sweaty, and itching; they're horrible.

— I thought you'd be too old, says Denise.

Carmel laughs her angry one.

— What? she says.

— Well, says Denise. — I read it somewhere. I thought only younger women got breast cancer.

— I'll tell that to the specialist when I go in to him next week, says Carmel. — For fuck sake, Denise.

— I'm sorry, says Denise. — I just thought —

— Denise, says Carmel. — Ask me what's the biggest risk factor when it comes to breast cancer.

Denise looks at the grass. She takes her battering.

— I'll tell you, Denise. Increasing age. And if that's a bit complicated for you, it means growing old.

— Sorry.

— Yeah; me too, says Carmel. — Sorry, Denise. Where would I be without you?

It's Carmel and Denise. It always has been. Paula's the sister in the middle. She's never really liked Denise. She loves her, but she doesn't like her. Carmel does. Denise's thickness has always irritated Paula but Carmel has never minded it. In a way, it suits Carmel. Denise is Carmel's sidekick. Paula never would be. But Carmel has told them both at the same time. Paula's grateful. It's strange, but that's how she feels.

— You haven't noticed, girls, says Carmel.

They look at her.

— No ashtray.

— You've given them up.

— Yep.

— Why? says Denise.

— Ah, fuck, says Carmel. — It seemed like a good idea.

— Well done, says Denise.

Paula stands up again. She bends down to Carmel and puts her arms around her. She puts her chin on top of Carmel's head. Carmel's arms are around Paula, pulling her nearer.

— Where d'you hide your fat, Paula? says Carmel.

They laugh.

— It's a secret, says Paula.

Carmel grabs a wad at Paula's waist.

— Found it.

The shampoo smell is in Carmel's hair. Strawberry, or bubblegum — it's a kid's smell. Paula puts her hand on the back of Carmel's head. It's getting a bit awkward. She's standing, Carmel's sitting. Paula has to bend her legs and keep them bent. It's as if Carmel knows, and she won't let go. Paula's legs are killing her.

She's falling over, onto Carmel. She is — there's something happening. Carmel's moving, collapsing under Paula.

— The fuckin' chair.

They're falling together. The chair isn't an old one, like Paula's. It's newer, light metal. It's falling to the side and Carmel and Paula go with it. Paula can't stop it. There's nothing to grab, she can't stand straight. She's going over, and Carmel's hanging onto her. She's on top of Carmel, on the grass. Her face is near the ground. She'd forgotten what grass really looked like.

The chair is on its side. Carmel is on her back. Paula is lying across Carmel, stomach on top of stomach. From the air they'd look like a fat X. They're both laughing.

— Get off, says Carmel.

But she doesn't want her to. She slaps Paula's arse, twice. She laughs again.

— There's a bit of a wobble there, all the same.

— Fuck off, you.

Paula's face is close to Denise's ankle and the chain. Denise's heel has actually cut into the ground. Paula can see it, like a bird's beak in the grass.

— How much was it? she says.

She leans out — she's still on top of Carmel — and she holds it gently.

— What? says Denise.

— This, says Paula. — Your chain.

She feels Carmel's stomach growing under her; Carmel is laughing.

— I can't remember, says Denise.

— Did he buy it for you?

— No.

Carmel is shaking; she's choking.

— You'll have to get off me, Paula, she says. — I'm dying.

— Don't say that, says Denise.

She's angry. Paula can hear it.

— Hang on, says Paula.

She heaves herself up. She feels her sore hand hop as she presses it into the ground. It's her wrist. But it's not too bad. She's on her knees, off Carmel. Carmel doesn't move.

— It's nice down here, she says. — It's damp, though. You can feel it.

She rolls onto her side. She smells the ground. They hear her; she wants them to.

— I might as well get used to it, she says.

— Carmel, says Denise.

— Don't worry, Denise, says Carmel.

She's on her knees now too, beside Paula. How will Paula explain the grass stains on her knees to Leanne, if Leanne's in when she goes home? She wants Leanne to see the stains. She wants the slagging. She wants the crack. She was always there for me.

— I'm not dead yet, says Carmel.

— Good girl, says Paula.

— I'm not really seeing him any more, says Denise. — An'anyway.

— Jesus, says Carmel. — That came out of fuckin' nowhere.

— Just so you know.

— Thanks, Denise. Can I have him?

Denise is crying.

— What happened? says Carmel.

— It's not that, says Denise. — It's *you*.

— Fuck that, says Carmel. — It's only a tit, Denise. I'll be grand. What happened with your fella?

She leans on Paula as she gets up. There's a lot of Carmel; she's taking the shoulder off Paula. She stands, and sits in Paula's deckchair. Paula doesn't bother with the chair that's on its side. She sits beside Carmel on the ground. Fuck the damp. She'll have stains on her arse as well.

— So, go on, says Carmel.

— He was getting a bit boring, says Denise.

— Did you dump him? says Carmel.

— Yeah, says Denise. — There was no point in taking it further.

— Taking it further, says Carmel. — What's that mean, Denise?

Denise doesn't answer.

— How was he boring? says Paula.

— Ah, says Denise. — He was only interested in his children. It was all he talked about.

— That must've been hard for you.

— It was no escape, an'anyway, says Denise. — It wasn't what I was looking for.

— That's fair enough, says Carmel. — There's no point in going to all that bother if all you do is end up chatting about each other's kids. What about the sex?

Denise shrugs.

Paula laughs. She's not mocking Denise, or angry. It's admiration. She doesn't know Denise.

Denise crosses her legs. Paula watches the heel come out of the ground. There's a big bit of muck still stuck to it.

— The ocean's full of fish, says Denise.

They laugh.

— For fuck sake, Denise, says Carmel. — Have you looked at some of the fish?

— Some of them aren't that bad.

Paula leans over to Denise. She holds Denise's foot, the one dangling over the ground. She lifts it slightly. She flicks the dollop of muck off with her finger. They're gorgeous shoes. She lets go of Denise's foot.

— There.

— Thanks, says Denise.

— Did you tell him he was boring? says Carmel.

— Ah no, says Denise. — That wouldn't have been nice. He didn't kick up, anyway.

— Maybe he thought you were boring as well.

— I don't think so, Carmel.

— You're lots of things, Denise, says Carmel. — But you're not boring. Not these days, anyway.

— Did I used to be boring?

Denise looks at Carmel over her sunglasses. She drops her head. She pulls the glasses down on her nose. Paula hears her bracelets banging into each other as they drop down on her arm.

— No, says Carmel.

Her knee presses Paula's back. Paula leans back onto it.

★ ★ ★

— How's Star? she says.

— She's alright, says John Paul.

He's sitting in front of her. His elbows are off the table. He's looking straight at her.

She's brought him to the café. She hasn't seen her pizza fella since, the man whose arms she'd fancied. It's just as well, she thinks. She's relaxed here. They smile when she comes in. She smiles back. She's a customer. She's welcome.

He walked with her from the house. He said nothing on the way. It's another of those weird days. It's sunny and warm, then it's suddenly dark and there's torrential rain that makes the windows wobble.

It's raining now, belting down. She can see it hop on the ground outside. They're sitting at the window but John Paul has his back to it.

— How're the kids?

— Good; yeah.

He nods. He doesn't smile. His coffee is the same as hers, one of those lattes, in a glass. It looks strange in front of him. Too feminine. He hasn't touched it yet.

She sips hers. She tastes the coffee coming through the milk.

— Lovely, she says.

He picks up his. He drinks. She sees him swallow. She hears it. He puts it down. There's some milk on his top lip.

He wipes it off.

He nods.

— D'you want a cake or something?

254

— No, she says. — Thanks; I'm grand.

She points at the glasses.

— And I'm paying for these, remember.

— Okay.

She picks up her glass again. It wasn't a good idea, coming here. It might have been better at home. Easier. All she wants is to know him. Even a bit. He came to her. He rang her doorbell, nearly two years ago. But he's still the same stiff stranger.

— How's Leanne? she asks.

He moves. He sits back. He's nearly touching the window. His head must feel the cold from outside in the glass.

— How d'you mean? he says.

— Well, says Paula. — She seems to be getting on — I don't know. Fine. And I know you're in touch with her. So —

— She's in a good place, he says. — Today. You know, yourself.

She believes him. There's something about him. She's in a good place. He knows the bad places. He doesn't waste words.

She nods. She starts to smile — the tears grab her face. She's glad she's not facing the rest of the café. She quickly wipes her eyes. She swallows back a gulp. She wipes her eyes again.

He says nothing. He does nothing.

She picks up her coffee.

— Sorry, she says.

She puts the glass to her mouth. She's not sure she'll be able to swallow.

She's fine.

She puts the glass back down.

— I've been worried, she says.

He nods.

She wants to cry again. It isn't good. She's letting it fall. She won't be able to come back here.

— She's strong, he says.

She nods.

— Like you, she says.

He says nothing to that. He doesn't move.

She wants to run. She wants to hide and die. She wants to free him, and Leanne and Nicola and Jack.

— How —?

She stops.

— What? he says.

— No, she says.

She smiles. It's good; she can.

— D'you not want to — I don't know. Kill me?

— No, he says.

— Are you not angry?

— Sometimes, he says.

She makes herself; she looks straight at him.

— It's for me to deal with, he says.

— I'm sorry, she says.

— Yeah.

He nods.

— How? she says again. — How do you stay so calm?

— I don't, he says.

— You do, John Paul. Look at you. You're like a statue. I don't mean in a bad way. But you know what I mean.

— I do the yoga and that.

— Is that all it takes?

— No.

— So?

— I've no big answer.

— Give us a little one.

If it was a film he'd put his elbows on the table. He doesn't.

— I think a lot, he says. — I plan. Make sure I know what I'm doing.

— I'm all over the place, she says. — I can't stay still for more than a few minutes.

— You're doing alright.

— It's killing me, she says. — I mean, it's better. No contest. I'd never go back. But I have to keep, just — running away.

He nods, once.

He's elegant. It's not the clothes. It's him. The strength there that isn't muscle. The independence. There was none of that there when he ran away. Where did he get it? What happened?

— First, he says. — No.

He shakes his head; he dismisses what he's said.

— It's not a list, he says.

— Go on, John Paul.

— I don't have answers.

— Just, please. Say what you were going to say.

— You keep running away. That's what you said.

— Yes.

— You're not.

— I am.

He shakes his head.

— You're doing alright. You're facing it.

— It doesn't feel like that.

— Maybe it doesn't, he says. — But think about it. If you were running away you wouldn't actually be running. You'd have stopped. You wouldn't be bothered. You wouldn't be here.

He's right.

— You're keeping yourself busy, he says. — You have to.

She nods.

— So do I, he says.

He's said nothing new but she had to hear it. He should hate her; he shouldn't be here. But he is. That's why she believes him. That's why, maybe, she believes herself.

— You should give the yoga a go, he says.

— Yeah, she says. — I was actually thinking about it.

She has to ask, but something else runs in front of the question.

— You don't have your asthma any more.

— No, he says.

— How come?

— Don't know. Grew out of it.

She looks at him. She pushes herself; she has to ask.

— Why are you here, John Paul?

— Why are you?

— I'm your mother.

— There you go.

— I haven't been a good mother.

— No, he says. — You haven't.

Fuck, that's cruel.

— But I don't have another one.

He's looking straight at her. His face hasn't changed. His voice is the same.

There's nothing in his eyes.

It's as good as she'll get.

— Was it all bad? she says.

— No.

He picks up his glass. He won't talk until he puts it back down. She watches him drink. He puts the glass on the table.

— I wanted the kids to know they have a granny, he says.

He looks at her.

— It was Star's idea.

She nods. She smiles.

— That's nice, she says. — That's really nice. What about her own mother?

— What about her?

— Was she out of touch with her as well?

— No.

— Oh. I thought, with her mother being a heroin addict and that.

— No.

— God, though. It can't have been easy for the poor girl, growing up like that.

She hears what she's said. She looks at him. But there's nothing there, no sneer or smile.

— Who am I to talk? she says.

— It's a free country.

She doesn't know if she'll come here again.

She keeps falling for it. The happy ending, the Hollywood bit. But this man will never say I love you. Not to Paula. She'll never be able to say it to him. It'll always hang there. She'll always be the beggar.

— D'you think Leanne will be alright?

Leanne is already a safe subject.

— Yeah, he says.

— She's in a good place. You think.

— Yeah.

— That's great; that's brilliant. Did I tell you about your Auntie Carmel?

— What about her?

— You remember your Auntie Carmel?

— I remember Carmel, yeah.

— She has cancer.

— That's bad.

— Terrible.

It's easy, as long as they talk about nothing. Leanne and Carmel are nothing.

She wants to go home. She'll leave him alone.

— What kind? he says.

— The breast, she says. — She'll have to have a mastectomy and the other one — chemotherapy.

— She might be okay, he says.

— Yeah. Please God.

It's easy.

— How is she?

— Yeah, she's grand; she's great.

She's in a good place.

— You know Carmel, she says.

But he doesn't.

— She's all set for the fight.

— That's half it, he says. — The attitude.

He nods at her glass.

— D'you want another one? he says.

— No. I don't think so. Unless. You?

— No, he says.

He puts a hand on his stomach.

— Too much milk, he says. — It kind of sits there.

She knows something about him. The man, her son. He doesn't like too much milk.

Maybe there'll be more.

The tattoo is still there, on his arm. The Liverpool thing. She paid for it years ago, for his fourteenth birthday. She thought it would work. She'd give him the tattoo and he'd forgive her and love her for ever.

She points at his arm.

— D'you still like them, John Paul?

He doesn't look down.

— They're on the way back.

— Is that right? she says.

She's not sure what he means.

— I'm thinking of going to Istanbul, he says.

— Why?

He smiles. She wants to grab his face.

— Champions League final, he says.

— Liverpool are in it? she says.

— Yeah.

— Ah, lovely. In Istanbul?

— Yeah.

— That's, which one? The capital of Turkey.

— No.

— No?

— Ankara's the capital.

How does he know that?

— But it's Turkey, she says.

— Yeah.

— Will it not cost a fortune?

He shrugs. He's loose. He's almost boasting.

— What if you go and they don't win? It'd be terrible, so far away.

— They'll win, says John Paul.

She smiles. She could go with him. She could buy him a jersey. She could buy one for herself, PAULA on the back. Liver-pool, Liver-pool!

She wants to lean across and touch his arm, where the tattoo is. She just wants to hold him. To hold him.

It wouldn't work. He's all angles; he's hard. She'd end up with a puncture, the air fizzing out of her.

She just wants to hold him.

— I've got to get back, he says.

— To Star?

She holds him.

— Work, he says.

— Of course. I'm an eejit.

She stands up. She'll pay at the counter. She touches her face. She's okay. She's fine. She's not too hot.

— This was nice, she says.

He's standing up. He's looking out the window. It's stopped raining. He hasn't heard her.

She gets Jack to show her. She sits at his computer and she types in Mastectomy. She looked it up in his dictionary first. She has it spelt on a bit of paper. She finds each letter and taps. She checks to see the word building up in the box on the screen.

She clicks Search.

She can't take it in. The adventure is quickly over. Surgical removal of a breast. Surgical removal of the entire breast. Mastectomy lingerie. Mastectomy alone compared to lumpectomy combined with radiation. There are too many horrible words. And just too many words.

She doesn't want to give up. She looks down the page; she scrolls. She gets her eyes close to it. She reads. She waits for it to open. But there's too much. She's afraid to go further.

But she does.

She clicks open the first site. The types of mastectomy. Jesus, there's types. Axillary Node Dissection. Sentinel Lymph Node Biopsy. Not one word — she understands none of it. Invasive cancers. Separate incision. Lymphedema. Her eyes fall away from the words. She's stupid. She sits there.

She's checked herself for lumps. There weren't any; she found none. But how does she know? She can't even read properly. How can she trust her fingers, herself? She's never done a test. She's never had a smear. She's not even sure what a smear is, exactly.

She doesn't want to know.

It's just fuckin' stupid.

Cancer Facts 7.5. She's half out of the chair. She straightens up. She concentrates — she tries to. It's Carmel, not her. Preventive mastectomy (also called prophylactic or risk-reducing mastectomy) is the surgical removal of one or both breasts in an effort to prevent or reduce the risk of breast cancer. She reads it again. She understands; she thinks she does. You have a mastectomy to reduce the risk of cancer. But Carmel already has cancer. It's to stop it from spreading further. So why doesn't it fuckin' say that? Where can it spread to? Carmel's being killed by her own breasts.

She's drifting away, making it up. She's always at it.

She looks at the screen again, properly. She really has to get her eyes tested. She can feel the water behind them now. She has to lean right up to the screen. She can feel the heat on her face. Preventive mastectomy involves one of two basic procedures: total mastectomy and subcutaneous mastectomy. She's learning nothing, but meaning is breaking through. She's fighting with the words, with the fuckin' snobs who wrote them. In a total mastectomy, the doctor removes the entire breast and nipple.

Oh, sweet Jesus. Poor Carmel. It's the word there. Nipple. So harmless, and sexy. And funny and lovely. It's one of the clicky words. She clicks. A new page pops up. Dictionary of Cancer Terms. And there's Nipple. It's a cancer term. She can feel her own, protesting. In anatomy, the small raised area in the center of the breast through which milk can flow to the outside. What's cancerous about that? They can't even spell Centre.

She touches her nipples, through her sweatshirt. She looks behind her — poor Jack would die.

264

The doctor removes the entire breast and nipple. He does in his arse.

She's being stupid.

She's not.

She's not. This is all disgusting. The coldness of it. You can't just click these things and throw them at a screen. The doctor removes. Just like that. The doctor removes the entire prick and bollix.

She's at it again. Making it up. Fighting the facts. Because she can't understand what she's trying to read. Because she won't accept it. The doctor removes. It's happening in a couple of weeks. And the doctor's a woman. Carmel told her — she's lovely. In a subcutaneous mastectomy, the doctor removes the breast tissue but leaves the nipple intact. Tissue is another of the dictionary words. She doesn't click. Her breasts aren't tissue; they never fuckin' will be.

She's stupid. She's lying in bed. She'll try again tomorrow. She can do it in the morning, after she gets back from cleaning the Killester house. She won't give up.

She won't sleep.

Getting angry at words. It's just stupid. Hiding her ignorance. She's no help to Carmel. Just running away again.

She swings from side to side, even in the bed — she can feel herself. She'd get up now and go into Jack's room and turn on the computer and drag her eyes over and across those words again. She'd do it — and she'd feel sick and furious before she was even sitting down. She knows what's happening. She knows what she's up to. And that's not fair — she's not up to anything. John Paul was right. She isn't running away. She did, this afternoon. But she knew already, as she cursed the computer and tried to slam Jack's door; the carpet square in his room is new, like fuckin' grass, so she couldn't slam it properly. She knew she'd be coming back.

She's not going to sleep. She could get up. But she won't. She could read. But that would mean getting up and turning on the light. She doesn't have a light beside the bed — that's something else for her list. And she doesn't want to read. She'd be sick if she saw words packed onto a page. She can feel it, just thinking about it. In her stomach, in her throat. Nipple.

She thinks of Carmel being cut. It's hard to imagine, Carmel asleep, letting it happen. But it's going to happen.

— I might bring me own knife, Carmel said, when they were talking, the last time, three nights ago. — It's a very good one.

— Stop, said Denise.

— It is, said Carmel. — You should see what it does to chicken.

She's sure Carmel's asleep. Snoring away, keeping everyone else awake.

Why would she think that? She's joking. But why would she think it? Denise is the thick. Carmel's the joker. That's the way. Paula's the alco. It's been that way for years, *was* that way. Denise is gormless. Carmel's bitter. Paula's hopeless.

Carmel isn't asleep. Paula isn't hopeless. Denise is having the time of her life.

Paula sits up.

Her mobile is on the floor. She leans out and down, and gets it. She hears herself groan — she keeps forgetting; it's just a habit.

She selects Text Messages. She taps the keys. *Hw r u?* She fires it off to Carmel. She lies back. She puts the phone beside her. She turns the pillow. She lies back again. She puts her hands outside the duvet.

The mobile buzzes. She finds it under the duvet. She was right. Carmel's awake. *Go 2 slp u fuckn eejt.*

She laughs.

She replies. *Thnkng of u.*

Carmel's straight back. *Thnx.*

She puts the phone back on the floor. She lets it drop.

She'll sleep now. She might.

— How's Carmel?

— She's grand, says Paula. — Yeah; she's great. You know.

They're in Rita's sitting room.

— It's a terrible thing, says Rita.

— Yeah.

— Hanging over her like that.

— Yeah.

— And it could happen to any of us, Paula.

— For fuck sake, Rita.

— Don't mind me, says Rita.

— No, I was rude, says Paula. — Sorry.

— She's your sister, Paula, says Rita. — You can be as rude as you like. Will you tell her she's in my prayers?

— I will, says Paula. — She'll like that.

— She can shove her fuckin' prayers, says Carmel.

It's the same day, later. They're in Paula's kitchen.

— Rita's sound enough, says Paula.

— I know, says Carmel. — I know. And I shouldn't be fussy where the prayers come from.

Carmel has the date. She knows when she's going into the hospital. The beginning of June.

— Will you be able to wait?

— I don't have much of a choice, says Carmel. — It's not like the fuckin' hairdresser's. I can't go up the road to the next one.

— Okay, says Paula. — Okay.

They're alone, together. There's no Denise.

— She'll be off riding some dark handsome stranger, says Carmel.

— She's actually gone to the doctor with Harry, says Paula. — He's having his ears syringed.

— Lovely.

— He was afraid to drive the car after. Something about his balance.

— You couldn't make it up, says Carmel. — Could you?

— No, says Paula. — She'll be here later.

— He'll probably keep the fuckin' wax, says Carmel.

— Ah Jesus.

— Make earrings for his loving wife.

Paula has Marks and Spencer's stuff for them. She bought it today, before going on to work. And three new plates, three glasses, two bottles of wine. The red for Carmel, and Denise prefers the white. It's in the fridge. When Denise goes over and opens it, she'll see it's nicely filled. It's Friday night. There's a chicken. There's mince, and a box of eggs. There's yoghurt. There's ice-cream, in the freezer. And pizzas. And, back on the table, there's a brand new corkscrew. Paula bought it today. She got the cork out of Carmel's bottle with it, no bother. The bottle's on Carmel's side of the table.

— You must be nervous, a bit, says Paula. — Are you?

— A bit, yeah, says Carmel. — I'm fuckin' terrified.

Paula gets up and hugs her. Carmel's arms go around Paula. They stay that way for a good while.

— I'm an eejit, says Carmel.

Paula lets go of Carmel.

— Stop that, she says. — Why are you?

— It's only an operation, says Carmel.

— It isn't only anything, says Paula.

— D'you know what it reminds me of? says Carmel. — And it's weird.

— What? says Paula.

— Being pregnant.

— No.

— Yeah, says Carmel. — The waiting. Knowing it's going to happen but not knowing exactly when.

— But you know now, says Paula.

— But it still feels a bit the same. I've even packed a fuckin' bag. I have it at the door of the bedroom. Jesus, Paula, what's that shite Jack's playing?

— It's not Jack's, says Paula.

— What is it?

— It's the White Stripes. I'll turn it off. I'll change it.

— Is it yours? says Carmel.

— Yeah, says Paula.

— For fuck sake.

— Ah, lay off, Carmel. I like it.

She puts the CD into its box. Carmel comes over and picks up more boxes.

— Are all these yours?

— No, says Paula. — Some of them.

— Have you no good stuff?

— Like what?

— Stop being thick. The 70s.

— That's thirty years ago.

— It feels like fuckin' yesterday. What's going on, Paula? Is this something menopausal, or what?

She's holding up Queens of the Stone Age.

— That's Jack's.

Paula's blushing. She can feel her face burn. She'd wanted Carmel to notice the stereo. But she hadn't. It's no big deal. Every house has one, or two or three of them.

Carmel holds up another one.

— Jack's? she says.

— Yeah, says Paula.

How to Dismantle an Atomic Bomb.

— Like shite, says Carmel. — It's yours.

— Yeah.

Carmel hands it to her.

— Stick it on, she says.

She goes over to the table, sits down again.

— I've never really listened to music, she says. —
Even the old stuff. I don't really care. The first couple
of seconds is enough.

— I was like that, says Paula.

— No, says Carmel. — You weren't.

"Vertigo" starts. Paula turns the sound down.

— I've heard that one, says Carmel.

— It's all over the place, says Paula.

She sits down.

— I love it, says Paula.

Carmel nods.

— D'you ever think of Wendy?

— Yeah, says Paula.

— Me too, says Carmel.

— She was lovely.

Carmel nods.

— What would she be like now? says Paula. — D'you
ever wonder?

— Still lovely.

— Yeah, says Paula.

— She'd be, what?

— Forty-four, I think.

— Jesus, says Carmel.

They laugh.

— Wendy liked her music too, says Carmel. —
Didn't she?

— Yeah, says Paula.

— The bedroom wall, says Carmel. — The pictures she stuck up. It wasn't just Donny Osmond and them.

— She loved Led Zeppelin, says Paula.

— D'you have any of theirs?

— No, says Paula. — Jack might.

— Really? says Carmel. — Are they still big?

— I think so, yeah, says Paula.

She doesn't think they've talked like this before. They're like two people getting to know each other — their first date. Or two old friends who haven't seen each other in years.

— That was your man, Ozzy Osbourne, wasn't it?

— Led Zeppelin? says Paula.

— Yeah.

— No.

— Well, that's sorted, says Carmel. — I won't go under the knife thinking that Ozzy Osbourne was in Led Zeppelin.

— Stop.

— I didn't really know her, says Carmel. — The age gap, you know.

— That's only natural, says Paula. — In a big family.

— I was gone before she was really a teenager. And I stayed away.

Paula says nothing.

— Fuckin' regrets, Paula, says Carmel. — That's the worst part of this.

— We all have regrets.

— Just — look it. Listen.

— Sorry, says Paula. — Go on.

— I'm not being morbid, says Carmel. — I'm trying not to be, anyway. And I know my chances are good. And even if the operation isn't, what's it — it's too late — I know I won't be dying there and then, on the table.

Paula says nothing.

— Unless something goes really wrong. There's a power cut, or the doctor has a game of golf she has to get to, or something.

Carmel sits up.

— But anyway. I'm optimistic. I am. But fuck it, I'm not stupid.

She stops. Paula knows. She isn't finished.

— Dead, says Carmel. — That's the word. You have to get used to it. And you can't help looking back. It seems to be natural, you know.

Paula nods.

— Yeah, says Carmel. — And the good things kind of glide past you. You can take them for granted. But the bad things, the regrets. They fuckin' sting.

— I know, says Paula.

Carmel is looking at her.

— Yeah, she says. — You know exactly what I mean. Sorry, Paula. You become a bit full of yourself when you're dying.

They should cry. But they don't. Carmel nods at the stereo.

— It's shite.

— Fuck off.

Carmel pours some more of the wine.

— So, says Paula. — What stings?

— Things I said, says Carmel.

She shrugs.

— It's stupid, she says. — You can't be going around regretting every fuckin' word. And if I wasn't sick I wouldn't even be thinking about it. But I was a bitch, wasn't I?

— No.

— Sometimes.

— Yeah.

— See?

— We all are, says Paula.

— Yeah, but I'm good at it, says Carmel.

— That's true.

— But that's not really it, says Carmel. — Not really what I mean. I don't think I'm a bad person.

— God, no.

Carmel saved Paula's life, before Paula knew she wanted to be saved.

— No, I'm grand about it, says Carmel. — But I'm going to be nicer.

Paula laughs.

— Fuck off, says Carmel. — I am. Regardless, you know. But it's other things I really regret.

— Like?

— The things I didn't do.

— Like?

— I just wish I'd done more.

She slaps her stomach.

— I got old too fuckin' early. I let myself. Look at me.

She slaps herself again. She lifts her jumper, grabs hold of the flab. And Jack walks in. He's immediately very red. His face is blotched and glowing. It's too much for him. He knows about her cancer, her breast. And Carmel's always been good to him.

— Hi, he says.

He says it to the floor.

— Howyeh, Jack, says Carmel.

— Hi.

— Hungry, Jack? says Paula.

— No, I'm grand.

He turns. He's gone.

— Poor Jack, says Carmel, after they've stopped laughing. — He's probably starving.

— You were saying about regrets, says Paula.

She's at the tap. She's filling her glass.

— There's not much to say, says Carmel, — that isn't obvious. I wish I'd lived a bit more.

— Like Denise.

— No, not like Denise.

She takes a drink. She lowers the glass.

— Okay, she says. — A bit like Denise. But, not really. No real regrets there.

She's started to peel the label off the wine bottle.

— Nothing dramatic, she says. — Just, things. Like, I never go into town. I decided I didn't like it, years ago. And I don't know why. Because I did like it. D'you know what I mean?

— Yeah, says Paula. — I think so.

— You go into town.

— I have to, says Paula. — To work.

— I know, says Carmel. — But you still go in. And it's not just town. It's not even town. It's — I don't know. It's the attitude. You know. There's nothing good. There's something wrong with everything. I'm not really like that at all.

— I know.

— But it's the way I've been. Nothing worth seeing, nothing worth doing. I go to nothing. And now I'm afraid to.

— Why?

— I don't know. I want to be close to home. In case.

— What about Bulgaria? says Paula.

— What about it?

— You said you don't like going into town.

— Yeah.

— But you go to Bulgaria. It's not on the Dart, Carmel.

— Yeah, but that's different, says Carmel. — We did that because everyone else is doing it. It is a good investment, though.

— But you've been there and other places, says Paula. — I don't even have a passport yet.

— Yet, says Carmel. — You see, that's it. You said Yet. You're going to get one. We know you are. You're fuckin' amazing, by the way.

Paula says nothing; it's happened too fast. She's not sure she heard it.

— If it was me, says Carmel, — I wouldn't bother getting a passport. I'd think of reasons not to.

She nods at the stereo.

— It's not too bad, she says.

Paula smiles.

— Will I stick in the food or wait for Denise?

— Don't wait for that one. She's probably riding Harry's doctor.

— The new you, yeah?

— I forgot.

She takes a sip.

— Yes, she says. — Let's wait for Denise. She'll probably be starving.

— After all the exercise.

— Exactly.

— I've a few things in the fridge that don't need cooking.

Paula stands up. She hears a key in the front door. She hopes it's Leanne. She hopes it isn't. She doesn't know — it's dreadful. Shame sweeps across her, and she can't stop it. She shouldn't have asked Carmel and Denise here. There's too much to show them. Leanne's in the hall — and it could be anything; she could be in any state. Paula wants to shout, to run out there and slam the door.

— That's Leanne, I think, she says.

Carmel sits up a bit. She's still a wagon. But that's not fair. Carmel knows. Paula's seen Carmel ripped apart by her own children.

She goes to the fridge. She opens the door. She hides behind it.

She doesn't.

She's getting the dips, and carrots. She's trusting Leanne; she's letting it happen. And the cold from the fridge is good. It knocks the sweat off her face. She'd love to climb in, just for a minute.

She shuts the door with her elbow.

Leanne's there. She's already sitting at the table.

Paula's afraid to talk. Every word will betray Leanne — she knows it. And Leanne will know it. Carmel doesn't matter. It's not about shame; she doesn't care. It's about her voice, what Leanne will hear.

— Jesus, Leanne, she says. — You must've heard me going to the fridge.

Leanne shrugs and does a face.

— I wouldn't eat that muck, she says. — What is it, an'anyway?

— Food for oul' ones, says Paula.

She puts the box on the table, and the carrot sticks.

— Ah Jesus, says Carmel.

— I'm getting you crackers, says Paula. — Shut up.

She smiles at Leanne. She doesn't look at the bottle, at Leanne's hands, at the little bits of label paper on the table, around the bottle.

She opens the press. She gets down the crackers. She throws them across to Carmel.

Leanne has the glass Paula left on the table for Denise.

She stands up. She brings the glass with her. She goes to the tap.

She feels it when she picks up the bucket. Her back. She's already walking crooked, to give it room, avoid admitting it.

She's not sure.

It was nothing dramatic. She just picked up the bucket and felt it, at the bottom of her spine, to the side there.

It's happened before. It goes away. Like a threat, something that'll come back when it wants to. A nerve, just gently tapped. It's horrible. It's playing with her.

She feels like a cripple already. The last time, it hurt every time she put her foot on the stairs. She can feel herself now, shifting all her weight away from the twinge. She feels fat and breakable; her belly is sticking out. The pain lights up every other pain. Every wound and break she's had, going on and off. Reminding her. Catching up.

It's Wednesday night. She has to work. It's a good while since she's been afraid that the fridge won't be filled. She's earning more than she ever did. But the back is there, the twinge. I can do this. I can bring you down.

She shifts the bucket to her other hand. It's full of water. It's always heavy — it's going to make her snap. It's up into her breath.

She stops. She bends her knees. She puts down the bucket. Now, she bends her fuckin' knees. Forty years too late.

There's no tax, no stamps. It's money into her hand. If she stops working, she never worked. She's never been happy with it, but it's all there ever was. And all there is. If she doesn't do it, other people will. She knows, she sees them. It's why they're here. Go back to your own fuckin' country. That's not her; that's not Paula. There's plenty of work. She won't be waiting long. But she doesn't want to lose the extra money for supervising, or the name, and the years that went into getting it. She's near the bottom of the heap. Tonight, she knows it. She feels it.

She leans the mop against the wall. She opens the top button of her jeans. That's a bit better.

It's like the wiring, across and up her back, through her ribs and up, to the back of her neck — it's like the wire has been tapped and the pain is singing through the wires, humming, loudly, softly. A bird has landed on the wire. It won't get off. It keeps opening and closing its claws.

Opening, and closing.

She picks up the bucket. She can't stand straight. The bucket's too full. She gets it to the lip of the sink. She empties it. She dips the bucket slowly. She doesn't want to spill the water.

A week on her back and the job is gone. The house jobs aren't enough.

There's other work. There's real work, with stamps and pensions. But how does she get one of those jobs; how does she explain? She hasn't worked since 1975? What does she say? She doesn't know.

She wipes the sink. There's grit from the water around the sides. She rinses the cloth. She squeezes it. The action, from her hands, arms, shoulders — there's no quick jab.

She wipes the sink again. It shines; it's grand.

She steps away from the sink. She picks up the bucket. She bends her knees. A tap, on her nerve. It's there. A claw. She tries not to be too nervous.

Everything is hopping. Everything is sweating. Every hole and dent. Every thump and kick. All of Paula's

280

past is in her back. It's there, ready, breathing. One last kick from a man who died twelve years ago.

She has to put the buffer away. She'd forgotten; she wants to cry. She has to balance the bucket and mop on top of it. She pushes from her left side — she tries to save the right.

She feels it when she presses the button for the lift. Just lifting her arm, she feels it stab, and go. She's into the lift. She presses for the basement. She lifts her arm — it's fine. The door closes. She feels the movement, the shake, drop. She adjusts the bucket, resettles it on the buffer.

The lift stops. The door opens. She has to pull the buffer out. There's no room to turn it and push. The door starts to close. She does it before she thinks — she shoves the door back with her shoulder.

It's fine. She's okay.

She pulls the buffer. She starts to pull. She feels it; it's there. But she has to pull.

She's out of the lift.

Her mobile rings.

She digs into her pocket. Right side — the pain shoots up, but stops before it really starts. Her hand is shaking.

— Hello?

— It's me.

Nicola.

— What, love?

— Did you hear? says Nicola.

— Hear what?

— About Kylie Minogue, says Nicola.

— Ah, lovely, says Paula. — I'd love to go. With the girls, is it?

Will she leave her alone now?

— What? says Nicola.

— The Kylie concert, says Paula.

— What concert? It's not a concert.

— I've to go for the Dart, love.

— She has breast cancer, says Nicola. — Did you not hear?

— Kylie?

— Yeah.

— That's terrible.

She's always liked Kylie Minogue.

The bird lands — she puts her hand to her back.

She remembers one morning, dancing in the kitchen with Nicola — I SHOULD BE SO LUCKY — LUCKY, LUCKY, LUCKY — and she held up John Paul, a couple of inches, so he'd be the same height — I SHOULD BE SO LUCKY IN LOVE — around and around the kitchen. Her arms ached — she remembers. And when it was over Nicola asked her what was the stuff on her sleeve. It was blood. She hadn't noticed it. She'd gone to bed in her clothes the night before. She'd fallen asleep holding a wet cloth to her face.

Nicola just said something.

— Sorry, love. I lost you there.

— I said, will Carmel be okay? says Nicola.

Paula can hear Nicola's impatience — her mother, the eejit.

Go away, Nicola.

— About Kylie, you mean? says Paula.

— Yes!

— I'm not sure she even likes Kylie, says Paula.

She feels the claws.

— I have to go.

She presses the red button. She leans on the buffer. She tries to lean out of the pain, to get under it. The mobile goes again. She doesn't answer. The ringing stops.

She tries not to let Nicola annoy her. But it's been happening. Nicola's the one who's furthest from her. It didn't feel like that before, but now it does. Nicola reared the younger ones as much as Paula ever did. She picked up Paula and washed her. She fed Leanne and Jack. And after she left she still looked after Paula.

She puts the mobile back in her pocket.

She stands away from the buffer. She pushes. She's fine. She hears and feels the double buzz. Nicola's text. She'll read it when she's finished.

She pushes the buffer around the corner. There's the corridor, and the storeroom. She could leave the buffer outside. She won't — she can't. She's the boss. It's her job, putting away the buffers and buckets that the other cleaners leave outside the door. She's last out, for €30 a week extra. She knows exactly what that can buy, and what not having it will mean.

The metal double-doors need a pull. The lock's a bastard. She's never sure when she has it. It's just luck; there's never a click. It gives tonight. She feels it come.

She turns on the light. She stands there for a while.

She feels bad about Nicola. But it's hard. Nicola sees no difference between Paula now and Paula the way she was ten years ago, five years, last year. Nicola was never a child; she never could be. Paula's fault — she knows, she feels it. It's in her back there, too. She could never feel guilty enough.

There are five buffers. They're in a line, like dodgems, against the corridor wall. Paula rolls her own in first. She feels the dust against her face. It's funny. No one cleans the room that holds the cleaning stuff. She goes out, and brings in the next. She pushes with both hands. She straightens her back, a bit.

One more buffer. Then the hoovers and the wheelie-buckets. She's not puffing now. She's not afraid to breathe. It's still there, though. The bird creeps along the wire.

Nicola will never trust her. She'll always be checking. Paula doesn't drink. She's nearly ready to make that claim. But she can't say that to Nicola. Because she'll see Nicola's face. Not disbelief, or sarcasm. Just sadness. And she'll keep checking the shelves. She'll keep looking in the fridge when she comes into the kitchen. That's why she bought the fridge for Paula, although she doesn't know it. She can walk right in and open it. She's not looking for alcohol. She knows it won't be there. She's looking for the mixers. Can I have a cup of mixers, Mammy? Paula will always be helpless, and hopeless. There's nothing she can ever do about it.

284

It's hard to take. It's hard not to hope. Leanne has seen the change in Paula. Jack has seen it. He's a bit afraid, but he's seen. She thinks John Paul has. Carmel, Denise, Rita Kavanagh. Even her mother, the last time Paula went to see her — Did you do something to your hair? — before she shut down again and stared across Paula's shoulder. Paula had done nothing to her hair. It suits you.

Paula is one of Nicola's children. It'll never be different.

She hates it.

She shuts the storeroom door. She's careful. She caught her skin in the door a few months ago. It took a chunk right off the side of her hand. She checks — she pulls the handle. It's locked. She can go home.

She remembers Nicola's text. She'll read it on the Dart.

She's happier than Nicola. That's probably true. Alcoholics can stop drinking but what is there for the children of alcoholics? Is it always too late? Probably. She doesn't know.

She's outside the building. She feels each step as she goes down. There's a jab, waiting — the little claws. She can't relax her body. She can't walk evenly. Her stomach is pushing out again. She sees the bridge at Tara Street. She's in trouble if the escalator isn't working. She can't face all those steps.

The Kylie Minogue thing. God love her, she's gorgeous. She's always liked Kylie. It's kind of heart-breaking. But Nicola phoning, she was letting Paula know that she hadn't thought of it. It'll be all over the papers, and on the telly, pictures of Kylie, her famous arse, experts going on about her chances of recovery, diagrams of mastectomies, other famous girls who survived or didn't. Carmel won't be able to avoid it. Nicola thought of it — Paula didn't.

Sitting down on the train, bending her back — what'll happen? It's one of the newer carriages. The seats aren't nice; you can't sit back. She's better off sitting up straight. She takes the mobile from her pocket. She sits. She's fine.

She phones Carmel.

— Are you coming home from work? says Carmel.

— Yeah.

— On the Dart?

— Yeah.

— Well, if you mention Kylie Minogue, I'll be waiting at the station and I'll smack the face off you.

— People are worried about you, says Paula.

— Oh, I know, says Carmel. — And I've had to cancel my tour of Asia and Australia. For fuck sake.

— They mean well.

— Ah, I know, says Carmel. — How're things with yourself?

— Not too bad. My back's at me.

— I'll swap with you, says Carmel.

— No sympathy for me tonight, Carmel, no?

— Hang on, says Carmel. — I need a bowl. My heart is fuckin' bleeding.

— Fuck off.

— Is it bad?

— It's thinking about it, says Paula.

— Take it easy, says Carmel.

— Yeah. Did my Nicola phone you?

— No. Why?

— I just thought.

— No.

— Grand.

She sees Nicola's car outside the house. She's not in the mood. The back's enough to be dealing with. She doesn't need Nicola. The guilt, the uselessness.

Leanne's in the front room.

Paula speaks softly.

— Where is she?

— Kitchen, says Leanne.

— By herself?

— Yeah.

Leanne's watching one of those reality things. Celebrity Fuckin' Eejits. Paula stands there for a while. Leanne points at the screen.

— He wants to get off with — not her. Her.

— Oh.

Paula goes into the kitchen.

— On your own?

Nicola's sitting at the table. There's a mug at her elbow. She's filling out forms or something. She's always working.

— Yeah, she says.

She doesn't look up.

— Where're the kids?

— At home, says Nicola. — With Tony.

— Ah, yeah.

— He is their father, says Nicola.

287

Paula looks at her. She puts her jacket on a chair.

— Is everything okay?

— Yeah.

— Nicola?

— What?

— Is everything okay?

— Yeah.

She'd love Nicola to say No. It would do so much. The vulnerability, and the trust. She'd be Nicola's mother. She could rest. Her back wouldn't matter.

Nicola picks up her forms and papers. She taps them on the table. She slips them into a plastic folder. She stands up. She stretches, a long time, her arms way up. She's gorgeous. Her tummy there, where her blouse has come up out of her trousers. The little mark where she once had her belly-button pierced.

— Tired?

— Yeah.

— Me too. More tea?

— No, says Nicola.

Paula picks up the kettle. It's warm but light. It needs more water. She waits for the twinge; she half expects.

She fills the kettle. She talks to the window.

— So, what has you here?

— Well, if I'm not welcome —

— Lay off, Nicola. You're always welcome. But it's night and Leanne's in there and I think Jack's upstairs —

— He is.

— And you're in here on your own. Why?

— I just thought, says Nicola. — On the phone, earlier.

— What?

— You sounded a bit strange.

— It's my back, says Paula.

She's annoyed, too late. She jumped in too quickly with her excuse. She's done what Nicola does; she's killed it.

She puts the kettle down. She presses the switch.

She turns.

— I thought the back was going on me again, she says. — Like before. When you phoned.

— Is it alright?

— I think so.

— You didn't answer my text.

— My back; sorry.

Nicola moves towards her.

— Let's have a look.

— Carmel's grand about Kylie, by the way.

— Take off your top. Did you phone her?

— Yeah, she's grand.

— You're all twisted.

— I know, says Paula.

She feels Nicola's fingers on her back.

— Where's it sore?

— Lower. Right. Yeah, there.

— Will I rub it?

— It can't do any harm, says Paula.

— You can lie on the couch.

— I don't want to disturb Leanne.

— She can sit on your head, says Nicola. — Go on in. I'll make the tea.

— No, says Paula. — I'll make my own tea. I'm not a total cripple.

She puts her hand on Nicola's shoulder. She feels a jab as she lifts her hand. She doesn't let it stop her. She doesn't let it run across her face.

She feels Nicola tighten, under her fingers. She sees Nicola staring at her arm — as if they're getting into a fight. She feels her bones relax. She sees her look at Paula now, and smile. They're both trying. They're trying to meet. And they know it.

— You're not to come running every time you think there's something wrong, says Paula.

Nicola fights back the objection; Paula can see it.

— D'you understand? she says.

— Yeah. I do.

— I'm grand, says Paula. — D'you believe me?

— Yeah.

She doesn't, but Paula won't say that.

She's tired. She's heavy. The pain is still threatening. She woke up with it, the minute she moved and knew she was awake. It's been there all day.

She didn't really sleep. She feels that now, around her eyes, and in her lungs.

She woke up low. There's nothing she can do about it. She walked to the shop earlier. It's a lovely day; that much got through. She bought herself a Bounty. She smiled at the East European young one in the shop.

She can't remember eating it. She did eat it. The wrapper's in the bin. She runs her tongue behind her teeth. There's no chocolate there, no taste.

She lies on her bed.

She came up for something. It doesn't matter.

She's in the hall. She's holding her jacket.

She's in the back garden. She's in the grass. It's nearly up to her knees. She bends down; she's careful. She grabs some grass. It feels hard in her hand. Her wrist is sore, her whole arm. She lets go of the grass.

She sees the wine bottles. Beside the step, at the back door. She remembers. Carmel and Denise, the red and the white. She doesn't remember putting them there.

She's in the kitchen. She hears the kettle. She hears rain on the window. Her mobile is ringing.

She's in bed. It's dark outside. She sits up — did she go to work? She can't breathe. She gets up, she turns on the light. She remembers. She went to work. She came home. She turns off the light. She gets back into bed. She's wide awake.

She wakes up. She's on the couch. It's bright — the street light. The curtains are open. She tastes drink — dry and sour — in her mouth. She swallows — it's gone. She hasn't been drinking; she's awake. The telly's off. She came down to watch it. She thinks she did. She's cold.

She's in the garden. The wine bottles are empty. She puts one to her mouth. She must have rinsed it. And washed it. No taste on the glass.

She goes back in. She shuts the door. She locks it. She still has the bottle. She looks at the clock. It's four in the morning, just after. She puts the bottle on the table. She picks it up. She can't leave it there. Jack will see it, and Leanne. She goes back to the door. She unlocks it. She puts the bottle back out, beside the other one. She bends down.

She goes back in. She locks the door.

The smell, the stale drink — the dead air is around her. She'd climb in. She'd lick every broken piece and bleed happily to death. Especially the green glass. She'd bleed green and lie down.

There's a man talking to her.

— The wasps are a curse, aren't they?

He's beside her.

— They are, yeah, she says.

He leans across her, so he can drop a bottle into the green hole.

— Sorry; excuse me.

She looks at his bottles. They're in a cardboard box he's able to hold in one arm. A couple of wine bottles, and four beer ones, she thinks. A Dolmio sauce bottle, not properly rinsed. Two little brown medicine bottles. No cans.

— It's a sign of the summer, he says. — I suppose.

— Yeah, says Paula.

He gets out of her way. She drops Carmel's bottle into the hole. She drops Denise's. She scrunches up the plastic bag and puts it in her pocket.

She doesn't know why — she takes the brown medicine bottles from his box.

— Oh, he says. — Thank you.

— No problem, she says.

He's nice.

He's right about the wasps. They're zipping around, or just hanging there; they're nearly in her breath. She goes across to the brown bin. She feels the broken glass under her feet.

He's wearing nice shoes. They're black and they're polished.

She drops in the brown bottles. They don't break; she can hear that.

— Any more? she says.

— No, he says.

He turns over the box.

— I'm not drinking enough.

— D'you drink coffee? she says.

Jesus Christ.

He's about sixty, she'd say. He shaved himself this morning. He's blushing. So is she. What sort of a knacker is she? She hasn't even washed yet. It's a fuckin' bottle bank.

— Yes, he says. — I do.

His name is Joe. He has four children and three grandchildren. He worked in the Department of Health. He took early retirement. He's thinking of doing a degree next year, in politics or Greek. His Nike hoodie belongs to his son. He left it behind when he visited last Sunday with the grandchild, a girl. Sorcha. He has a mobile home in Wexford.

— Courtown?

— Not far. Cahore.

— Lovely.

He'll go down there a good bit, now that it's looking like summer. His children use it most of the time. Three of them are married. The other one's a bit wild. He came to this bottle bank because the one nearer his house was full. He didn't want to leave the bottles there in the box. They'd have ended up being broken. The coffee is excellent. His wife left him eight years ago.

— And you, Paula?

— Well, she says. — My husband's dead.

— Oh.

— Ten years. Actually, eleven.

— That's hard.

What is she fuckin' doing?

— I've four children as well, she says. — Two married, two still with me at home. One in school, doing his Leaving next year. And I've four little grandchildren. I'm ahead of you there, Joe. Three little girls and a boy.

She likes his hair. It's a bright kind of grey and it's longer than it should be, and it looks strong. His tie looks stupid with the hoodie.

— And do you work, yourself, Paula?

— Yes, I do, Joe, she says. — I clean some offices. I'm kind of in charge.

She can tell. He's not put off. He's quite excited.

No, he's not. She is.

She's not. But she likes him.

294

— Where's your wife? she says. — Ex-wife; sorry. Are
yis — are you divorced?

— No, he says. — Not formally.

He doesn't mind the question.

— She lives in Kerry now, he says. — We're the best
of friends.

You are in your bollix.

She smiles.

— That's good.

— And your husband, he says. — How did it —?

— He got shot, says Paula.

— Oh, God.

— By the Guards.

He's not so relaxed now. But he's not running away.

— An accident? he says.

He doesn't believe that; she can see it.

— No, she says. — It was deliberate.

She picks up her coffee.

— He wasn't a nice man, Joe, unfortunately.

She likes the way she's talking. Unfortunately. But
it's a bit mad.

She takes a sip of her coffee. She's careful. She's
being watched.

He isn't good-looking. He probably never was. But
he's nice. There's something steady about him. She can
see it, even in the way he's sitting. He's lonely. She can
see that. And a bit awkward.

He's brave enough. He asks her another one.

— Was it, sorry — was it robbery?

— Yes, she says. — Well. No. It was worse, really.
Kidnapping.

— Oh, dear.

— And it got even worse, Joe. He killed a woman.

That's it, anyway. It's out in the open. She's not shaking too badly.

— That must have been difficult, he says.

He even smiles.

— I'm sorry, he says. — That must sound a bit feeble.

— No, no, she says. — It was. Difficult.

She wants to run. This is mad.

— We weren't living together at the time, she says. — But it was terrible.

— I can imagine.

No, you can't, Joe.

— Yeah, she says.

— This was eleven years ago?

— That's right.

— I think I remember something —

— It was on the News. And in the papers and that.

— It must have been.

— Yeah, she says. — Outside the house and all. Even though he didn't live there.

— I hope you had the grass cut, Paula.

He is a nice man. She laughs. He laughs.

— I'm only joking, he says.

— I know, she says. — And, no. The garden was a bit of a mess, so it was.

He has no fuckin' idea.

— So, she says. — What about you? Was your grass cut when your wife walked out on you?

Jesus.

296

— God, sorry.

That sounded vicious. She's taking over from Carmel.

— Well, he says. — I was actually cutting the grass. As it happens.

He laughs — he makes himself.

— Somebody had to, he says. — But she didn't like it, apparently. And I thought that was a bit unfair.

— Hang on, says Paula. — She left you because you were cutting the grass?

— No, he says. — That would be ridiculous. I actually went in for a glass of water. It was a hot day.

He's still angry. She can hear it. We're the best of friends. Yeah; maybe.

He picks up his cup.

— She'd packed a bag, he says.

— What's her name?

— Oh. Mary.

— Sorry, she says. — Go on.

He puts the cup on the table.

— Isn't this a little bit strange, Paula?

— I suppose it is, she says.

For fuck sake.

— But go on, anyway, she says.

— I probably misled you when I mentioned that I was cutting the grass.

— I don't know, she says.

— A minute ago you told me that your husband murdered someone. And now I'm telling you about my wife's departure. What's your surname, Paula?

— Spencer, says Paula.

They laugh.

— It's because we don't know each other, she says.
— That's why. It's easy.

— You might be right, he says.

— What's yours?

— Sorry?

— Your surname.

— Oh, yes. Prescott.

— Like the dry cleaners.

— No relation, he says. — But I have been told I'm a bit dry.

— She told you.

— Yes.

Get over it.

She'll give him another minute.

— Anyway, he says. — Dry or not. She was going.

— Another man, says Paula.

— No, he says. — A woman.

— What? You and —

— She left me for a woman.

— Fuck off.

The words shock him; she sees it.

— Sorry, she says.

This is fuckin' ridiculous.

— It's just, she says. — I'd never have guessed that. He nods.

— Yes, well, he says. — Neither would I. I'd still be standing there. But, luckily —

He snorts. She half expects to see snot on his top lip.

— She put me out of my misery.

— Jesus.

She'd never have guessed. She's not sure why not, because she's often thought about women and women. It's never seemed wrong or even strange. She's often thought how easy it would be.

But this is weird, the whole set-up here.

— Tell us, she says. — Why are you telling me this?

— Well, he says. — I have to say. It's the most interesting thing about me.

— Fair enough, she says. — My husband was shot. Your wife ran off with another bird. We're fuckin' fascinating.

— We are, he says. — We are.

She's dying to tell people, Carmel, Leanne, even poor Jack. Not about his wife; that's nobody's business. Just that she's met him. I've met someone, by the way. She can hear herself. Just a friend, like. Nothing serious. She gave him her mobile number. He doesn't have one. They're meeting again. They're going for a walk. They're meeting at the Causeway Road. She'll walk there. It's not that far.

She keeps thinking about him in his kitchen, and his wife walking out the door. Mary. And she keeps following Mary to her car — she'd have a car — and she puts the case in the boot and she drives off to Kerry. And Paula's in the back, trying to see her in the rear-view mirror. Why is she leaving? Why did she leave? How do you become a lesbian when you're fifty? She was the same age Paula is now, or thereabouts. He'd have mentioned it if she'd been much younger.

She's not mad about walking. It's never made much sense. It was his idea. And that's fine. It's safe. His hand won't go for her leg. She laughs at that, alone. She'd noticed his hands. They were small. No dirt in the nails when he picked up his cup. They were cleaner than hers.

But the wife. It can't have been out of the blue. He comes in from the garden for a glass of water and his wife's turned into a lezzer. What kind of a man has that effect? What does he have to do?

She's married to a dead man and she's day-dreaming about a man who'll be dead in a few years. He's sixty, for fuck sake. She doesn't fancy him. Not at all. There are old men she could fall for, no bother. Not old, just a good bit older than her. Sean Connery, Leonard Cohen — she saw a picture of him in the paper a few months ago; he was seventy. She likes that old footballer, Frank McLintock. And there's Paul Newman. And Proinsias De Rossa. She saw the King of Spain on telly and he looked lovely. She hasn't told anyone, but she thinks the new Pope is a ride. She watched Sky News for a few days after he was elected, just to see if there'd be more about him.

There's the bus crash the day before they meet. A school bus, on a road in Meath. Five girls are killed. Four of them from the same school, all from the same little place. A close-knit community, the man on the radio says. She watches it on the *Nine O'Clock News*, when she gets in from work. The bus is overturned, on a straight stretch of road. There are two other cars, crashed into each other. There's a picture of some schoolbags, thrown from the bus, on the side of the road. One of them looks like Jack's — she tries not to be stupid. There'll be piles of flowers there soon, and teddy bears. People in the village talk to the reporter. They try not to cry as they speak. One woman blesses herself. They heard about the crash on the radio. Other kids called home on their mobiles. Jesus, the thought. Your children on the bus. Coming home for their tea, says a man on the News. To do their homework.

It's another of the cold days. She wear Jack's jacket. He gets out of his car when he sees her coming. She doesn't know what make the car is. It's green. He takes a big umbrella out of the boot.

— I should have called for you, he says.

— No, she says. — It's grand.

They walk towards Sutton and Howth. The rain stays off. It was belting down all last night. It's still on the ground. They talk about the crash.

— There was a man on the television last night, he says.

He talks as he looks ahead. She looks at the side of his face. His wrinkles look deliberate. The skin on his neck is looser than hers. His shirt is clean. He must have ironed it himself.

— He mentioned the children coming home for their tea.

— I saw him, says Paula. — He was — what he said really brought it home.

— Yes, he says. — I thought so.

He looks at her. He's not as tall as Charlo.

— A nightmare, he says.

— Yeah.

They say nothing for a while. They just walk. She'd prefer to be at home. She thinks she would. They go past the palm trees. The tide's out. He's looking across at the island.

— Do you play golf, Paula?

— No.

For fuck sake.

— Do you?

— Occasionally, he says.

— That means you're no good at it.

He smiles. That's nice.

— There you have it, he says.

He's got a plain jumper on, under his North Face jacket. He's wearing a tie under his jumper.

He points the umbrella.

— There's a couple of oystercatchers.

— The birds?

— You're not interested?

— Not really.

— Well, look, he says.

And he points again.

— There's an old shopping trolley.

She laughs.

— I know the names of virtually all the birds that inhabit Dublin Bay and you're not impressed.

— No.

They're both a bit lost. He's blushing.

— Well, she says. — I know the names of all the household bleaches and floor cleaners. D'you want to know them?

He laughs. He looks at her. He laughs again.

— How far do we go? she asks.
— Sutton?
— Okay. And back?
— Well, my car's back that way.
— Okay.
Jesus.
— What's your wife's partner like?
— What — sorry?
— Did you ever meet her?
He's pretending he's slow.
— Ah, he says. — Yes. I did. She's very attractive.
— Is she middle-aged as well?
— Yes, he says. — I suppose so.
She points at the houses across the James Larkin Road, up the embankment.
— I clean one of them, she says.
— Really?
— Yeah. Mondays. It's gas, she says. —Your wife and that. You never know what's happening, really. Behind closed doors.
— Charlie Rich, he says.
— Who?
— Charlie Rich sang "Behind Closed Doors".
— You like the music, Joe?
— I haven't listened to much music in years. I used to. I went to gigs.
He grins.
— D'you know the White Stripes? she says.
— No.
— None of your kids?
He shrugs.

303

— Maybe your wife likes them.

He eventually smiles.

— I went to them last summer, she says. — Up in Marlay Park.

— An outdoor gig.

— Yep.

— You're a great girl altogether.

She eventually smiles.

— They were brilliant.

— Did it not rain?

— No, she says. — It wouldn't have mattered. I'm going to Coldplay in a couple of weeks.

Will he want to go too? Is that what he thinks, that she's asking him? She can't see him filling black bags. Squashed into the minibus with the African women.

— I've heard of them, he says.

— They're good, she says. — But they're not as hard as the White Stripes. Do you get to see her much?

— I told you, he says.

— No, you didn't.

— Yes, I did.

He looks at her.

— No, she says. — When?

— I told you. The most interesting thing about me is the fact that my wife ran away with another woman.

— Oh. Yeah. Sorry.

They get to Sutton. It doesn't rain. They turn back. She'd like a coffee — she'd love a gin and tonic, four or five of them — but she's not sure she wants to stay with him for that long. She wants to get home. He doesn't suggest it, anyway, a coffee and a bun or anything.

They chat. Or they don't. They say nothing. It rains a bit and that's good, because they talk about it. And he gets to hold up his umbrella. She walks under it, beside him.

She lets him drive her to the house. She's not fuckin' walking. He stops the car. He turns off the engine. She doesn't invite him in. She can tell, she thinks — he wants to get away.

— Well, she says. — That was nice. Thanks.

— Yes, he says. — Thank you.

— Well —

— Can I phone you?

— Yeah, she says. — That'd be great.

She opens the door. He doesn't lean across to kiss her. Thank God — she doesn't want that. His hand is on the keys. He's ready to start the car.

— Bye, she says.

— Goodbye, he says.

She closes the door. It doesn't shut properly. The seat belt's stuck. She does it again.

He's gone.

She watches the car turn the corner. She kind of misses him, although she's glad she's on her own. She'd like to see him again. It's hard, after so long alone. But he's nice. He *is* a bit dry — Mary's spot-on. His birds of Dublin Bay. Pointing his umbrella. He likes her, though. He listened to her. He laughed. He looked at her once, and she could tell; he wanted to hold her, probably grab her. He wanted to fuck her — ta-dah. That's kind of nice, although it's weird as well.

She mightn't see him again. But Denise is right. The ocean's full of fish. She'll start hanging around the bottle bank. All she needs is more bottles. There's all sorts of bottles — sauce, medicine. She's not looking. She's not desperate. He likes her, though. She saw that.

It's ridiculous.

It's nice, though.

She turns on the radio. It's the end of Joe Duffy. It's a young voice, a girl. And Paula remembers — the crash yesterday, in Meath. The girl is talking about her best friend, who's dead. She's on a mobile, Paula thinks — she can hear voices and noise behind her. She's probably at the school. The girl talks about them laughing, at the school sports last week. They did the three-legged race together. They fell over. She's clear, she's lovely; she knows her friend is dead. It's heart-breaking but it makes Paula smile. The kid on the radio is just so brilliant and alive.

It's over. She turns off the radio.

Leanne looks rough. Paula says nothing. She tries not to look too carefully. She tries not to smell the air. There's nothing she can do.

She has to wait. That's all.

She has to hope.

You were late in last night. She'll say nothing. I didn't hear you come in.

Leanne is dressed for work. That's something to clutch. She's going to work. She got up. She'll be going out the door.

306

She's scratching her arms. Paula watches her as she stands looking out the window, waiting for the kettle.

— I'm going to the doctor tonight.

Leanne has turned. Her face is blotched. Her eyes are wet and red.

Paula catches up with Leanne's words.

— Why? she says.

— Hay fever, says Leanne.

Paula tries not to sound too happy.

— God love you. Is it back?

Every year since she was little. Pollen, dust-mites — they all go for Leanne.

— I thought with all the rain, says Paula. — It isn't even warm.

Leanne shrugs. She's miserable. Her eyes are full.

— Those Zirtek tablets worked last year, says Paula. — Didn't they?

Leanne shrugs.

Paula says it — she can't stop.

— I didn't hear you come in last night.

Leanne stares at her. Wet, red eyes.

— Why? she says. — Were you passed out?

— Sorry.

— Yeah, says Leanne.

She picks up her bag as the kettle clicks. She walks past Paula. She doesn't slam the door. Paula hears her heels on the path outside.

She knew she was going to say it. She could feel it; she wouldn't resist. She just had to say it. I don't trust you.

Ah, Jesus.

You've let me down.

She watches the steam from the kettle. She makes herself move. She goes to the sink. There's nothing to wash.

Nicola rings. It's later. Paula's on the bus. They chat for a bit. Nicola wants to say something. Paula always thinks that.

— How are the girls?

— Grand; yeah.

— Not long now to the holidays.

— Yeah; Jesus. Still more than a month, though. Look it, I have to go.

— Okay. Bye, love.

— Talk to you.

Paula puts the phone back in her pocket. She smiles at the Chinese young one who's looking across at her. She's upstairs. She likes what you can see from up here. Behind the garden walls, through upstairs windows.

It's three days. Joe hasn't rung her. That's grand. It's a bit disappointing.

The bollocks.

Her phone rings again. She looks at the name on the screen.

John Paul.

The jungle drums are out. He's going to give out to her.

She's sick of her fuckin' children.

— Hello, love.

— Alright?

— I'm grand. And yourself?

Calm down, calm down.

— Good; yeah. D'you want to come to the house?

— I'd love to.

— Cool. We've moved.

— Cool.

Did she just say that? She's falling apart, but this is lovely.

— Where to? she says. — I don't have a pen.

— I'll come and get you, he says. — It's not far from where we were. Sunday; yeah?

— Lovely, she says.

— Three o'clock, about.

— Lovely.

It's later; lunchtime. She's home again. She texts Leanne. What's the text for Sorry? *Sy? Sry?* She writes the full word. *Sorry. Xx M.* She fires it off. She waits for the buzz. The bitch won't answer. She leaves the phone on the table.

She hears the key. Jack walks in. He walks back out.

She puts on U2. She turns it up. She'll impress the Poles next door, although they probably won't be there. They come home late. They go off early. Sunday's the only day she really hears them. She sees them go out on the street, in their good clothes. They're the only ones heading off to Mass. She plays it loud anyway. It'll kill everything — the guilt, her deafness. She can go to the table and check her phone, because she can't hear it.

She picks it up. No text.

She's at the press, looking for sugar. She finds the packet of seeds. Empress of India. The flowers look gorgeous. Vibrant flowers on deeply coloured foliage. The planting instructions are on the back. She throws it in the bin.

She lies on the bed for an hour. She doesn't close the curtains. She isn't going to sleep.

She goes to work. It rains on her. She doesn't care. Only, her feet. They're cold — they're wet. There's a leak in her left shoe. More money she doesn't have.

Her back is fine. She's grand again. She remembers — her thumb. It's gone too, that pain. It's been gone for a while. She's been flinging the buffer around the place. She'd forgotten about it. She looks at the thumb, and she feels her wrist. There's no pain there now; nothing.

It's payday. They'll have a takeaway. Leanne could be home by now; it's after seven. She checks the time on her mobile screen. No text. She's not sure if Jack's working tonight. She could phone Leanne. She should. But it could backfire on her. Are you checking up on me? Leanne was going to the doctor. Paula could text her. *Hw doc go?* She's not sure. What's the rule? Can you text someone again if they haven't answered the first time? She'll have the Kung Po King Prawn. She likes that. Leanne always has the chicken curry, with chips. She hates rice. *Tkaway 2nite?* More checking up. One fuckin' mistake. One worry, said out loud.

She's not being honest.

She unplugs the buffer. She hears herself grunt when she bends. She winds the flex around the handle.

She was vicious. There was something there. She wanted to hurt Leanne, to let her know. I don't trust you. She wanted the smell on Leanne's breath. It would have been a relief. The inevitable, out of the way. It's what she expects, for herself. It's a matter of time. It'll happen to Paula. It'll happen to Leanne. She was always there for me.

She pushes the buffer to the lift.

She hates herself. It's true. She's shit. She's useless.

Fuck that. She can beat it away.

But it's true.

There's chewing gum on the floor of the Ladies. She'll have to get down on her knees. Some slut just dropped it straight out of her mouth. A woman in an office — for fuck sake. She gets it up with her house key. She drops the grey gum into her black bag. She washes the key. She washes her hands.

She's on the Dart. She holds her mobile. She's hungry. A man gets on at Connolly. Paula gets her knees out of his way. He sits across from her. He reads the *Herald*. He holds it up to his head. She sees the back page. Liverpool have won that European Cup. CHAMPIONS. They won it last night. John Paul will be delighted. She'll text him. He didn't mention it when he phoned earlier. And he obviously didn't go to Istanbul. But he'll be delighted. Flashing his tattoo. *Euro cp, wll dne. XxM.* She fires it off. At least some things are working out. She puts the mobile into her pocket. She can take it out when he texts her back. She needs the drama.

It's only in her pocket when it rings. The music from *Miami Vice*. Vanessa, Nicola's little one, did it for her

— Paula hasn't a clue how. She looks at the screen. It's not John Paul. It's a private number.

— Paula?

— Yes.

— It's Joe.

— Hello.

She feels the heat in her face.

— How are you?

— Grand, she says. — On my way home from work.

— Were you working late?

— No, she says. — It's my normal time.

— Of course, he says. — I didn't think.

The train stops at Clontarf Road. The man with the *Herald* gets off. She can stretch her legs. She can slump.

— So, he says. — I was wondering. Should we meet? For a drink, perhaps?

— I'm an alcoholic, Joe, she says.

The train's moving again.

It's what she's wanted to say. It's all she's wanted to say. The carriage isn't empty and she couldn't care less. There's no shame.

— Are you still there, Joe? she says.

— Yes, he says. — I'm here. I've a glass in my hand, actually. I was looking for somewhere to hide it.

She laughs.

— There's no need, she says. — I'm fine.

— You're, is it, recovering?

— Yeah, she says. — Kind of.

— Good.

— I haven't had a drink in a good while, she says. —
Well over a year.

— Good, he says. — A walk.

— Ah, look it, she says. — I work hard, Joe. A walk is
too like more work.

— The pictures. Last offer.

— Lovely.

— There's a German one on in the UGC, about the
last days of Hitler —

— I hope you enjoy it, Joe, she says. — I'm going to
The Interpreter.

— Alright, he says.

— I like Sean Penn, she says.

— Fine.

— He reminds me of my husband.

The train's at Killester.

— Still there, Joe?

— Just about, he says.

— Just so you know.

The train's moving again.

— Sunday? he says.

— Can't, she says. — I'm going to my son's.

She loves the sound of that. And it's happening.

— Monday? he says.

— Grand, she says. — After work.

There's the little envelope on the screen when she
stops talking to Joe. It's from John Paul. *Ta. Jp.*

The house is empty. The telly's off. She takes off her
jacket. She goes upstairs. She has a look in Jack's room.
His jeans are on the floor, and a T-shirt. He's gone to
work. She goes to Leanne's door. She stands there. She

wants to go in. She wants to get down and look under the bed. Pull back the duvet, feel the sheet and mattress. But she doesn't.

She goes downstairs. She waits for Leanne.

She's walking up Marlborough Street. It's about four o'clock. She's on her way to see Carmel, in the Mater Private. Carmel had her operation yesterday. The mastectomy. Denise phoned Paula last night. Carmel was grand; she was comfortable.

She's a bit hot, walking. She comes to a Spar. She takes out her mobile. *Nd anythng?* She sends it to Carmel. But she doesn't wait. Carmel might be asleep. There'll be more shops on the way. She keeps going.

She gets to Parnell Street. She crosses, to Hill Street.

Comfortable. It means nothing. She's heard them say it on the News. It means that whoever's been shot isn't dead. She'll be happier when she sees Carmel. She's sure she will. It's gas to think, her sister's in a private hospital. She can't help it; she wants to see what it's like. She'll tell Carmel about Joe. She might. What is there to tell? They went to the pictures. They're going for a drive next Saturday, up the mountains. She can hear Carmel, if she tells her. Bring your condoms, Paula.

She'll tell Carmel. A bit of excitement. A bit of crack.

She's on Temple Street when she hears and feels the mobile. A text. She opens it. *1 tit. Hpy Brthdy.*

She laughs. She won't delete this one. She can't wait to see Carmel now. She goes across Dorset Street at the lights — they're changing. She runs. A car honks, twice. She doesn't look. It's only some messer.

It's her birthday. She's forty-nine. She bought a cake earlier. It's in the fridge. They'll have it when she gets home.

Also available in ISIS Large Print:

Love & Other Impossible Pursuits

Ayelet Waldman

Ayelet Waldman is an uplifting discovery: a fantastically enjoyable new writer with no pretensions and a genuine storytelling gift **Sunday Times**

Is Emilia the wicked stepmother incarnate? Passionately in love with her husband, Emilia has a secret, guilty loathing for her precocious little stepson, William — a 40-year-old in a five-year-old's body, whom she picks up from nursery every Wednesday afternoon. He is lactose intolerant, she feeds him dairy products; he mustn't get cold, she pushes him — accidentally — into a pond in Central Park. How can she forgive William for living, when her own cherished child has gone?

A candid, raw, humorous and emotional novel about family in today's fractured society.

ISBN 978-0-7531-7682-5 (hb)
ISBN 978-0-7531-7683-2 (pb)

The Rules of Perspective

Adam Thorpe

It is April 1945, and the small provincial town of Lohenfelde is about to be overrun by the Allied Third Army. Huddled in the vaults of the Kaiser-Wilhelm Museum are Heinrich Hoffer and his three colleagues. Their petty rivalries and resentments surface quickly in this claustrophobic confinement, and the vaults become a stage for an intense psychological drama of secret histories and shared terror.

Above the ground, picking through the rubble, is Corporal Neal Parry, who wishes he was studying art and not dodging snipers. When he finds an exquisite painting in what remains of the museum vaults, he is immediately reconnected with a lost world of beauty and order: the world of art. It is this small 18th-century oil that is the poignant link between the young American soldier and the four charred corpses he finds at the same time.

As the narratives interweave, the story of the painting reveals the hidden story of Herr Hoffer and his three associates — and in doing so uncovers other, darker mysteries.

ISBN 978-0-7531-7525-5 (hb)
ISBN 978-0-7531-7526-2 (pb)

The Laments

George Hagen

Hagen's exploration of the nature of identity and life's inevitable compromises is jauntily entertaining
Guardian

When Howard and Julia Lament secretly adopt Will, a baby switched at birth in a bizarre hospital debacle, it marks the beginning of a journey that takes them from Rhodesia to the Middle East, Britain to the New Jersey suburbs — for no matter where the Laments set up home, the grass always seems greener on the other side of the ocean. As the Laments discover that living somewhere doesn't necessarily mean belonging there, Will grows up struggling with his sense of identity in the shadow of his anarchic twin brothers, Julius and Marcus. Yet when disillusion and mishap threaten to tear his family apart, it is Will who fights to hold them together.

ISBN 978-0-7531-7507-1 (hb)
ISBN 978-0-7531-7508-8 (pb)

Eleanor Rigby

Douglas Coupland

a powerful and moving examination of a life lived negotiating loneliness   **Independent**

skilful plotting and appealing characters   **Telegraph**

funny, unexpected and fragile   **Guardian**

Liz Dunn is 42 years old, and lonely. Her house is like "a spinster's cell block", and she may or may not snore — there's never been anybody to tell her. Then one day in 1997, with the comet Hale Bopp burning bright in the blue-black sky, Liz receives an urgent phone call asking her to visit a young man in hospital. All at once, the loneliness that has come to define her is ripped away by this funny, smart, handsome young stranger, Jeremy. Her son.

ISBN 978-0-7531-7375-6 (hb)
ISBN 978-0-7531-7376-3 (pb)